Stef C.R.

The Love Penalty
ISBN 13: 979-8-8692-7479-3

Copyright © 2024 Stef C. R.

All rights reserved. No part of this book may be reproduced in any form except for the purpose of brief reviews or citations without the written permission of the author.

This is a work of fiction in which all events and characters in this book are completely imaginary. Any resemblance to actual people is entirely coincidental.

Cover designed by Lorissa Padilla.
Book edited by Ciara Lewis.

Fuck it, this one's for me.

Author's note

While this is a hockey romance with a guaranteed HEA, this book does include mentions of death (off page) and explicit content.

Note to my family: *please skip chapters 25, 26, 28, 29, and 32.*

Playlist

Coolest fucking bitch in town - Haley Blais
Wildfire - Cautious Clay
ceilings - Lizzy McAlpine
Slingshot - Zach Seabough
I Love That Sound - Michael Bernard Fitzgerald
Stuck in The Middle - Tai Verdes
Slowing Down - The Backseat Lovers
raw - LOONY
Alcatraz - Oliver Riot
Everything Is Just a Mess - The Brook & The Bluff
All Is Well - Hans Williams
Inside Friend - Leon Bridges
Brakelights - Omar Apollo
Hey Lover! - Wabie
Thinking (11:44) - Felly
I Think I Like When It Rains - WILLIS
Love & War in Your Twenties - Jordy Searcy
Next to You - John Vincent III
You Are In Love (Taylor's Version) - Taylor Swift
I Wanna Be Yours - Arctic Monkeys
Electric - Alina Baraz

ONE

Olivia
September

HAVE you ever had that feeling that things are about to change? I don't know if things are about to become better or worse, but I know with certainty that this season is going to be different. Maybe that's just wishful thinking.

I've only been on the ice for twenty minutes and my legs are already killing me. I should have skated more over the summer break. Instead, I worked two jobs so I could save money for the upcoming season. As a hockey officiant at the EHL level, I get paid per game, which means my income is highly variable. There are some months where I get to officiate more than fifteen games, and others where I only officiate one or two.

That means I need to either find a part time job during certain months, or work extra hard during the offseason so I can have savings to fall back on. Since I chose to work myself dead this summer, I haven't had the chance to join any stick and puck practices or participate in beer league games as I normally would.

I am out of shape and all the gear on me is making me uncomfortable. My hockey pants are frayed and my gloves have big holes in them, but I've been frugal all summer. Maybe once I find out my officiating schedule I can afford some new gear.

I've never been an amazing hockey player, but I have always loved the game. It's something my dad and I had in common. Every time our NHL team in Minnesota would play, my dad would turn the TV really loud, grab us both frozen dinners, and we would watch the game together. On paydays, he would get pizza and pop. I've kept that tradition going even now that he's gone, although eating pizza and watching games by myself is really fucking sad.

"Liv, you're up!" Amelia's shouting breaks me out of my thoughts and I hop the wall to take her spot as the center. I despise it when she calls me Liv. I despise nicknames in general.

I'm slower than usual and I definitely should have stretched before playing in this beer league tonight. Mark sends a puck my way, and just like every other pass tonight, I miss it. My frustration is building. I haven't been this bad since I was in middle school and my dad would take me to stick and puck practices and get me to join little leagues.

"Chin up, Livie!" Amelia says as I finish my shift and take a seat on the bench again. I swear if she calls me anything other than Olivia one more time I will snap.

"Everything okay with you?" Mark asks as he takes a seat next to me. "You seem distracted tonight. Can't say I've ever seen you miss a pass, you're usually wiping the ice with us."

His comment surprises me and I huff a laugh. "I'm fine, just tired and out of practice, I guess."

"Have you been working two jobs over the summer?"

I nod. "Yeah, unfortunately."

"How's your grandma doing?" Mark asks as we both scoot down the bench and more people shuffle on and off the ice.

I roll my eyes. "She's fine. Same old, you know, refuses to move in with me, says she's fine living with her two other seventy-year-old roommates, baking cookies, and crocheting all hours of the day."

Mark laughs, and it startles me so much I jump in my seat a little. I always forget how loud he can be. He's unfiltered too, and always asks me personal questions. Not that I'm judging the guy or anything, I'm sure he's a wonderful person, but he is just not my type. He's too chatty, too bubbly, and too loud. I'm pretty sure I've said all of this to his face before, but he's pretty relentless and insists on getting to know me. He always asks me to *hang out*, and I always give him the same answer: not interested.

It's not that he's not handsome, because he is. He's got dark brown hair and brown eyes with pretty, long lashes. He's 5'11", which is about three extra inches taller than me, and he has a nice smile. I just can't get over his personality, and the fact that all he wants is to hook up.

While I may not be the most affectionate and open woman out there, hooking up has never been my style. I need an emotional connection before I can take that extra step with a guy. My last and only boyfriend was in college and after that nasty break-up, I haven't been inclined to date much. Besides, with my traveling and hectic schedule during the hockey season, I don't have time to date.

After another forty minutes of epic failure on the ice,

I'm in the locker room, packing everything up and getting ready to leave.

There are only a handful of girls in our amateur league and the tiny arena we play at doesn't have a women's locker room. That means we have to share one with all of the guys. I'm so used to being around naked guys by now that I've learned how to keep my head down so I don't accidentally get flashed when they get out of the shower. While I've become insensitive to the nakedness around me, I don't want to reveal myself, so I always skip the shower and take one at home.

I listen to the conversations going on around me but refrain from joining in. Truth is, I've never been great at making friends and keeping them. While I am friendly with most of the people in this locker room, my quiet and lonesome personality always makes me the odd woman out. I used to go out with them in the beginning, until I realized I was too awkward to insert myself into the conversation and none of them made the effort to include me. So instead of quietly sitting at a table with a bunch of people around me, I'd rather sit at home and maybe get lost in a fictional world.

Once everyone files out of the room, I see Mark hovering around. "Some of us are going over to The Logan for a drink, do you wanna join us?" he asks me, wiggling his eyebrows.

I sigh. "Not tonight, Mark. I need to get some sleep."

"I'm sure a couple drinks can help with that," he says, getting so close to me I can smell the sweat coming off every pore. "Besides, you can stay over at my place if you don't want to drive."

His hand reaches up and pushes my sweaty locks away from my face. "I also have a working shower that we can jump into, together," he says, licking his lower lip in a gesture that I think he means to be sexy, but in actuality, it makes him look like he's drooling.

I internally cringe, and I'm sure he can see it on my face. I've never been able to hide my expressions, and right now my face probably says *ew, what the fuck?*

My hand reaches up to his and I lightly slap it away. With a huff, I say, "Not happening, Mark. Please stop suggesting it."

He backs away and I can see the irritation on his face. For a moment I think he is going to walk away and leave it be, but as he reaches the locker room door he turns back to me and says, "You know what Olivia? You might be hot but you're not worth the chase. Have fun hanging out by yourself all the time, I'm sure it's super fun."

I hold still until I'm sure he's gone, then breathe in and out, trying to calm my racing heart. I shouldn't care what Mark of all people thinks of me, but I can't help feeling hurt by his comment. Probably because he's right, I'm not worth it. I've never been worthy of anything or anyone.

My mom left when I was ten.

My boyfriend dumped me because I wasn't smart and ambitious enough for him and his family.

And my dad...well I can't really blame him for dying. I probably didn't deserve him either.

My father, Carl Wilson, always had a great opinion of me. He worked so hard as a mechanic and always made sure to be home on time to spend time with me after school. I was his whole world and after seeing how excited I was about hockey, he made it his mission to give me every opportunity to play. He'd always say, "'Squirt, some day, you're going to play women's hockey at the professional level!'"

The farthest I got was playing Division I in college. The closest I will get to the professionals is by officiating. When

I was 16 and realized I needed to get a job and help my dad pay for my hockey gear, I decided to start reffing. I got certified and started out in a little league.

More than a decade later, I am officiating at the EHL level and have my sights on the NHL. I know it won't be an easy road, there are very few women officials for a reason. It's a cutthroat job market to begin with, but being a woman in the world of men's hockey is brutal. Not only am I not respected by the players and coaches, but also by the fans. One bad call on the ice, and the entire arena is suddenly against me.

But I've always had thick skin, and if I am going to make it to the NHL, I can't let that kind of stuff get to me.

I lift my hockey bag over my shoulder and decide it's time to head home. There is no televised hockey tonight since we're in the offseason, but I'm excited to get home, away from people, and curl up on my couch with a romance novel. As I start driving, I get a call from my old mentor, Jack, who I haven't spoken to in a year. I wonder what this could be about.

TWO

Olivia

I FIRST MET Jack six years ago, after I graduated college and decided I wanted to officiate hockey games for a living. I signed up for a referee camp and he happened to be my instructor. He's one of the sweetest guys I've ever met and has always made me feel part of his family. His daughters are a few years younger than me, but we've always gotten along. We haven't spoken in the last year because I have been too busy with the EHL gig and my other side jobs. I tend to fall off the face of the earth sometimes.

If it were anyone else, they would probably be offended if I didn't answer their calls or talk to them in so long. But Jack knows me, and he's in contact with my grandma, the only person I talk to regularly. So he knows I'm not dead.

I answer the call and it connects to my car speakers. "Hi Jack."

"Olivia, why don't you answer your phone? I called you five times. I have news," he says in a soft, chiding tone.

"Sorry Jack, I was at a beer league and my phone was in the locker room. What's up? Is everyone okay?" I say with some concern. He wouldn't be calling if it wasn't important. My mind is already thinking of the worst possible scenario. Did something happen with his wife, Bonnie? Is he sick? Is he dying?

Before panic can overtake me, Jack says, "Everyone is fine, I am calling with good news, honey."

"Oh. Okay..." I say and wait for him to continue.

After a moment, he says, "There is an open position for a young AHL referee in the Midwest region," he pauses for another moment and I feel my heart racing so fast, "and I recommended you."

He says this matter of fact. As if he didn't just hand me a huge opportunity like it was nothing. I am so excited that I need to pull over and process this conversation.

"Wait, wait... what?" I all but screech. "What kind of position? What's the pay? Would they really take me without much EHL experience?"

"Slow down, honey. Here's what I know so far. One of the young referees that was supposed to officiate this season had some kind of accident over the summer. He'll recover, but he's in no condition to skate for a while. That means there's an opening. I heard this from some of my old contacts at the AHL, so I immediately recommended you. They want to have a meeting with you at the end of this week. What do you say?"

I am so shocked, I don't even know what to say for a full minute. "Of course I will meet with them!" I blink back tears, because *holy shit* this is exactly what I needed.

"Now, as a young referee, you'd still get paid per game, so it's not a salary position, but the pay is better. You'd get to travel around the Midwest, so you'll at least get out of Minnesota for a bit."

"That sounds great, Jack. Truly, I don't even know how to thank you."

"You can thank me by buying me a drink when you're in Wisconsin for a game," he says, laughing softly. "I'll forward you an email with all the details for the meeting. And call me every now and then, yeah? I don't want to call your grandma every time I need an update about you, that woman talks my ears off for hours."

I can't help but laugh, and okay, maybe some tears do escape this time. This man has been a father figure to me these last six years. "I will call more, I promise. Thank you!"

"Alright kiddo, have a good night."

"Goodnight." I hang up the phone and grip the steering wheel as hard as I can. I drop my head on it with a huge sigh of relief and anticipation.

Suck it, Mark, it will be super fun to hang out by myself in all the cities I'll get to travel to.

⚒

A WEEK LATER, I wait for Jack to pick up the call. After four rings, he finally does. I can't contain my excitement when I yell "JACK, I got it, I got the job!!"

"Honey, I will have to bill you for my hearing aids now," he says and I laugh uncontrollably.

"I am really proud of you, Olivia. I'm sure your dad would be too." My laugh softens into a sigh and I nod along even though Jack can't see me. My dad *would* be proud.

"Thanks, Jack."

"How are you celebrating?" he asks.

"I got some donuts and I'm on my way over to see

grandma and tell her the good news in person." I enter my car and place the donuts in the front seat.

"That sounds wonderful. I have to go, Bonnie needs me to help with something, but send me your schedule, please. Especially for when you'll be in Wisconsin."

"Will do, Jack." We end the call and I make the drive from downtown to my grandma's townhouse in the suburbs.

When she sees me walking towards the house, she starts smiling and waving her hand around. I love my grandma, but she can be so dramatic sometimes.

"Oh my God, look who it is. You must be my long lost granddaughter, because I don't even recognize you. How much weight have you lost?"

I cut in before she can go down the rabbit hole with all the questions. "Hi, Grandma, it's me. No, I haven't been abducted by aliens. No, I haven't been kidnapped and held hostage," I joke and she narrows her green eyes at me, the same dark shade as mine. "I'm sorry I've been AWOL recently, I've just been working a lot."

"Tsk, all that work, but no fun?" she taunts.

"Well, the reason I am here, with donuts no less," I say and show her the big box I picked up at the bakery, "is that all of that hard work finally paid off." I stand tall and take a deep breath, then tell her, "I got a job in the American Hockey League." I have to spell things out for her, she's always been terrible with abbreviations.

"Eeeeek!" She yells out right before she crushes me in a hug, donut box between us. "Honey, that's amazing, I am so proud of you!"

"Thanks, Grams." I hand her the smushed box and we walk into her kitchen. My grandma, Elizabeth, lives with her two best friends—Ethel and Marianne. They are all in their late sixties and early seventies and having the time of their lives in a three-bedroom townhouse. Grandma and Ethel are both widowers who never felt the need to remarry, and Marianne has always been something of a lone wolf. They've been living together for more than a decade now.

When my dad died ten years ago, I was eighteen and ready to go to college. Grandma suggested I push it back for a year and that she'd come live with me, but I couldn't do that. I needed to keep going, keep playing, keep living, otherwise the grief would swallow me whole. So I went off to college and grandma took care of the house while I was gone. Growing up, I was always a bit ashamed of our house. We didn't live in the best neighborhood and the house was a bit run down, but it has been in our family for a few generations, so at least we didn't have to pay a mortgage.

Every summer I would come home and take care of anything that needed improvement. I didn't accomplish much since every penny I made from working at restaurants and cafes needed to go to food and hockey equipment. I also had my dad's life insurance check, but his will specifically requested I used it for my college tuition. He wanted me to succeed, so that's what I strive to do.

After college, once I realized I wasn't going to make it further in women's hockey, I came back. I've been living here since, but lately it's felt less and less like home.

Once I tell my grandma everything about the new job, I head home and make a plan for the future. My path to the NHL won't be an easy one, but I am determined. As a young referee, my contract is with the AHL, but after some experience, I can extend that to the five year NHL contract. Basically, I would be paid by the National Hockey League, but work for the American Hockey League. At the end of the five year contract, I would either be promoted to the NHL, or I would become a veteran referee.

Veteran referees don't officiate at the NHL level, so my only course of action is to be the best I can be and get that five year contract. I check my schedule for the coming season, and I am booked solid officiating lots of games in Wisconsin, Minnesota, Vermont, Ohio, and Michigan.

I open up the information about my first game. It looks like in a few weeks I will be officiating the home opener game for the Grand Marquee Manticores in Michigan.

THREE

Robbie

SEPTEMBER WEATHER in Northern Michigan is the best. It's warm enough that I can still wear shorts and a polo and even go out on the water, but at night it gets cold enough that I can start a bonfire like the one tonight. Some teammates that I consider close friends are with me at my parents' cabin, enjoying the last night of freedom before training camp starts tomorrow.

"Yo, captain! When are you gonna retire?" Ashton, the team's hot-headed forward, yells from the deck as he's bringing a cooler to us by the fire pit.

"Who said anything about retiring?" I mock glare at him.

He rolls his eyes and smirks. *Bastard*. "Come on, you know you're getting old. Are you gonna let any of us get a chance at captainship?"

"I think you mean *captaincy*, and no, I won't," I say, smirking back.

I've been the captain of the AHL Grand Marquee Manticores for the last five years. As the number one draft pick fourteen years ago, fresh out of high school, I spent a couple of years with Chicago's AHL team before getting called up to the NHL. After two years there, a trade to Detroit was in the cards. I was having my best year here in my home state, and everyone said I had so much potential. Right as we made it to the playoffs that year, I tore my ACL and had to sit out for the rest of that season. The team didn't win the Stanley Cup, but I don't think they blamed me, either. There was just a lot going on that season and everyone was a bit sloppy.

After my recovery, I had a pretty bad season and with my contract coming to an end and was sent down to the AHL team. I couldn't complain much though, as the Manticores played in my home town which meant I got to see my huge family all the time. I improved a lot with the team, so much so that I got called up to the NHL quite often. But after another ACL injury followed by a gruesome recovery, it was pretty clear that I wasn't going to be able to play at the same level as I had before. Five years ago I was offered the captain position and that really solidified it for me. I would never play in the NHL again, but I've made my peace with it.

"What about that nonprofit organization you and Alex were talking about?" Elias contributes. "I thought you were considering that."

I sigh. Of course my best friend would know exactly what's on my mind. Ever since Eli got acquired from Finland two years ago, he and I have been really close. He's an exceptional goalie and, with his track record, he'll be called up to the NHL any day now.

"I don't know, man. It sounds amazing, and you know

there's nothing I'd love more than to coach youth hockey and volunteer," I say.

"But?" he asks pointedly.

"But it sounds like a lot of work to start a nonprofit from the ground up. I wouldn't have time for something like that unless I truly retired."

Jordan whistles. "Damn, are you seriously considering it?"

"Maybe," I say, adding another log to the fire. "Probably not this year though, I need to be here for Elias' last AHL season. We all know he's moving onto bigger and better things." I smile at my best friend and give him an affectionate head pat. He just gives me a deadpan look, but my smile is so infectious he can't help but grin back.

"We'll see. I haven't heard anything, and last time I checked, our NHL team has two very good goaltenders. Unless one gets injured or something, I probably won't get called up," he says with a small pout.

"Nah, you're too good to stay down here with us," Ashton says as he sits in a camping chair and starts chugging a beer. What a caveman.

"How can you possibly throw them back like that and not feel like shit at training?" Jordan asks him with a disgusted look on his face.

Ashton lets out a loud burp, pats his abs and gives Jordan a look of pure innocence. "Well, you see, Grandpa, I'm 25 and have my whole life ahead of me, unlike you three ancient fossils." He grins and ducks out of the way as I throw an empty beer can at his head.

"Don't put me in the same box as these two, I'm still in my twenties," Elias supplies.

"Yeah, late twenties. My dude, you're almost over the hill," Ashton says with a head shake.

"What does that mean? 'Over the hill'?" Elias asks, confusion written all over his face. Sometimes we forget there's a language barrier between us.

"It means you're past your prime. Old. Ancient," Jordan explains sourly.

"Fuck off, Ash, I am not 'over the hill,'" Elias says with a small Finnish accent. He doesn't usually speak with an accent, but it comes out sometimes when he gets angry. And if he's really pissed, he'll start swearing in Finnish.

We all take a seat in our camping chairs and the three of them continue bickering. My mind is back on my conversation with Alex and how much of a compelling argument he made for starting the nonprofit together. We went to high school together and basically grew up playing hockey. He was the captain of the Manticores when I got sent down, and when he got traded to Quebec, I took over the position.

Alex retired last year and moved back to Grand Marquee with his wife, Malia. I've gotten to hang out with them this past summer and he mentioned that he wants to start an organization that focuses on youth hockey and helping those who can't afford equipment and lessons. It sounds like the perfect job for me. So, am I seriously considering this? Retirement?

"Pass me another beer, Grandpa." Ash's voice breaks me out of my thoughts.

"You need to respect your elders, young man." I point at Ashton with a piece of wood as I feed the fire some more. "And trust me, you don't want to be hungover for the game tomorrow."

"Eh, it's just training camp, we have another month before the season officially starts," he says.

Jordan scoffs. "Man, you haven't been here as long as we have. Now is the time for you to show your skills, when the

NHL will actually let us play in the pre-season games. Go out there, show them you can score, make plays, show them all that potential we know you have. Every little thing counts, especially what you're putting in your body."

Jordan, our defenseman, is right. He knows more than any of us how important this time in the offseason is. He spends most of his time training and analyzing hockey, bettering himself in the hopes he'll get called up more often.

Ashton considers the advice for a moment, and before he can open his fifth beer, Elias snatches it from his hand and puts it back in the cooler. We might be a bunch of jocks, but we know how to look out for each other.

FOUR

Olivia
  October

THE BUS RIDE to Grand Marquee was excruciating. I should have brought my headphones, but I somehow managed to forget them. While I did bring two romance novels with me, reading them kept making me motion sick. I made a mental note to prioritize my headphones and some audiobooks next trip.

The weather in West Michigan is not too bad considering it's the middle of October. It's chilly enough that I am wearing a sweatshirt and jeans, but at least I don't need a hat yet. My coffee-brown hair sits in a high ponytail and my face is makeup free as I walk around downtown. The hotel I'm staying at is within walking distance of the arena, and there is plenty to do and see.

The city is known for its craft beer so I stop at a local brewery for some samples and appetizers. The place is crazy packed for a Thursday night. I arrived a few hours ago and the game is not until tomorrow night, so I can indulge a bit. From looking at my schedule, I'll be in this city to officiate quite often, so I might as well find some favorite spots.

I leave Saturday morning, but I plan on stopping by the bagel place near the hotel before heading to the bus station. It seemed pretty fancy, they even had gluten free bagels and vegan cream cheese, which I don't think I've ever seen in my hometown.

From my seat at the bar, I can see most of the restaurant. There are lots of high top tables and booths, but also a stage for live music and entertainment. I don't see any instruments, so that's probably not the reason the place is so busy. The group at the long high–top table next to me is loud as hell. I can't help but look over to see what all the fuss is about. After all, people watching is a favorite pastime of mine.

There are ten of them, all laughing and having a good time. They look like one big happy family. The bartender breaks me out of my perusal as he places a delicious looking burger with fries in front of me. I've never had a peanut butter and jelly burger, but I'm nothing if not adventurous. I take the first bite and my eyes immediately roll back in pleasure. The combination of sweet, savory, and a hint of spiciness from the fresh jalapenos and chipotle sauce hits the right spot.

After another couple bites, my attention is once again drawn to the group next to me. There's an older couple sitting next to each other. The man is at the end of the table, leaning in to the woman on his left and whispering something in her ear. They seem so happy.

Everyone is wearing business casual clothes, and it makes me feel underdressed. I look down at my sweatshirt and I see I've spilled ketchup on it. I sigh and rub at it with a napkin.

I take a sip of my IPA and let my eyes wander to the table again. There's a second couple, and they look to be younger, probably in their mid-thirties. She's wearing a beautiful dark yellow dress with a burgundy cardigan that compliments her dark brown skin and brown eyes.

A very tall, very blond guy that looks about my age and with an incredibly athletic build catches my eye. He's handsome in a very Nordic way. I notice him talking and gesturing to another guy that sits at the other end of the table. This one has a similar build, but darker skin and hair. Next to him, her back to me, is a much shorter blonde girl. She's leaning on the table, pointing fingers at the viking. To her left are two more guys, both with tall and imposing figures. The one farthest to the left turns around and catches my stare.

I quickly look back down to my food and hope he didn't think I was a creep. I peek another glimpse at them, and he's still watching me. I expect him to frown and tell me to mind my own business but he grins and winks at me.

Oh.

Oh no.

I finish my beer and try to flag the bartender down, but he's busy. Before I can start waving around at him, I sense someone stepping up next to me at the bar. I turn around, and it's him. The guy from the table. He's taller than I initially thought and looks to be about 6'2". His eyes are dark blue and his face is speckled with so many freckles I can't even count. He looks very handsome with his sharp jaw and dark red hair, and that grin is dangerous.

"Hey, I'm Ashton," he says, extending his hand.

I take it so I'm not rude, but don't smile back. "Olivia."

"Can I buy you a drink?" he says, unphased.

"I was just about to leave, actually."

"Ah, that's too bad. I would have liked to get to know you better," he says, and if I was interested, I would admit that was pretty smooth.

"That's okay, I'm not from around here, so it's not like you'd have made a lasting friendship anyway," I say bluntly.

I can tell I caught him by surprise by the way his eyebrows raise and he gives me a crooked smile. "You are something else, aren't you?"

"Suppose so," I say, not breaking eye contact.

He raises his hand and for a second I'm confused, but then I realize he's signaling for my check. "Well, it was nice to meet you, Olivia."

"You too, I guess," I say and furrow my brows.

He laughs and gives me a lingering look before turning to leave. As I watch him go, I realize the whole party at the table has paid and is ready to leave. As he approaches them, I see the last guy in their group, the one whose back was to me and I couldn't make out his features. He's as tall as Ashton, but his shoulders are a bit broader, his waist narrower. His dark blond hair is wavy and long enough that strands fall in his eyes as he looks down. He and Ashton are talking and Ashton nods toward me before leaving through the door. I'm not fast enough to look away, because when he lifts his head, our eyes lock.

His are light blue and sparkling with mischief. I wonder what he sees in mine. Whatever it is, it has him staring at me for a beat, lips parted, and I am frozen. Because right there by that door is the most gorgeous guy I have ever seen.

FIVE

Robbie

THE ENERGY in the locker room during the home opener is unlike anything I've ever experienced. Everyone is pumped and ready to get on the ice and start the season off strong. Our team hasn't made it to the playoffs since 2017, the year before I was made captain. While we've been doing our best since, we've had a long streak of bad luck. Every time we come near the playoffs, we get tons of injuries or our best players get called up, and we are left to struggle.

This year though, we are desperate to make it. I know I am, at least. Especially if I'm seriously considering retiring next season and pursuing other opportunities.

We're all geared up and ready to go and we saw how pumped up the crowd was during our warm-ups. Everybody is excited to see us win tonight on our own ice. Most fans are here to see Elias and some of the newer prospects from Sweden, which is understandable. These kids are the future.

"Ready to crush this?" I ask Elias. He's quiet for a beat, his head is back against the locker, his eyes are closed, and he's taking controlled breaths. It's part of his ritual, I suppose, helps keep him focused. Elias has always been the quiet type. At first we thought he was too shy, especially coming to a new country and experiencing what I'm sure must be some culture shock, but he proved us wrong. As soon as we got to know him better and he let us in, he showed us exactly how excited, fun, and caring he can be. He'd do anything for his friends, and we'd do the same for him.

"I was born ready," he replies with a grin, puts on his mask and stands up. It's time to get ready for the "high five alley." Before every game, the starting line and goalie go out an entrance separate from the player tunnel where there are fans to high-five us as we enter the ice. Today though, since it's the season opener, we have the entire team lining up by jersey number to be introduced on the ice.

Ashton is first to go since, to no one's surprise, he's #1. While he might be a conceited little asshole, Jordan and I took him under our wing a few years ago. He was 22 at the time and was traded to us from the Vermont Vortices. With a big personality and a loud mouth, we made sure to keep him out of trouble. Now he's 25 and one of our best forwards. So much so that he's usually one of the go to guys that gets called up to the NHL when there is a need. He's fast and puts up a lot of points. Ashton, Jordan, and I usually work well together and share the first line on the ice.

A few other teammates are introduced, and then it's Jordan's turn. His jersey is #20 and he swears it's his lucky number. I've known Jordan the longest, for about seven years now. We met at training camp and hit it off immediately, so I invited him to my family's cabin before that season started. He's a Michigan native just like me, and as we were bonding we realized we actually went to the same high school. He was just two years younger than me so we never ran in the same circles, but he knew who I was. His sister Tangela is now married to my brother Michael, so in a way, Jordan is family too.

When they call number #31, I skate out and wave at the fans. The venue is packed even tighter than it was during warm-ups and that gives me a huge vote of confidence. I look around and notice that the referees and linesmen are out here already and talking to the coaches and crew. Half our team is out on the ice and the announcer continues to call out numbers. Elias skates up and lines up with the rest of us, his jersey proudly showing #35.

Not long after, the whole team is out here. We wave once more at the fans, and everyone but the first line heads to the bench. Elias takes his spot in the home net and the rest of us stay in a line and take off our helmets for the national anthem. Since we're playing the Finchton Foxes, another US team, we only get to hear one anthem tonight. Their skill set is very similar to us and I don't think they've made the playoffs in recent years either. However, we have something they don't: a damn great goalie.

We get in the center ice face-off position, and now is my time to shine. The referee, Bob, is someone who's officiated many of our games over the years and we have a great professional relationship. I nod at him and say, "Welcome back, Bob. Hope you had a good summer."

"Cut the chit chat, Elliot," he says with a smile and I return it. He tells us to get in position, and as soon as he drops the puck, I immediately send it to the side with a backhand. Jordan catches it and passes it along, but it gets intercepted by a Foxes player. We go back and forth a few times, until Ashton finally gets a hold of it and starts sprinting towards the Foxes net, with me on his heels. He encounters a defenseman and passes the puck to me. I catch it and wind up for a slapshot. The puck hits the net in the top right corner and the buzzer immediately goes off. And just like that, we lead 1-0 in the first 5 minutes of the period.

The next fifteen minutes go quite smoothly, even if we don't score any more goals. Surprisingly, no penalties have been called yet tonight. Elias has made some amazing saves and the crowd is wild for him. They've been chanting his last name so all we hear as we head to the locker rooms for intermission is, *"Kalias!, Kalias!, Kalias!"*

As soon as we're all in the locker room I say, "Great job guys, let's keep up the momentum. Elias, you're killing it out there. You're a wall, man." I pat his shoulder pad and smile widely around the room. Everyone is buzzing with excitement, and the coaches are all content.

"What's wrong with you, Ashton?" one of our teammates asks.

"What do you mean?" he asks, confused.

"You didn't visit the penalty box at all today, what's up with that?"

Ashton rolls his eyes and ignores the question. That's strange, he's usually ready to tear into someone with comments. I go to sit next to him and quietly ask him "Everything good?"

He looks at me with a slight furrow in his brow. At first I think he won't answer and I get ready to leave, but he stops me and quietly says, "I don't know, man. Maybe I'm ready to be more mature or whatever. What you guys said at training camp really sunk in. I don't want to be stuck here until I'm in my thirties and never go to the NHL."

His eyes go wide as soon as he says it and he stammers, "Not... I mean—shit... not that I think you're stuck... I just—um..." I put him out of his misery and place a hand on his shoulder, giving him an understanding look.

"It's fine man, I get it. I'm glad you're taking it more seriously, whatever the reason is," I smile and pat his shoulder again and can feel the relief as his frame sags.

"I'll need your help though, keeping me honest, keeping me in check. I know you already do a lot, but I would really appreciate it."

"Anytime, kid."

"Thanks, Grandpa," he smirks and I walk away shaking my head.

"Alright guys, the second period countdown is up, let's go out there and have some fun," I say, clapping my hands and putting my gear back on.

WE SWITCH nets for the second period. The team fans out, taking their starting positions as I move to center ice. "How are the kids, Bob?" I say, coming to a stop. But I don't get a reply. When I look up, I see that it's not Bob with me at the face-off. It's a woman. I'm so distracted for a moment that I miss her calling the five second count.

She says, "You're off the face-off!"

I just stare dumbly and say with a laugh, "What?"

Her posture goes rigid, but she doesn't look at me. She's in position, puck in hand, and says more firmly this time, "I said, you're out of the face-off, Elliot. Now I suggest you move before I give you a second violation and a penalty for delay of game."

Shit. Okay, point taken. I move over and let another player take over the face-off. I'm still a bit distracted, so I miss the puck coming to me. I grit my teeth and swear to myself as I sprint down the ice with my teammates to regain control. Something nags at me amid the action, this woman seems familiar. But how?

Once my shift is over, I sit on the bench and I know my eyes should be tracking the puck, but instead they're on her. Referee #13. I see an opening as a teammate heads over to the bench, and I jump over to take his place, except the puck comes towards us. Both he and I turn to catch it and we hear the whistle go off.

Referee #13 skates up to the box and calls out the penalty. "Manticores, #31, two minutes for too many men on ice."

Fuck. I can't even deny it, we definitely messed up. I'm disappointed in myself, I should have known better. As I skate by her to the box I turn to look at her and say with a smile, "Sorry, ref, won't happen again."

She looks up and pierces me with those dark green eyes. Wait. I do know her. Or at least, I've seen her before. She was at the brewery last night talking to Ashton. As we left the place, I looked back and saw her there, hair up in a ponytail, inquisitive green eyes glued to mine. I feel like we're stuck in that same trance now as I skate by her.

She looks away first but I still catch a small smile as she says, "I'm sure it won't."

✕

MY PENALTY in the second period really hurt us. While I was in the box, the Foxes managed to score on a breakaway. I feel like I let Elias down, he shouldn't have been in that defenseless position to begin with, and I tell him so during the second intermission. He says it's fine but I could tell he wanted a shutout tonight. We just need to do better in the third period.

We head out again and the game takes a turn. We're playing more physically, delivering clean checks to the Foxes, letting them know we mean business. After five long minutes in the offensive zone, Jordan takes a shot from the blue line and it's so unexpected, the Foxes goalie doesn't even see it coming. And just like that, we take back the lead 2-1.

The team maintains defense and once I come off the bench for my shift, I'm in a great position. Ashton is out there and snatches the puck, passing it to me. I'm on a breakaway toward the Foxes' net when, out of the corner of my eye, I see one of them skating fast at me, but I'm quicker than him. So I prepare to take the shot, but right before I can, I trip on the stick he throws at me and go down hard, knocking into the goalie and taking the net off the post.

The whistle comes immediately and my new favorite referee skates up to make sure I'm alright. I get up quickly, showing I'm not in any way injured and she makes the call, "Grand Marquee Manticores, number #31 awarded a penalty shot for tripping."

Yeah, definitely my new favorite referee.

Sorry, Bob.

I take up my spot at center ice where Miss Referee placed the puck for me and start meandering slowly towards the opposing net. At the last second, I quicken my pace and the rest happens in a blink. I fake a shot to the left, goading an immediate reaction from the goalie. As he moves off his line, I redirect and put the puck in the bottom right corner of the net with ease.

The crowd erupts into cheers and the score is now 3-1, baby.

SIX

Olivia

THE FINAL BUZZER goes off and the Grand Marquee Manticores win 4-1. After the penalty shot, Ashton, the guy I met last night, scored the final goal with 30 seconds remaining on the clock. He'd recognized me and kept trying to make chit-chat during the small breaks when the ice crew was cleaning up the snow, but I kept trying to evade him. Truth is, I'm not here to make friends, I need to remain fair and objective at all times, and that's exactly what I am trying to convey to these players and coaches.

Brian, the Manticore's head coach, was one of the nicest guys I've met so far. He said he was excited to have me here and looks forward to working together this season. The Foxes' coach took one look at me, saw I was a woman, and promptly continued to ignore me. Whatever, that's fine. I knew some of these guys would have no respect for me, which is why I need to assert myself and make them respect me.

The home team stays on the ice to celebrate their win and wave at the fans. They give the kids closer to the bench pucks and sticks and fist bumps through the railing that separates them. As I start heading off the ice, I turn and take one more look at the group celebrating. I see #31 jumping in the goalie's waiting hug and they look so ridiculous I snort out a laugh and shake my head. Ashton catches me watching and winks at me.

After changing in the referee-appointed locker room, I take my leave. Down the hall is the home team locker room and I quickly walk by it, but I still hear the end of the captain's speech.

"Great job out there tonight, team! I know we've had some struggles in the past, but I am confident this is our season! We're gonna make it to the playoffs, mark my words." They all holler and cheer him on, and I keep moving.

If they keep playing the way they have tonight, they have every chance of making it. The first line is really strong and their goalie is so good, it's like he almost has precognition. He senses where the puck will go and catches it effortlessly, it's incredible to watch. The only reason he got scored on was because they were one man down and the defense was not in position.

As I make it out of the arena, I see a restaurant nearby and decide to get some food and celebrate my first AHL game. The streets are filled with people that have just come out of the game—lots of red, white, and black jerseys, courtesy of the Manticores' fans heading out to bars or their cars. The restaurant is full as I walk in and there are even some people waiting for a table. The host asks me, "How many?"

"Just me."

"There is a 30-minute wait for a table, but I think I see

an empty spot at the bar if you'd rather sit now. It's all the way at the end and close to the kitchen so it'll be loud," he explains.

"I don't mind, I'll take it," I say, my stomach already growling. I usually eat something light a few hours before the game so I don't feel sick on the ice, which means I'm always hungry afterwards.

I make my way through the restaurant over to the bar and admire the decor. The place has a game theme, from video games, to board games, and even arcade. There is a PacMan machine, which you don't see often, and many others I don't recognize. The wall opposite the bar has an entire shelf of board games, from the classic Monopoly and Catan, to the more obscure, or newer board games. I notice that only the people at the booths on the far side of the restaurant are playing games, and the tables are bigger than normal. I wonder if I'd need a special reservation to get those tables and play.

The rest of the walls have posters and art that are video game specific. There are some really nice Zelda and Mario pieces. Underneath, a small plate shows the local artist's name and the price of the print. They're cheaper than I would have thought for the quality of the design.

I take the only empty seat at the bar, all the way at the end, by the kitchen. There are two bartenders, both running around and filling orders as fast as they can. I scan the QR code and look at the menu on my phone, and after about five minutes, one of them heads over my way with a water glass.

"Sorry for the wait, what can I get you?" he asks, leaning in and resting his forearms on the bar, giving me his full attention.

"Can I get the fried avocado nuggets and the bacon and blackberry jam grilled cheese?"

"Sure thing, anything to drink?"

"Some kind of IPA. You can pick."

"I'll get that order right in."

"Adventurous, I like it," a deep voice says behind me. I turn around on the bar stool and come face to face with the Manticores captain. His dark blond hair looks almost brown since it's damp from his shower and he looks incredibly handsome in a blue dress shirt that makes his eyes pop. My mouth is dry as I take him in. My gaze runs over him and I notice his crisp and tight dress pants. *I bet his ass looks amazing.*

That thought makes me blush and I snap my eyes right back to his. I swear he can read my mind because he gives me a smug smirk and says, "You wanna take a picture? I can even turn around, give you the whole view."

I narrow my eyes at him and lift my chin, "No, thank you, I've seen enough." I turn back around to face the bar and right at that moment the bartender places a tall glass of beer in front of me. I pick it up and take a big gulp. What is going on with me? Why am I getting so flustered? Better yet, since when do I ogle and flirt with hockey players? I take a deep breath and tell my gut to settle down. With any luck, he probably left.

"Hey Robbie, your order is almost ready, it's just gonna be a few more minutes," the bartender says and turns around to fill another order.

Well, so much for him leaving. He steps up to my right, leaning in sideways on the bar, his back to the kitchen door, facing me. I can feel him taking me in, although I don't give him the satisfaction of acknowledging him.

After what feels like an eternity, but is probably only

about 40 seconds, I face him and ask, "Can I help you with something, Elliot?"

He gives me an amused smile, his blue eyes sparkling, "My friends call me Robbie."

"We are far from friends, Mr. Elliot," I deadpan.

"Ouch. Mr. Elliot is my father, please don't insult me," he puts both his hands on his heart and feigns hurt. "And I know we just met, but trust me, we'll be friends," he says with an easy smile.

I scoff and shake my head, "I'm here to do a job and be impartial, not to make friends, Captain."

He tilts his head and observes me for a moment, then says, "I don't think the two are mutually exclusive."

"Wow, big words for a hockey player!" Why the hell did that just come out of my mouth? I'm making assumptions and stereotyping this guy when I don't know anything about him. I take a peek at his face and see his smile fading. Well, now I feel like shit.

"Sorry, not sure why I said that," I admit sheepishly.

"It's fine. Hey, did you order the chronic fries? They are delicious," he deflects and looks around the bar and plays with a straw wrapper. Did I really hurt his feelings with that comment?

I swallow and say, "No, I got the grilled cheese." He nods and looks everywhere but at me, and the loss of his attention hits me harder than it should. I was actually enjoying the conversation. Until I ruined it. Why am I so bad at this?

I mentally kick myself and ask, "So, why don't you think the two are mutually exclusive?"

He takes a moment, still folding the straw wrapper until it's a small square in his big hands. I notice that he doesn't like to stand still and for some reason that makes me smile. He finally looks up at me and says, "Because, you being objective and impartial has nothing to do with friendship. You can still have a friendly relationship with players and respect them the same way they respect you, and not have to rule in their favor. Take Bob for example, I've known him for the last five years, and we have a great friendship even though he's sent me to the box dozens, if not hundreds of times. He shows me pictures of his vacations and kids, and I tell him about my life too. We don't hang out outside of the game, but that doesn't mean I don't see him as a friend."

I listen intently and nod. He makes a good point, but I'm not Bob. Bob's probably someone who's good with people. He continues to watch me, waiting for a reply or a reaction. When he doesn't get one, he continues, "I think you made all the fair calls on the ice tonight, and I don't hold anything against you. In fact, I'm glad you're here. You did a great job asserting yourself and making the players respect you out there. We need more women in the hockey world."

I blink at him a few times but still don't say anything. Because what should I say? The truth is I've been wanting to hear that from someone who is not my grandma or my mentor, someone with an outside perspective. Hearing it from him makes me tear up a little, because for whatever reason, I respect his opinion. He's been in the game for so long, he knows what the pressure is like. I look away before he can see tears forming and because I don't know how to take a compliment, I quietly mumble, "Thanks."

I don't know if he hears it, because the next moment, the bartender shows up with my food and a to-go bag for him. "You're all set, Robbie, have a good night."

"Thanks, man," Robbie says with an easy smile. The

bag is dangling from his left hand and his right is still leaning on the bar as he's facing me.

"Well, Miss Referee, it was nice meeting you. I look forward to our next game," he taps the bar twice with his fist and another smile and starts to turn to leave.

Before he can, I swivel in my seat and say, "Don't call me that, I don't like nicknames."

That makes him turn back and I notice his puzzled look, "What should I call you then?"

"Olivia."

SEVEN

Robbie

OLIVIA.

I haven't been able to stop thinking about her since that night two weeks ago at my brother's restaurant, The Arcadian. After a game, I usually grab some food and head home to my two cats. My house is only a ten minute drive north of downtown and by the time I shower at the arena and pick up the food, the highway is nice and clear.

I didn't expect to see her there, and I definitely didn't expect to start a conversation with her either, but I felt this pull that I could not ignore. Her hair was in a braid that was resting on her shoulder, and she had wisps of wavy hair around her face. She was wearing only the littlest bit of makeup and she looked ethereal. Her green eyes were so piercing, I felt like she was seeing right down to my core.

Not only is she incredibly attractive, but she's smart too and I love that she isn't intimidated by me. Most people are, due to my size and the fact that I play a fairly violent sport.

If anything, I should be intimidated by her. She seems tough as nails and she asserted herself with poise during the game. Some of the players on the Foxes team kept snickering and making small comments about her being a woman, but she shut them down immediately by reminding them that she is a game official and has every right to throw someone off the ice if they are being disrespectful.

In the past two weeks, we played five games, three at home and two away. The second away game was in Cleveland and I saw Olivia again.

During the game I said hello to her a few times but only got a nod in return. She was most definitely ignoring me and my attempts at making friends. I'm still not sure why she's so averted to it. Maybe it's because she thinks it'll be perceived as favoritism, but I can't say I've ever had that issue with any of the refs I am friends with. If anything, they crack down on me even harder when I'm being a dickhead and make stupid mistakes on the ice.

After the game, I decided to skip the shower and head straight to the hotel as I was feeling more tired than usual. While Ash, Eli, and Jordan decided to go out, I was in need of a bed. It was pouring rain the whole trip to Ohio and my right knee was flaring up like crazy. I left that part out when I told the guys I was headed back to my hotel room. The last thing I needed was for Ash to make even more fun of me for being old.

Drenched to my bones after making the awful decision to walk the five minutes to the hotel, I entered the hotel lobby only to run into the back of someone. I must have knocked into her pretty hard because she started to fall, but at the last second, I put my arms around her torso and pulled her back into me. Her bag fell off her shoulder to the lobby marble floor and we both stood there for a moment.

My arms were still around her and I slowly pulled them away. "Are you okay?" I asked.

"You smell really bad," she mumbled.

When she turned around I was met by Olivia's scrunched up face and a panicked gleam in her eyes, like she couldn't believe she just said that out loud. She relaxed a bit when she realized it was me. And yes, I did smell really bad since I forgoed the shower. I also probably looked like a wet dog after my encounter with the rain.

I gave her a lazy smile and looked at her more closely. She looked sweaty too, like maybe she didn't shower either after the game. Her hair was in a low ponytail and her green eyes were roaming all over my face.

"You don't smell that great either. Did the ref locker room not have a working shower?" I teased her with a smile.

She rolled her eyes and bent to pick up her bag from the floor before saying, "I usually skip the locker room showers, or wait until all the guys leave."

I never thought about the fact that she has to share locker rooms with other guys. I grimaced my apology and she smiled. She actually smiled. Not more than a pull of her lips to the side, but it was perfect. And it was for *me*.

She looked like she was about to leave so I did my best to keep the conversation going, "Sorry about running into you like that."

"It's fine, I was kind of just standing there, distracted by my phone."

"Are you staying here as well?" I moronically asked.

"As opposed to what? Sleeping under the bridge?" she quipped with amusement in her eyes. I could get behind this feisty Olivia.

"You never know. I don't like to make assumptions."

She shook her head but asked, "Are you headed up?"

I nodded and took this for what it was. An invitation to ride the elevator together.

Once we got in, all I could hear was the water dripping off of me and the buzzing of the panel. For the first time in a while, I felt nervous. I didn't want to say something dumb and spook her away. By the time I figured out a topic of conversation, the elevator dinged, letting me know we were at her floor. She stepped out and said over her shoulder, "Goodnight, Robbie."

"Goodnight, Olivia."

TONIGHT IS ANOTHER AWAY GAME, this time against the Vermont Vortices. I always despise playing against them. They are a bunch of meatheads, and that says a lot coming from another meathead. They always start fights for no reason at all and fake injuries left and right to draw out penalties against us. It's ridiculous.

On the bright side, Olivia will be here tonight. For some unknown reason, I want to impress her and show her I'm not only good at my job, but that I am a decent person too. And maybe, just maybe, I can get her to be my friend.

EIGHT

Olivia

THE ARENA IS PACKED to the brim, which I didn't expect. I did some research and found out that Vermont didn't have a professional hockey team until about four years ago when the Vermont Vortices formed as a lone independent franchise in the AHL. They have been doing fairly well and even made it in the playoffs last year, but they are too hot headed for their own good. They spend a lot of time in the penalty box for taking cheap shots at the opposing team and fighting.

On the one hand, I am ready for some excitement tonight, but on the other, I dread having to assert myself yet again in front of a new-to-me team. So far in the season, I've officiated two Grand Marquee Manticores games and I am starting to learn their quirks, who to keep an eye on, who spends the most time in the penalty box, who starts fights. I've also officiated two games for the Finchton Foxes, and while the coach still looks at me like I have leprosy, the captain and some of the other players have been respectful towards me and easy to talk to. I also officiated a game for the Chicago Bobcats which went surprisingly well. I think that is the first game ever in a professional setting that did not have a single penalty called.

The buzzer goes off, indicating that it's time to start and all of us officials head out on the ice. We skate around, making sure the nets are in the proper position, and get everyone ready for the puck drop. As soon as the national anthem finishes, we get in the center ice position.

"Hi, Olivia," Robbie says in that deep voice of his that I haven't been able to get out of my head since that night at the restaurant. Or the night in Cleveland when he bumped into me and steadied me with his strong arms. I glance at him and find that easy smile on his face, dimples on display and all. I see he has a bit of stubble since last time I saw him. *C'mon Olivia, don't get distracted by his perfect stupid dimples now. You have a job to do.*

"Elliot. As soon as I blow this whistle, you have five seconds to get in position or you're out of the face-off."

"Yeah, Elliot. Stop flirting with the fresh meat, and play the game. I already know I'll wipe the floor with you, but you should at least put up a fight," one of the Vortices players says. Did he just call me *fresh meat*? While that gets my blood boiling, I let it go. The game hasn't even started and I'd rather not make an enemy out of this guy right off the bat. I notice his jersey is #42 and realize he's one of the Vortices forwards, Dustin Mitchell. Based on my research, he spends the most time in the penalty box. No wonder.

Before Robbie can reply, I blow the whistle and since the Manticores are the visiting team, Robbie places his stick on the ice. Right before I drop the puck, Mitchell jumps the gun and places his stick down too, smacking Robbie's out of position. I snatch my hand back and straighten up.

"Out of the face-off, Mitchell," I call out. I can hear the crowd booing already but I'm not going to let this slide.

"The fuck? What for?" he yells out.

"I'm not here to explain hockey rules to you. Move, before I give you a delay of game penalty."

"Goddamn bitch," Michell fumes.

"Hey, watch your mouth," Robbie unhelpfully interjects. I take a deep breath before my feelings get the best of me and I kick them both out. Before Mitchell can reply, the Vortices captain sends him out and replaces him.

And so it begins. We successfully start the face-off this time, and the game is afoot. I spend a lot of time dodging pucks and players, while staying alert and keeping an eye on any ensuing penalties. The linesmen are in charge of calling out offsides and icing and dropping the pucks for any of the face-offs that do not occur at center ice.

Almost five minutes into the game I see one of the Vortices players trip Ashton, so I blow the whistle and call the penalty.

"Vermont Vortices, #15, two minutes for tripping."

The booing that follows is something I expect and have learned to ignore. I know these fans are mad because I've put one of their players in the box. They don't care about the rules of the game, they only care about winning, and I can understand that from an objective standpoint. What bothers me is when the players take out verbal attacks on me. It's one thing for them to say, "that was a stupid call," versus them saying, "you're stupid." Most players and coaches know how to differentiate between the two, but not the Vortices. On his way to the box, #15 yells at me "What are you even doing here? Do you even know what hockey is?"

I ignore him as I get in position to continue the game. At the face-off, the Manticores get the puck and keep the pressure on the Vortices for the first minute of the power play, until Robbie gets a perfect pass and scores. Number 15 comes out of the box and skates by me on the way to the bench. I definitely hear the bitterness in his voice when he calls me a bitch.

There's a small break as the ice crew is out, so I skate up to the Vortices captain and say "Captain, can you get #15 under control? If he verbally attacks me again, I will have him back in the box." I maintain eye contact with him and can see he's annoyed by me, but at least I gave him a warning. If he can't control his teammates, that's on him.

"Yes, ma'am," he says with a nod and skates away. The game is about to reset and I see Robbie skating up to me.

"You okay? Is that guy bothering you?" he asks with concern.

While I'm touched he's noticed and is concerned, this is exactly why I told him we can't be friends. "I know how to do my job, Elliot. How about you focus on yours?" I say and skate away from him, but not before I catch the look of surprise and hurt on his face.

THE SECOND PERIOD goes about the same as the first. While I haven't been any more verbally abused this period, I've also noticed a change in demeanor from the Vortices. They've played extremely physically and have drawn at least two boarding and two tripping penalties. The Manticores are starting to get frustrated too and Ashton has spent the last four minutes of the period in the box for high sticking a rival player. The score is still 1-0 for the Manticores.

I drink some more water and use the restroom before having to head back on ice for the final period. On my way out, I see Robbie lingering in the hallway by the referee locker area.

"Olivia, hey," he says with a serious look on his face while blocking my path. The man is giant, especially on those skates.

I let out a frustrated sigh, because what the hell is he doing? Accosting me at my job? Doesn't he have some speeches to make in front of his team or something?

"What now?" I say, annoyed.

He grinds his teeth and I see a muscle tick in his stupid perfect jaw. He looks nice with a bit of stubble, and his lips look full and soft. Inviting.

Damn it.

Damn him.

I need to stop checking him out.

"Look, I'm sorry if I offended you out there. I wasn't trying to suggest you weren't capable of doing your job. The opposite, in fact. I just," he sighs, running a hand through his sweaty hair. "I wanted to make sure you were okay," he says, looking chastised.

I hold his gaze when I say, "I accept your apology, but like I said, I'm fine. I don't know what you think this is," I gesture between us, "but out there you don't get to question me or my calls. You can disagree with them all you want, but you are a player and I am an official. That is the end of our professional relationship. I don't need you to be worried for my sake."

His shoulders slump, but he nods. His gaze searches my face, and whatever he sees there must placate him because he says in a quiet voice, "Understood, Miss Wilson. I won't bring this up again."

Whatever tether was between us snaps as he walks towards the ice.

NINE

Robbie

WHAT THE HELL *am I doing?*

I've been asking myself that question ever since I met Olivia. I don't know what it is about her, but I am in way over my head. And the worst part is, she doesn't even want anything to do with me.

You are a player and I am an official. That is the end of our professional relationship.

I can't even lie, it stung to hear her say that. In my mind, I thought we were on our way to becoming friends. I thought I would impress her tonight with my charming personality and some light banter, and then I would ask her out for a drink afterwards. I have so many questions for her.

Why did she choose to become a referee? Does she play hockey? Who's her favorite player? Favorite team?

That conversation we just had was the bucket of ice water I needed dumped on my head to bring me back to reality. She's right, too. She doesn't need me intervening in any conflicts, and I don't need to be thinking about her when I'm out on the ice. I need my head in the game.

"Hey man, are you good?" Elias asks as we get on the ice and prepare for the third period.

"Yeah, just got distracted for a moment." I shake myself out and give him a smile right before he skates away to get to the net. I see Ashton and Jordan skating up to me.

"Got any plans after the game?" I ask them.

"Bedtime," Jordan says at the same time Ashton replies, "Going out."

I shake my head, but before I can chastise him, he says, "In my defense, I've cut way back on the drinking. And I'm only going out to see some old friends in town." Since he used to play for the Vermont team, he knows a lot of people in the area. Even some of the Vortices players are old friends of his. Not the nicest guys in the world, but they're not the scum of the earth like Mitchell, so I guess there's that.

"Alright man, just be safe," I say.

"Thanks, Grandpa," Ashton says as we get in position to start the period.

⚒

THE LAST PERIOD has been shit, but we are almost done with only 2 minutes left on the clock. The linesmen call so many offsides and icings that we barely have time to gain momentum on the play. Ashton gets another 2 minutes in the penalty box for holding Mitchell, and Jordan gets checked so hard he has to go down the tunnel and effectively sit out the rest of the game. Hopefully he's just rattled and it's not a concussion or anything worse.

Vortices player #15 got a minor penalty for verbally abusing Olivia, and after he continued to do it, he got ejected from the game. While I understand her frustration with him, I think that was a bad call. Now the rest of his team is angry and fueled up.

Since we iced the puck, the play starts in our defensive zone. At the face-off, the Vortices get control of the puck and they pass it to Mitchell who is close to the net. He catches it and shoots at Elias, but the rebound bounces off. As Elias dives for it, Mitchell slashes at his stick and knocks it out of his hand, then shoots the puck in the net.

Olivia immediately blows the whistle and all hell breaks loose. She calls out goalie interference and announces no goal, but Mitchell is not having it. He's yelling out that the goal was valid and pushes Elias. That's all we need for us to jump on him. No one touches our goalie.

Elias falls into the net and we take Mitchell down almost immediately, but more Vortices players join the scuffle. The linesmen are there to break us up, but this fight has been brewing all night and we are not stopping. Mitchell and another guy drop their gloves and start fighting with two of our Manticores, one of them being Ashton.

Ash and Mitchell are both circling each other and taking cheap shots, but when Mitchell's fist makes contact with Ashton's jaw, he gains the advantage and takes him down, getting a few more punches in. Olivia and the other ref start to lead both of them to the penalty box. She has a firm hand on Ash and he's clutching his nose, which may be bleeding.

I'm skating behind them so I can clearly hear Ashton and Mitchell swearing and yelling at each other but I don't hear what Olivia says to Mitchell. Whatever it is, it makes him rip out of the other ref's grip and turn, fist raised up as if he's about to hit. I can't tell if he means to hit Ashton or Olivia. Regardless, I can't allow either of them to be hurt any more by this asshole, so I step in. Right as I do, I feel his fist collide with my face and my head snaps to the side. I can taste the blood in my mouth, but as much as I want to retaliate, I decide to take the high road. There are so many penalties being handed out after this fight, there's no reason for me to get one too.

Before he can take another shot at me, the two linesmen and the ref escort him to the tunnel. He's out. Olivia takes Ashton to our tunnel as well, then returns to discuss the penalties being handed out.

We get two penalties courtesy of Ashton for fighting and unsportsmanlike conduct. The Vortices get three penalties on account of Mitchell for goaltender interference, fighting, and unsportsmanlike conduct.

A minute and a half left in the game and we are 3 vs 2 on the ice. In this scenario I usually have Ashton and Jordan here with me, but with them out of the game, I have another forward and defenseman assist me in the play. The Vortices pull their goalie to get an extra player and make it even, but thankfully, we keep the pressure off of our net. I score an empty net goal and we manage to run out the clock for the remaining thirty seconds. When the buzzer goes off, the victory, if we can even call it that, is ours.

TEN

Olivia

TONIGHT'S GAME had more penalties and fights than usual. The other officials and I discuss this in the locker room as we take off our equipment and get ready to leave. I wait until the guys have finished with their showers and then take mine. There is so much adrenaline still coursing through me, I feel like my whole body is buzzing.

While I shower, I can't stop thinking about the interaction with Mitchell. One second, I was telling them both to stop talking and to just leave the game, and the next I saw Mitchell whirling around, ready to hit. I can't know for certain if he was going to hit me or Ashton, but from his angle and position so close to me, I can only assume that hit was meant for me. Except Robbie was there. Why would he jump in like that?

I can't imagine he'd do it to protect me. Not after I told him I could handle myself and that he could basically fuck off. But he did protect me, whether it was intentional or not.

For that, at least, he deserves a proper thank you and maybe an apology. I kept thinking the worst of him, but the truth is, he's a really decent guy. I've noticed that he always has his teammates' backs, and if anyone runs into the refs or linesmen, he's there to make sure they are okay. Maybe having someone like that as a friend would not be the worst thing in the world.

By the time I am all packed up and trying to leave the arena, my mind is made up. I need to talk to Robbie.

I don't have any way to contact him so I decide to wait outside the arena by the player's entrance. The players usually take longer to finish up as they sometimes have a team dinner inside the arena, but that's not always the case. I'm hoping I didn't miss him.

※

AFTER TWENTY MINUTES and lots of odd looks from players and coaches exiting the arena, I finally see Robbie come out.

"Robbie!" I say, loud enough he should hear me. But he doesn't. He also doesn't look around, he just takes off at a fast pace. I follow him and call out once again, "Robbie, can we talk?"

He's looking at his phone and shaking his head, and with that motion I see he has headphones in. Well, so much for hearing me, I guess. I pick up the pace, but the man has long legs. I almost have to jog to catch up.

I'm still a few feet away when I notice he slows down at a crosswalk and looks up just in time to see the light for the pedestrian turning green. What he doesn't notice is the car running the red light and heading straight for him.

I drop my bag and start running. I reach out both my

hands to grab him right as he's about to step out in the street. I use all my strength to grab him by his jacket, pull him back and spin him around to face me all in one motion as the black van barrels past.

For a moment, we're both frozen, just staring at each other and breathing hard. My hands are still clutching his jacket and I let go slowly, my eyes still glued to his face. Holy shit, that was close. *What was he thinking?*

"What the hell, Robbie? You almost got splattered by that car. Why don't you watch where you're going?" I say angrily.

He still seems to be in shock because he hasn't uttered a single word yet. He's just staring at me with those wide blue eyes. The corner lamppost is illuminating his face, and I can see how pale he looks. *Jesus Christ.*

I look down and see that he dropped his phone so I pick it up. The screen is shattered into so many little pieces and it looks dead. That means his headphones stopped working too, so I at least know he can hear me now. I take a deep breath and hand him the phone, wincing, "Looks like you'll need a new one."

His hand shakes as he reaches out to take it. He's still dazed because all he says is, "Yeah," as he pockets his broken phone.

As soon as his hand reemerges from his pocket, I grab it and squeeze it tight. I keep my eyes on his dazed face as I release his fingers. Then I grab my bag and turn to face the crosswalk, saying, "We need a drink."

Or five, so I can erase the image of you almost getting hit by a car from my mind.

⨯

THE RESTAURANT we walk to is only a few blocks away from the arena. The place is not too packed, so we're able to get a booth fairly quickly. We sit across from each other and I scan the menu code and scroll through quickly to see if anything sounds good. I look up and see Robbie looking at me. I'm about to ask why he's not looking at the menu when I remember his phone shattered to bits. He still hasn't said anything and his eyes seem a bit unfocused. I can tell that incident rattled him. I take pity on the poor guy and move to sit next to him on his side of the booth.

I lean in close and show him my phone screen, "Are you hungry? What do you want to order?"

He clears his throat and blinks down at me a few times before finding his voice. I expect him to say something like a burger or pizza, but he says, "Thank you, Olivia."

We continue to look at each other and I'm starting to realize how dangerous it is to be so close to him. He smells good, clean, with a hint of cucumber. His dark blond lashes are long and his light blue eyes hold me to the spot. While earlier they were unfocused, they are now clear as the sky. I can feel him observing me closely as well, eyes bouncing all over my face, but lingering on my lips.

Does he feel this invisible bubble around us? It feels like we're two magnets circling each other. Right now, our poles are so opposite, we're bound to attract. Before I can do something stupid like let him kiss me, the waitress comes over to our table.

"Can I get your order in? Drinks?" she says while blatantly checking Robbie out.

I look back at him and notice he's still lost in that field, not paying attention to anyone but me. I swallow and turn to the waitress, "Can we get two of your best IPAs and the sampler appetizer platter, please?"

"You got it," she says as she walks away.

"Hope you don't mind," I turn and say to him, realizing I don't know his typical drink order. I bring my knee up and let it rest by his thigh. He's wearing slacks with a nice cream button up and a dark wool jacket on top. In contrast, I am once again in faded jeans and a sweatshirt with a light windbreaker. I take it off and I throw it across the table onto the other booth seat. I gesture for him to do the same, except instead of throwing it, he neatly folds his jacket and places it beside him.

"Hey," I say, to grab his attention again, because damn if I don't want every drop of attention this man can possibly give. I'm not sure what changed tonight, but seeing him take a punch for me made me greedy. I want to yell at him to never do it again, and beg him to kiss me, because his full lips look so enticing right now. Even with a split lip, this man is drop-dead gorgeous. If anything, I want to kiss him to make it better. *What is wrong with me?*

"Hey back," he says, shoulders slumping a bit as he leans back in the booth to rest his head, but his eyes never leave mine.

"Are you okay?"

"I think so. Thanks to you." He manages a small smile and it nearly breaks my heart. Robbie looks exhausted, like he's been carrying the world around on his shoulders and all he got in return was a near brush with death. I want to make him feel better, but I don't know how. We're not friends, we're barley acquaintances, and I'm not great with most people. But if he can put up with me and my icy attitude, the least he deserves is some compassion.

"How are your teammates doing? Ashton, and the other one that got hurt?" I ask.

He blows out a breath and pulls his hand through his hair, messing it up.

Good Lord, he looks delicious.

"They're okay. Jordan was just a bit dizzy when he went down the tunnel, but he's fine, no concussion. And Ashton was mostly just pissed off at how Mitchell interfered with Elias, our goalie."

I crack a smile. "Your goalie's name is Elias Kalias?"

He shakes his head with a small smile and says with a sigh, "His friends call him Eli, but yes. He's foreign, so we try not to judge him too hard."

I laugh and shake my head. "The four of you seem really close. I take it that applies off the ice as well?"

"Oh yeah, we're thick as thieves."

"Pillow fights, sleepovers, robbing banks together?"

He nods along seriously, "The whole shebang." And then he does something.

He grins.

Oh, that grin.

His straight teeth and cute dimples are on full display. This should be illegal.

The waitress brings over our beers and we both take a few gulps before resuming conversation. I really thought this would be awkward if we ever did hang out, but it's surprisingly easy to talk to Robbie. Maybe that's why I blurt exactly what's on my mind, "Why did you take that punch for me?"

I think my bluntness may have shocked him because he pauses mid drink. It takes him a second to place the glass back on the table and glance back at me. "I, um—I didn't do it for you. Not exactly."

He didn't? That's good, right? But then, why?

Oh…

Oh.

My face is beet red with embarrassment and I avoid looking at him as I say, "Oh, of course. You were helping your friend. Sorry, I just assumed—"

"No, it wasn't just that." My eyes jump back to his face now. "I—of course I jumped in for you. I just mean I would have done it regardless if it was you, or Ashton, or the other ref, because that guy Mitchell is an asshole and no one deserves to be treated with such disrespect," he says hotly, "especially not you."

"You still think that? After I was so rude to you?" I ask.

"You weren't rude, you were establishing boundaries. I'm sorry I didn't accept that the first time around. You said you didn't want to be friends and I should have let it go. Instead, my ego was hurt and I kept pressing the matter," he clarifies.

"What if I changed my mind?" I say, my eyes not leaving his.

"About being friends?" he asks with a hopeful gleam in his eyes.

"Yeah." I swallow and wait for his reply.

After a moment he asks, "Why?"

"Self preservation?" I say jokingly.

"You don't have to humor me just because I had your back out there tonight. I'll do that any time, because it's the decent thing to do," he says seriously.

"I'm not humoring you. I get it now, Robbie. You're a good guy and I can see you'd be an amazing friend. Truth is, I don't have many of those. Definitely not ones close to my age. And it's hard to let new people in. My best friends are my seventy-year-old grandma and my fifty-five-year-old mentor, Jack. Isn't that depressing?" I scoff.

He smiles and cocks his head, assessing me, trying to see if I'm lying.

"I'm not kidding," I say.

His eyebrows raise and he whistles out, "Okay, mind reader. Well, in that case, I would be honored to be your friend." I can tell there's no hint of humor or deception when he says it. I just hope this isn't a mistake.

ELEVEN

Robbie

DO you know how sometimes things feel like they're happening in slow motion? Like everything slows and you can pinpoint the exact moment when a collision is going to happen? That's how this whole night has felt for me.

When Mitchell turned around and raised his fist, I could see it all so clearly, so I reacted as fast as I could. When I felt Olivia's hands grab my jacket and spin me around, I saw with clarity how much my life could have changed in that fraction of a second. When I looked into her gorgeous green eyes as she asked me to be her friend, that's exactly how I felt. Everything slowed and all I could see was *her*.

The rest of the night felt like a fever dream. We talked about anything and everything. She told me about her grandma and her mentor, and how they are really the only family she has left. I swear she's finding a way to make tiny cracks in my heart and slither in through them.

I told her about my messy family and my three best friends. I showed her pictures of my cats and she said she always wanted one but her dad was allergic.

I mentally file away every bit of information she gives me. I find her fascinating and beautiful. And I need to slow it down, because I just became her friend and the last thing I want is for her to run away if I tell her all my crazy thoughts about her. Like how I want to run my fingers through her long wavy hair and pull her in my lap. How I want to push her up against the wall and see how incredible she tastes. How I want to tell her all my secrets and life stories.

We stayed at the restaurant until it closed around 1 AM, and then we walked together to the hotel we were both staying at. We shared an elevator and exchanged phone numbers—I had to write hers down on a scrap of paper from the front desk—and said goodnight. I fell asleep thinking about the slant of her lips and the waves of her hair.

I'm not blind and neither is she. There's clearly some chemistry here, but I'm not about to mess it up by making a move and acting on my feelings. The last thing I would want is to make her uncomfortable. And besides, I want to continue talking to her, getting to know her.

BANG BANG. *BANG!*

I wake with a start. Someone is pounding at my door. I'm tired and bleary eyed as I make my way to the door and open it with a frustrated, "What?" before taking in the sight in front of me. Ash is sporting the world's blackest eye and his whole demeanor is different than his usual cocky one. He's looking at the floor as he says, "Hey Cap, can we talk?"

I gently grab his shoulder and pull him into the room. I grab the phone from his hand, since mine is broken, and tell him to take a seat while I use the restroom. I text Elias and Jordan to come over to my room if they're awake.

I go out and pull a chair so I can face Ashton where he's sat on the bed. "Ash, what happened?" I ask.

His shoulders are slumped and he's looking down at his lap, hands fidgeting. He shrugs. I swear to God, he's a child sometimes. But instead of chastising him, I tap his foot with mine. "Did you come here to brood or talk?"

"I don't know. What am I doing wrong, man?" he replies quietly.

"Who says you're doing anything wrong?"

"You, the guys, everyone," he sighs and I frown.

"Is this about your partying and us joking about keeping you in check? You know we're not serious about that crap, right? We see your crazy potential and we would never judge you for living your life how you want. We'd never turn our backs on you," I say.

"It might be said as a joke, but you're not wrong. It's just —I don't know," he sighs and runs his hands through the longer parts of his fade. "You all have your lives together and you know what you want out of life, and I'm just kind of aimlessly drifting."

He stands up then sits back down. "My only goal in life was to make it into the NHL, and what am I doing? I'm known as the guy with the most penalties and fights. A hothead. No one takes me seriously."

There's a knock at the door and I tell Ashton to hang on to his thoughts. I open the door to let Eli and Jordan in. They take one look at Ash's face and they immediately respond and fuss over him.

"What the hell happened to your face, man?" Jordan asks while taking the chair I was just sitting in.

Elias' face is stony and he stares hard at Ash. He approaches him, tilts his head back with more gentleness than I've ever seen him show, and grunts out, "Who did this to you?"

Ash is quiet for a moment but eventually relents and says, "Mitchell."

We all explode at once.

"What?"

"The fuck??"

"When?"

He pulls out of Elias' grip and lays back on the bed as he says, "Last night. A couple of old friends and I had plans to meet up for a drink after the game. I wasn't planning on having more than one beer, by the way. I already felt like shit after the last fight at the end of the game, so I was hoping to call it a night early. But then, more Vortices players showed up, including Mitchell. I was doing my best avoiding him, but then he started talking shit about you, Cap. He also said some nasty things about Eli. So," he shrugs, "I couldn't let that stand. I told him he's a piece of shit and all he knows to do is fight. He's not even that good of a hockey player. So then he punched me. I didn't expect it so I went down. Hard. I think I might also have a bruised rib from knocking into the bar."

"What happened next?" I ask. I am fucking furious. What the hell was Mitchell thinking, punching another player off the ice?

"The cops showed up and we all got thrown out of the bar and taken down to the station. I called Coach and he came down, listened to the statement I made."

"Did you press charges?" I ask.

He shakes his head, "No, Coach said to leave it at that. I think he plans to bench me for a few games though. I just can't help but feel like I majorly screwed up, when I didn't even touch the other guy."

"What did the police report say? Did any of the witnesses lie and take Mitchell's side?" Jordan asks. Good point, what if they plan to turn this into a vendetta to get Ash suspended?

"No, two of the guys that gave statements were my friends. I was there, they didn't lie."

"Okay. Good," I say, pacing the room. "I'll talk to Coach, make sure you're not benched for too long." He starts to protest but I stop him, "Just enough so that you're back to feeling one hundred percent. I won't have you play with a black eye and bruised rib, alright?"

He looks like a beat up little kid and I feel for him, I really do. Especially after what he told me earlier. "You're gonna be just fine. And as for your reputation, that will improve. You've been making great progress already and we'll support you, always."

He stands up and envelops me in a big hug, "Thanks, Grandpa."

ROBBIE IS THE BEST HOCKEY PLAYER IN THE WORLD

Robbie

Hi. So, quick question. How did you save my contact information on your phone?

Olivia

I added it as Robbie, but now I'm thinking I'll change it to that one annoying hockey player.

I think you mean Robbie is the Best Hockey Player in the World, thank you very much.

Ha. You wish. :)

Ouch. Way to hurt my feelings, prickly ref.

Prickly ref, my new tagline. I like it. I'll add it to my resume.

TWENTY-ISH QUESTIONS

Robbie

Let's play a game of 20 questions. What's your favorite food?

Olivia

What are we, 12? Idk, tacos. What's yours?

Carbs. What kind of tacos?

Are you really wasting a second question on food again? Tacos al pastor. I love pineapple. What is your favorite color?

Hmm, are you also one of those pineapple on pizza kind of people? Because if so, we can't be friends anymore. My favorite color is green :)

I see you've wasted another question on food related topics. Yes, I do enjoy it on my pizza. Don't knock it till you try it. What's your favorite song?

> Damn, you are cruel. That wasn't meant to be another question, just a follow up. My favorite song is AOK. What's yours?

>> Probably Work Song. What's your favorite TV show? And fair warning, there is a right and wrong answer here.

> *Sweats profusely* okay I'm going to go ahead and say Brooklyn Nine Nine. What is yours?

>> Okay, that's a better answer than I expected. I thought you'd say something like The Office (UK) and I'd have to block you. Mine is Schitt's Creek.

> I like your style, miss Olivia.

TWELVE

Olivia
November

TWO MORE WEEKS have gone by and I haven't seen Robbie. We text almost every day, which I didn't expect. He said he would text me the day after we exchanged phone numbers as soon as he got a new phone, but he didn't, and I didn't want to seem too eager for his conversation so I kept to myself as well. A few days later, it was Halloween. I got a picture with the two most adorable cats, both of them dressed up for the holiday. The first one, a black cat, had an orange bow tie around his neck, and the second, an orange tabby had a purple witch hat on his adorable little head.

Since then, I wake up every morning to cat pictures and lots of questions.

I flip through and see the game of twenty questions we've played over the last week over text and realize how much I've already learned about him. I know that he prefers black tea over coffee because he gets too jittery from it, that his favorite movie is *Kill Bill* because he has a big crush on the main actress, and that his favorite song is *AOK*. Now that he knows my favorite show is *Schitt's Creek* and my favorite food is tacos, he's starting to ask more important questions.

> Why did you get into hockey?

While it's an easy question for him to answer—he loved the game ever since he was little, and his parents made sure he got the best training and education—how do I summarize my answer without unpacking all my childhood trauma. Not because I don't want to tell him, but if I'm going to lay my soul bare, I'd rather do it in person.

I text him back.

> How about I tell you in person?

His reply comes immediately.

> I thought you weren't officiating this weekend?

It's kind of cute that he looks up my schedule.

> One of the refs has food poisoning, so they asked me to take his spot. I'm at the airport, getting on a plane to Chicago shortly.

Tonight's game is an hour north of Chicago and I'm actually excited to do some sightseeing. While the AHL covers my travel and stay for tonight, I paid extra and had my flight back changed to Sunday afternoon. That should give me two days in the city to explore. I tell Robbie all of this and he's immediately excited.

> Okay, I have so many ideas and recommendations.

I see the three dots appearing and reappearing a few times and now I'm a little nervous. After a minute or two, I'm surprised by an incoming call from Robbie.

"Hey," I say, a little flustered. "Hi," he says in that deep voice of his, "how long until you board?"

"Oh, another 20 minutes probably. Why?"

"So, I was thinking..."

"Uh-oh. That's dangerous."

"Ha-ha. Very funny," he says, and I swear I can hear his eyes rolling. I smile to myself. "I was thinking that I have the whole day off tomorrow since there's not a second game against the Bobcats and if you want, I can show you around the city," he says all of this rushed, like he's nervous I'll say no or something. *As if.*

I let him stew for a moment and say with a smile, "And what makes you qualified to show me around?"

"I lived in the city for two years while I was in the NHL. You know, before I got injured and tanked my whole career, of course," he says with a laugh that has just a small hint of sadness in it. I knew about his past in the NHL even before he told me. I may have googled him in a moment of weakness.

"Okay, I think that could be fun. As long as you take me to all the best food spots, I'm in," I say. I may have told him of my love of food and exploring new dishes.

"What am I, an amateur? Of course we'll hit up all the good food, maybe a speakeasy. How do you feel about crappy rental hockey skates?"

"Love them, of course."

"Perfect. We can skate at the ribbon. I know it's not even the middle of November yet, but they open the rink early."

"Ice skating, good food, and speakeasies. Sounds perfect," I chuckle.

"Good. Can't wait to see you, Olivia." The way he says my name has me catching my breath.

The gate attendant calls out that boarding is now open for my flight, so I say, "I gotta go, Robbie. See you tonight!"

"Have a good flight."

I DON'T GET to see downtown Chicago since the airport is outside of the city. The hour train ride north of the city is packed with people, some wearing Bobcats jerseys who are clearly headed early. The game doesn't start for another two hours, but my travel arrangements were made last minute so I can't complain—I'm just glad to be here. My hotel is within walking distance to the arena, so I quickly check in and head over to get ready.

My pregame ritual includes some much needed stretches and ample time to put on all the equipment. Most fans think anyone can do my job, some even make comments about it, but the truth is, it's really hard. Unlike most players that get a few minute shifts on the ice, the officials don't get to take breaks or rotate. We are on our skates the whole time. And unlike the goalie, we have to skate around the players and keep pace. Lots of times we have to dodge pucks and even jump out of the way to avoid collisions with players.

I stay in shape by playing hockey, keeping up with

cardio exercises, and doing *lots* of leg workouts. While I am a tall gal at 5'8", the rest of my body is fairly average. My legs are strong and toned, but my stomach is soft and I'm not exactly flat-chested. The uniform hides most of my curves though. I'm glad I chose to be a referee, but even with my size, I don't think I could break up fights among all these giant hockey players.

While I stretch, my mind keeps drifting away to Robbie. He must be here already. *Is he getting ready? What are his pre-game rituals? Does he listen to music like I do to get pumped up?* I'll have to ask him tomorrow.

"WELL, WELL, WE MEET AGAIN." I turn on my skates and see Ashton casually circling me, a big smile on his face. "How's it going?"

I'm skeptical as to why he's being friendly. Outside of that first night in Grand Marquee, he and I haven't really spoken much. Some quips were made here and there during games, but that's it. Even when he got into that fight with the Vortices, he didn't really speak to me as I escorted him to the tunnel.

"I'm good," I say wearily.

"Got plans tonight?" he asks unabashedly.

"Um, not really, no," I continue, but don't ask any follow up questions.

"Want to hang out?"

Excuse me? Did he just randomly ask me out?

"We've had this conversation before, Ashton. I believe I said no the last time as well?" I ask, eyebrows raised.

"Actually, I said I wanted to get to know you better, and you said, and I quote, *I'm not from around here, so it's not like you'd have made a lasting friendship anyway.* You didn't technically say no, you just assumed you'd never see me again," he says with a grin.

Well, he's not wrong. But that doesn't mean I want to date him. He seems like the kind of fuckboy you read about in books, maybe even has a girl in each city he visits. While attractive, I can't say he's my type. I don't even know if I have a type. My one and only boyfriend had light brown skin, brown eyes, and black hair that was always cropped short. And oh, yeah—an opinionated mother that kept intervening in our relationship.

I'm not bitter about that, not at all.

"Well, let me clear that up for you," I say, lifting my chin and smiling, "the answer is no." Then I skate away and notice Robbie looking at me.

Now, there is someone I am interested in. I don't know what it is about him. I find plenty of people attractive, objectively speaking, but there's something else that pulls me into Robbie's orbit. He's the exact opposite of my ex, from his appearance and stature, to his personality and career.

I've never really thought about what settling down would look like for me. My goal is to get to the NHL and that's what I intend to do. My ex couldn't handle that and he dumped me, and while I was heartbroken at the time, I understand now that he never would have supported me. He wanted a stay-at-home wife that would raise his children and host parties for his rich friends. That would never be me. I'm too antisocial and grumpy to put up with that. As for kids, when I do settle down, I would like them to have a father that cares about them more than he cares for his money and social standing.

As I skate by Robbie I make sure to give him one of my best smiles and say, "Hello, Captain." I don't wait around for a response, but I do notice the way his throat bobs on a swallow and the way his head turns to look at me.

THIRTEEN

Robbie

WE LOST 3-2 to the Bobcats, but I couldn't care less. *Okay, that's a lie.* I care a *little bit*. This should have been an easy game, but apparently the Bobcats have some overachievers on their team this season. But we did the best we could under the circumstances. I told Olivia to wait for me after the game so we could discuss plans for our day in the city.

I see her sitting on a bench by the player's exit area. Her equipment bag is propping her feet up and she's wearing thick black leggings and a sweatshirt that drowns her figure. Every time I've seen her she's worn a faded sweatshirt, and this one is a light gray and has the original six hockey teams and all their logos on it. I search her face and notice her eyes are closed and she's clutching her phone in her hands.

My chest constricts and I feel bad for making her wait when she's clearly exhausted. The hotel we're staying at is fifteen minutes away, so I unlock my new phone and order us a ride share. Then I slowly approach and sit down next to her. I gently bump her shoulder with mine and she opens her eyes. They focus in on mine, and I can say I am thoroughly, completely *fucked*.

She's so goddamn pretty it physically hurts. Her green eyes are dark and I notice a few freckles on her nose and cheekbones that I haven't before. Her lips part in surprise as she sees me there next to her but she doesn't straighten up. She continues to rest her back and head on the wall and I mirror her.

With a soft smile I say, "I made lots of plans for us tomorrow, but if you need rest I can adjust some of them." She starts shaking her head before I can even finish the sentence. "Are you sure? You look tired."

"I'll be okay. It's only ten right now, I'll get plenty of sleep as soon as I can get up and walk to the hotel."

"I ordered us a car. It should be here in five minutes," I say looking down at my phone.

"You didn't have to do that," she says, looking at me with gratitude.

I shrug and say, "You looked tired, so I got your back".

Oh shit, was that the wrong thing to say? Why are her eyes glassy, like she might cry? My own eyes widen, but before I can backtrack or say anymore stupid shit, I'm met with arms around my neck.

I've always loved hugs, but Olivia's hugs? *Incomparable*. She squeezes me tight like she won't ever let go and I can't help but reciprocate. I bring one hand up to her head and gently rub the back of her neck as she tucks her nose under my chin, right at the base of my throat. My other hand rubs small circles on her back and her grip turns from tight to melting. After a couple minutes of just holding her, I get a notification that our car is outside. "Car is here. Are you asleep?"

"Hmm, no. But I could be. You give nice hugs," she says in a tired voice. I have to say I didn't expect her to be so into physical touch. Or maybe it's just because she's tired and I shouldn't read too much into it. I give her one more squeeze and break us apart, then grab her bag and sling it over my shoulder. I offer her a hand and she takes it, and we walk to the car together.

The driver doesn't try to make small talk, which I always appreciate. So instead, I focus on Olivia. As soon as we get in the car, she puts her head on my shoulder and I swear I feel actual butterflies in my stomach.

Since when do I get butterflies? I am a grown ass man.

I like that she feels comfortable enough around me to let down her barrier like that. *She trusts me.* It makes me feel like the most special guy in the world.

"Olivia," I say, gently moving the hair out of her face, "can you stay awake? The hotel is very close, we'll be there shortly."

"I'm awake," she mumbles and I chuckle at her. "Don't laugh at me, I had a long day."

"I know you did. Are you sure you don't want to cancel tomorrow?" I ask, deep down hoping she says no, because I want nothing more than to spend time with her. But not if she's this tired.

My question makes her more alert, so she sits up fully. I instantly feel the loss of her on my shoulder and mentally kick myself for opening my mouth. She looks at me and narrows her eyes, "Are *you* trying to cancel tomorrow?"

"No, of course not," I say immediately.

"Okay, then we're good. So tell me, what did you plan?" she says mid yawn.

"Well, I figured we can head out around 7 and grab some breakfast."

"SEVEN?? Like, AM??" she says.

I laugh at her dumbstruck expression and say, "I take it you're not a morning person?"

"Nooo," she groans and her lips get all pouty and adorable. *Kissable*. Aw hell, not this again. I shake my head and stop looking at her lips so I don't do something stupid like grab her by the waist, pull her in my lap, and kiss the hell out of her. I want so badly to mess up her hair and run my hands over her thighs. I need to stop having these thoughts. She's just a *friend*. A brand new friend at that.

The car comes to a stop in front of our hotel so we get out and I grab her equipment bag from the trunk. She tries to take it from me now that she's more alert, but I playfully slap her hand away. She scoffs and says, "I can carry that myself, you know."

"I know," I say with a smile and start walking away from her. She shakes her head but follows me inside the lobby. We head to the elevator and she punches in her floor number.

"Okay, I'll be ready at 7 AM, but I will need coffee before I can even attempt to make conversation with you. And I will be very grumpy until I have breakfast." My eyebrows go up and I smile at her. She shrugs and says "Just a fair warning, I'm quite grumpy when hangry."

"Don't worry, I planned for everything."

"What else is included in that everything?"

"Hope you're not afraid of heights, because after breakfast, I'm taking us to the John Hancock tower and the ferris wheel. Then we have lunch at a ramen place, some shopping on Magnificent Mile, maybe an architecture boat tour.

Then we can end the night with dinner and a drink at a really nice speakeasy."

"Wow, that's a lot," she frowns and then goes quiet for a moment. We get to her floor and she leads me down the hall to her room.

"Is everything okay?" I ask, confused. I thought she was fine with me planning everything, but maybe I've taken it too far.

"I don't know," she says, peeking at me and then looking away before she pulls out her room key and fidgeting with it.

"You can tell me. If there's something you don't want to do, I can cancel it."

"It's not that—I just—" she fumbles with her words and there's some pink in her cheeks now. She sighs and says quietly, "I don't know if I can afford all of that."

Oh.

Right.

I didn't even think about what her financial situation could be like. Shit, the last thing I want is to make her feel uncomfortable.

I clear my throat and drop the bag at our feet as I face her, "I'm sorry, I should have asked before making all of these plans. I assume you would kick me in the balls if I suggested I pay for everything?"

"Don't you dare," she says, giving me a death stare.

I put my hands up and say, "Fair enough, I would probably feel the same if someone did that to me." Her expression softens but she looks a bit sad now. I am absolutely not letting her cancel this whole trip on me. "How about a compromise?" I hear myself say. My head is spinning with ways I can make this simpler and still take her to all these cool spots.

"What kind of compromise?" she asks hesitantly.

"Well, what if you pay for breakfast and I pay for dinner? And for lunch, instead of another restaurant, we just grab some hot dogs from a food cart? And we choose between the tower and the ferris wheel. And instead of a boat tour, we just do the architecture tour on foot?" I say all of this really fast and take a deep inhale while I wait for her reply.

She seems to consider it, but she is biting her bottom lip. It takes all my willpower not to reach out and touch it with my thumb. "I guess that would be fine. But I feel like you paying for an expensive dinner is not comparable to me paying for breakfast."

"There's no way I'm not taking you to that speakeasy. You will love it, trust me. And if you're that worried about it, we don't have to do a full dinner. We can just share something," I say hopefully.

She holds my gaze for a moment and gives a quick nod. "Okay. Thank you, for compromising."

"Of course," I say honestly, "I just want to hang out with you."

She gives me a small smile and a quick 'thank you' hug, then opens her hotel door. She grabs the bag at our feet and I say, "Goodnight, Olivia."

"Night, Robbie."

I smile wide the whole elevator ride to my room and have the best sleep I've had in a while.

FOURTEEN

Olivia

ROBBIE IS at my hotel door at 7 AM sharp. I have to admire his tenacity and punctuality, but this is still way too early for me. I'm a night owl and I would sleep until noon every day if given the chance. I'm sure my grumpy face reflects my thoughts, but Robbie is not put off by me. He gives me a bright, big smile that brings out the dimples I'm so obsessed with. The ones I've started to see in some of my dreams.

"Good morning, sunshine," he says, handing me a big cup of coffee. I frown, but take it from him and give it a sip. Of course he got my coffee just right, damn him.

"Morning," I say groggily and close the door behind me. We head to the train station and I steal glimpses of Robbie. He hasn't tried to make small talk since he knows I'm not in the best mood, but he also doesn't seem upset about it. He's got a smile on his face and sips quietly on his coffee as we walk side by side.

While I appreciate him giving me the space I clearly need to become a functioning human being this morning, he shouldn't have to compromise yet again. He already made a lot of changes to our plans that I feel bad about. The least I can do is talk to him.

"So, how come your besties have not been invited on this day trip?" I say. *Besties? What is wrong with me? Can I ever hold a normal conversation?*

He laughs and says, "Well, Eli was up this morning but he prefers to start his day in the gym. I asked if he wanted to join us later but he said he's meeting an old friend of his from Finland who is playing for Chicago's NHL team this season."

I nod, encouraging him to continue talking. He says, "Jordan is headed back to Grand Marquee early and visiting his parents. And I figured you probably didn't want Ashton around constantly trying to flirt with you." He looks at me to gauge my reaction to the last statement and I decide to tease him a bit.

"Hm, what if I'm in need of some flirting?" His eyes go wide and he looks away from me. I may have said the wrong thing. *This is why I don't hold conversations this early in the morning.*

He doesn't say anything for a while as we get on the train and find some empty seats. In the short time I've gotten to know Robbie through texts and small conversations here and there, I've learned that he loves to talk—constantly. So this silence from him is starting to worry me.

Then he surprises me by saying, "If you want me to call Ash and invite him, I will. It's just that, during some of the games, I got the impression you weren't really interested in him. But, if I was wrong about that, I apologize. I'm not trying to monopolize your time, but just for the sake of being honest—" he pauses and turns his head to look at me, "I was really hoping it would just be us today. Because I like hanging out with you, and getting to know you."

I feel like an idiot. What the hell was I doing, trying to steer the conversation towards flirting? He totally got the wrong impression too. I was hoping *he* would flirt with me, not offer to invite Ash. "I don't."

"You don't like hanging out with me?" he asks, confused.

What?

Oh God, I can't even follow the conversation properly.

I shake my head and drag a frustrated hand over my face, "This is why I don't hold conversations in the morning." I turn to face him in the seat and make sure my message is clear this time, "I don't want you to call Ash. I don't even know why I made that comment about flirting, it was stupid. I'm not even remotely interested in him, by the way." Robbie swallows and my gaze gets drawn to his throat. Is it weird to find a guy's throat attractive?

"Okay, I won't call him then," he says with a small smile.

"Good, don't," I say definitively and tap my fingers on my knee. "For the record, I really like spending time with you too. I don't usually do this—just befriend people. There's a reason I don't have a lot of friends, and I think some of it has to do with how socially awkward I am."

His hand covers mine on top of my knee and I can't help but stare at it, at the way his thumb caresses me. "I don't think you're socially awkward. I think you like to keep to yourself and you're quiet. Except for when you start to let people in. Last week, you sent me a ten minute voice note about how much you love hockey. I think you do just fine at making friends if they're the right ones."

I nod and turn my hand so that it now lays flat underneath his. We're both caught in this moment, just looking at our hands barely touching. I wonder what he'll do. Will he lace his fingers through mine? Will he continue to caress my hand? I don't get to find out because the train stops for one of the stations and we both involuntarily lurch apart.

ROBBIE WAS RIGHT. Breakfast was delicious, and it was definitely what I needed to get me out of my pit of hangryness. After walking around The Loop for most of the morning and getting another coffee, we then went to the John Hancock Tower. From the very top, we could see Lake Michigan and part of Illinois and Indiana. If it were a clearer day, we could have seen part of Wisconsin and Michigan as well according to Robbie. I've never been in a city as big as Chicago, and I have to say I love it. The bustle of it, the fact that there are so many options for food and stores, the gorgeous architecture, I love all of it.

After the tower, we walked around downtown and Robbie gave me as much information about the architecture as he could. My favorite building was definitely the Chicago Tribune tower, with its neo-gothic architecture.

We then went down to the pier and, just like Robbie said, there were hot dog carts. So we ate our Chicago dogs as we walked down the pier and saw the ferris wheel.

Without realizing it, the day went by and we now find ourselves at the ribbon to ice skate. The sky is getting darker as we are approaching dusk and it's the perfect time to skate. Not only do we get to see the skyscrapers at night, but there are tons of lights illuminating the ribbon.

"Are you ready for the world's crappiest skates to adorn your feet?" he asks with a big smile on his face.

"Absolutely," I say with a serious expression, "you promised me blisters and aching arches. You better deliver."

He laughs and bumps my shoulder on his way to the check in area. He grabs our skates while I get us a locker to leave our shoes in. A short while later, we are ready to hit the ice.

The ribbon is fairly busy, but since we are both professional skaters, we easily dodge kids and people that are learning how to skate. Robbie is skating backwards and taking pictures of me with the skyline as my backdrop and I shake my head at his shenanigans. He trips but catches himself and readjusts his balance quickly.

"Will you please be careful? If you get hurt and have to sit out any games this season, I will be mad," I say.

"Aw, you like seeing me play that much?" he asks teasingly.

"Oh no, you are a terrible hockey player. Just awful. I just won't have anyone to hang out with after games, that's all," I say while batting my eyelashes.

His mouth drops open in shock and he starts skating towards me. I don't realize his intention until it's too late and he picks me up by my middle and pretends like he's going to drop me. "You take that back right now, Olivia," he says, but he's still smiling at me.

My hands fly around his neck and I hold tight as I say, "Never." I give him a big smile back.

"Say I'm the best hockey player you've ever seen," he says, blue eyes sparkling under the twinkle lights.

"I'm sorry, but you are not Gordie Howe. I can't possibly lie to you like that," he twirls me, arms tight around my middle and I can't help but laugh and smile. I can't remember the last time I've been this happy.

FIFTEEN

Robbie

I CAN'T HELP but smile as I watch Olivia's reaction to the speakeasy I brought her to. While the Gilt Bar is a sultry upscale bar and restaurant, the best part about it is the secret library hidden in the basement. I called ahead and made a reservation since the place is incredibly popular, and now I get to watch Olivia's awed expression.

While texting a few weeks ago, she told me she loves books and that growing up, whenever her dad was at work and she had spare time, she would always be in the library. One of her favorite part time jobs was as a librarian. I couldn't get *that* image out of my mind for a while after she told me.

Olivia gapes at the decor of The Library. The lights are dim but we can clearly see the vintage art, the velvet booths, the fringed chandeliers, and best of all, the books that fill the surrounding walls. "This is incredible," she whispers.

"I told you we couldn't skip the speakeasy," I say and place my hand at the small of her back to lead her to our booth.

As we take a seat, she frowns and looks around. "Why didn't you tell me it was this upscale? I would have dressed a bit better." I take a look at her casual blue jeans and light brown cable knit sweater that she's had all day under a dark green windbreaker.

Oh darling, you look perfect.

Her eyes snap up to mine and her lips part in surprise.

Shit.

Did I say that out loud?

Before I can say anything else, the waiter takes our drink orders and leaves us to ponder over the menu. I clear my throat and look at the appetizers. Everything sounds delicious and I know I made a good choice coming here because Olivia groans and says, "Can I just live here?"

I chuckle and say, "Here, as in Chicago?"

She shakes her head, "No, here in this bar. Look at it, it's perfect. All of this food sounds amazing, and the books... the books, Robbie!!"

"I don't think you can live in a bar, but I can see you having a library room in your house."

"Maybe one day," she sighs wistfully.

WE FINISH our appetizers and are waiting for our dessert when I decide to bring up an earlier question. "So, you said you'd tell me in person. What made you choose a career in hockey?"

She rests her chin in her hand and offers me her full

attention and a small smile. "My dad," she says, "he was a huge hockey fan and wanted me to go pro. I had just got into college when he died in a car accident. I thought about not going and just finding something else to do with my life, but I couldn't. There wasn't anything I loved more than hockey, and I couldn't let my dad down."

"I'm so sorry. I can't even imagine what it's like to lose a parent so young," I say, thinking of my own family.

She shrugs but I can tell this is a heavy topic for her so I continue, "You don't have to tell me if you don't want to. If you're not ready to talk about it."

"No, it's not that. I don't mind telling you, it's just depressing," she gives me a self-deprecating laugh as she folds a napkin with her free hand.

I reach over and place my hand over hers, squeezing. "You can tell me anything, I promise I won't ever judge or make fun of you."

She swallows hard and squeezes my hand back before letting go, and she tells me everything about her childhood: her mom leaving when she was only ten years old, how hard it was to lose her dad at eighteen, and how she chose to become a ref.

"During my senior year of college, once I realized that I didn't really have what it takes to make it pro, I had to make some decisions. My major was sports marketing, but I hadn't gotten an internship the previous summer and the job market wasn't that great at the time. So as soon as I graduated, I signed up for a summer ref training camp. That's where I met my mentor Jack. I probably wouldn't be where I am today without his guidance."

I nod and say, "It's important to have connections and people to help guide you. My friend Alex wants me to start a nonprofit for youth hockey with him in Grand Marquee.

He and I have volunteered a lot during the offseason with some other groups in the state."

"That's incredible. Are you going to do it?" she asks.

I sigh, "I really want to. But to get it started from the ground up would mean I have to retire. If I'm doing it, I'd like to go all in, so I'm considering it."

She nods, "I can see you doing it. You have the patience and personality for it, and I'm sure you'd be a great mentor and coach."

Her answer fills me with pride and I smile at her, "What is your long term plan, then? NHL officiating?"

She nods and takes another sip of her drink, "Right now I'm just on a game-by-game contract with the AHL. I'm hoping if I do well I can get a five-year contract, then hopefully get into the NHL. It's definitely an ambitious plan, but I'm determined. And if it doesn't work out, I can always turn to coaching."

I don't know what makes me ask the next question, but I hear myself say, "Do you think you'll want a family?"

She tilts her head to the side and ponders it for a moment. "I think so, if I find the right person. I was almost engaged, actually," she says quietly, looking down at the table.

"Almost?" I ask, dying to know how any guy would get close enough to marrying this girl and fucking it up.

"I was seeing someone in college, his name was Weston. We started dating during my second year there. We were complete opposites to be honest, he was a finance major and came from money. His parents hated me from the start, his mother even accused me of being a gold digger one time.

"But despite his family, I really liked him and we made it work. As graduation was approaching we were discussing the topic of marriage and he mentioned that he had been looking at engagement rings. Of course he mentioned this during one of the dinners we had with his parents, so I was completely blindsided by the conversation.

"He had a job lined up at his dad's venture capital firm but I was at the point where I was questioning if I wanted to do sports marketing. So I mentioned that I wanted to find referee positions as more than just a part time job, and that was the beginning of the end for us. His parents all but said that, in order to marry their son, I had to become a stay-at-home wife or find a respectable job, and I was crushed. They still thought of me as an exploiter, that I was with him for money, and that my hockey was 'just a hobby.'"

She takes a deep breath and wrings her hands on the table. "So, we fought about it for a couple of weeks, and he wanted me to give up hockey. When I said no, he broke up with me. Just like that. No compromise," she says and blows out a breath.

"Do you regret it? Not marrying him?" I find myself asking.

"Not for a second," she says.

"You are incredibly smart and amazing at what you do. If he couldn't see that you are more than someone to parade around at office parties, then he's an idiot," I say heatedly. I am so angry for her. This incredible woman who has been through so much and came out the other side stronger than before.

"And Weston is a stupid name, too," I say to lighten the mood. She laughs at that and nods in agreement.

"What about you? Do you want a family?" she asks, and my answer comes immediately.

"Yes. I grew up with two siblings and lots of cousins. I think I would want a big family, if I find the right person," I say, mirroring her answer.

"I can see that," she nods. I think she means to say more, but our dessert arrives and we get distracted by a delicious chocolate cake.

WHEN WE GET BACK to the hotel, I give her a hug and hold on for more than I should, knowing I'll miss her the next few weeks.

LAST MINUTE

Robbie

I'll be in Minneapolis this weekend for back to back games but I didn't see your name on the schedule.

Olivia

I'm officiating a game in Wisconsin on Friday then I have Saturday off.

Any chance you'd want to come to the game Saturday and hang out Sunday if I stay an extra day?

Yeah, that could be fun. I could make it up to you for showing me around Chicago.

That was my pleasure, no need to repay me. Should I start looking around for things to do?

Actually, how about I plan this one? I know the area better than you.

Sounds like a plan. Can't wait to see you.

SIXTEEN

Olivia

I HAVEN'T STOPPED THINKING about Robbie for the last week. I dream about the way he hugged me and how perfect we fit together, like he was tailor-made for me. When I told him I couldn't afford all the things he had planned for us in Chicago, I wanted to crawl under a rock and never show my face again. It felt humiliating to admit that to him, and I truly expected him to offer to pay for everything or get upset with me and cancel the plans.

When I was dating Weston, I always insisted on paying for my own food and tickets, mostly because his family already thought I wanted him for his money and I needed to prove them wrong. Not that it mattered in the end, but at least I had my principles. But every time he would plan something too expensive and I would tell him no, he would get mad and cancel the whole date. In hindsight, I probably should have seen that for what it was: a major red flag.

I think again about the places Robbie took me and smile

to myself. It was perfect. *He's perfect.* For the past week we've been comparing schedules and figuring out which cities we'll be in together next. While I'm pretty meticulous with a planner, I don't always enjoy planning things ahead of time. I like to just walk around sometimes and discover new places and food. But Robbie is adamant about looking up everything there is to do and see and make some plans ahead of time. We once again reached a compromise that he would do the planning and I would just show up. Except for this Sunday.

I will be in Wisconsin for the first time this season to officiate a game on Friday and then plan to see Jack and his family and return home Saturday afternoon.

When I told Robbie, he immediately went into planning mode and got me a ticket to the Saturday night game. He also planned to get another night at his hotel and booked a flight home instead of leaving with the team bus after the game. Since he has the day off Sunday as well and can fly out in the evening, that means we get to spend the whole day together.

So, instead of him planning everything out, I decided to take it upon myself and show him around the town I grew up in. I want to take him to my favorite taco place, go indoor mini golfing, and maybe even take him to meet my grandma.

I know it sounds stupid, but I really want her to like him. Grams and I are so close, she immediately figured out I had a growing crush on Robbie and insisted I put myself out there and ask him out. But I can't. *Can I?*

What if all this is really just friendship to him?

I don't want to look like a fool.

What if he's got a girlfriend back home?

He doesn't seem like the type of person to stay single for long.

What if he's just getting close because he wants to hook up?

He doesn't seem the type to do that either—and while he didn't tell me any of his dating history during our heart-to-heart last time, he also said he wanted a family.

I'm overthinking again and I need to stop. I need to believe that he's a good person and that he won't break my heart if I let him in all the way. Otherwise I won't ever make progress. I need to talk to him and find an answer to all of these questions swirling around in my brain before I even attempt to ask him out.

And what if he says no?

Then all I can do is hope he'll still want to be my friend and move on.

※

AS SOON AS I ring Jack's doorbell, the door swings open and I'm enveloped in the biggest hug by Bonnie.

"Oh honey, I missed you so much! You are so skinny, have you been eating enough? I made roast chicken with potatoes and veggies and you need at least two servings," she says all this while crushing me to her, which is surprising for a woman of her stature. She's 5'2" with big round cheeks, lots of curves, and a short bob that's mostly silver with black strands peeking through.

I chuckle and say, "I'm okay Bon, although I will never say no to your homemade cooking." The woman makes the best food ever. I usually don't cook because, for one, I don't know how to, outside of the basic eggs and bacon, and, for two, I don't really have the time to cook.

"Well, come in then, it's cold out here," she says and grabs one of my bags. I didn't bring much with me since I'm only spending the night and then heading back home tomorrow, but my equipment is with me.

"Is that Olivia I hear?" Jack says from the living room where he's watching a game of hockey and sipping a beer.

"Sure is, honey," Bonnie says. "Why don't you join him for a minute? The chicken is still roasting. You two catch up and I'll call you when it's ready."

Jack stands up and gives me a hug, patting my back affectionately. I really missed him, and I feel bad for not reaching out more.

"Good to see you again, kiddo. How is the new job?"

I smile, "It's really good, I can't thank you enough for recommending me. Seriously."

He shakes his head but smiles at me, "I just nudged you in the right direction. You have a good head on your shoulders and you know how to use it."

I nod but worry my lip, which he notices immediately, "What's that face for? Any troubles?"

"Not really. So far coaches and players have been respectful and the insults haven't been too atrocious. But, there's this one team that I'm a bit worried about. The Vortices. While the captain seems decent, the rest of the players are misogynistic and unnecessarily violent on the ice." I blow out a breath. "I'm not sure what to do to de-escalate the situation sometimes."

"Well, I know this is going to sound strange, but maybe try to not engage as much with them. Sometimes you need to let fights happen and assess the mood of the game. Let's say the play has been going on for about a minute, and things are getting intense, and maybe you see a minor penalty; holding, for example. Sometimes, it's best not to call something like that for the sake of the game flow. I know you want to make the right call all the time because you're a people pleaser, but sometimes you need to make some choices in the moment, even if they anger the opposite team or the fans. Their anger is not your concern." Jack says all of this slowly, making sure the advice sticks with me.

"Dinner's ready!" Bonnie calls out from the kitchen and we both head to the table. I ponder the advice he gave me for the rest of the night and on the bus ride home. Maybe it's time to take a different approach when it comes to the Vortices.

⨯

THE MANTICORES WIN 4-0 the next day and all the players are ecstatic as they head out of the arena and toward the bus that will take them back to Grand Marquee. Except for one player. Beautiful blue eyes meet mine as soon as he spots me leaning against the wall by the players entrance and for a moment, my heart stutters. Is he getting more attractive every time I see him? He looks incredible. He's freshly shaved this time, and his hair is getting a bit longer and curling at his ears and nape of his neck.

He gives me his signature Robbie smile, dimples and all, drops his small duffel bag, and picks me up for a hug. My hands immediately move around his neck and I squeeze tight. We've talked every day this week over calls and texts, but I didn't have this. His presence, his warmth.

"Hey, I missed you," I say.

I can hear the smile in his voice as he says, "I've missed you too, Olivia." My feet touch the ground and the hug ends but I'm not ready to let him go yet. So I wait for him to pick up his bag, then link my arm with his and guide him towards my car.

"Do you want me to drive you straight to your hotel? Or should we get some food first?" I ask.

"Um, about that." I look up at him and notice that his cheeks and top of his ears are pink. "I meant to make the reservation on the way here yesterday, but got completely sidetracked. And then I asked about extending my room here downtown but they were all booked for tonight," he rambles on while I look at him, shocked.

"So, anyway, I technically don't have a place to stay, but I'm sure there's something between here and your house that we can find. Like a motel or something," he trails off as he takes in the expression on my face and his eyes widen.

"You're mad, aren't you?" he asks softly.

My hand drops from his arm so I can dig around for my keys and he frowns as he looks down at it. Am I mad? That he doesn't have a place to stay? No. I'm embarrassed about what I'm getting ready to offer, because there's no way I'm letting him stay in a crappy motel on my side of town.

"I'm not mad. I promise," I say, making sure to hold his gaze so he knows it's the truth, "I'm just a little caught by surprise. You can obviously stay with me tonight, I have a spare bedroom, I just didn't expect to show you my house. It's not exactly in the best shape, or neighborhood," I gaze down so he doesn't see the embarrassment and tears pricking my eyes.

"Olivia," he takes a step towards me and his hand reaches up to cup my face. Slowly, his fingertips make contact with my jaw and chin and he tilts my head up so I can meet his eyes. He looks sad. "I'm sorry," he says.

"For what?" I breathe out. I think. My mind is blissfully blank right now as I stare into his gorgeous eyes.

"For making you feel bad over something you have no control over. I didn't do this on purpose, just so you know. I truly did forget to make the reservation. And I completely understand if you don't want me in your house. We can find some other accommodation for me. But I need you to know, " he says, eyes sliding to my mouth for a second before returning to mine, "that nothing you could possibly say or show me would make me think any less of you. I wouldn't judge you for the condition of your house."

I relax more with his words. "Unless you lived in a cave or something. That would be weird and I would totally nope out," he jokes and it makes me smile. His thumb traces up and rubs the dimple in my left cheek. I lean my head into his palm more and he brings his other hand to my back, pulling me into a hug. I rest the right side of my cheek on his chest, right above his heart and I feel him softly kissing the top of my head.

"No cave, I promise. And I do want you there," I say quietly as he nods against me.

"Okay. How about we get some food to go?"

"Sounds perfect," I say as we break apart and get in my car but I don't miss the way his fingers linger on me, like he wants to hold me longer.

AFTER EATING pizza and having lengthy conversations about both of our games this weekend, we are both lazily lounging on my beaten up couch. Robbie is sitting at one end, his legs up on the ottoman, and I am sitting at the other end, my legs tucked underneath me, my head propped in my hand on the back of the couch as I watch him.

He's very animated when he gets excited about a topic, and that makes me smile. I've started to notice lots of things about Robbie that make my stupid little heart stutter recently. Like how he talks with his hands and always tilts his head a little bit to the left when he's giving me his full attention. Or how he always leaves generous tips when we get food or drinks together. But my favorite part about him is how his eyes light up and a smile takes over his face as he talks about his volunteer work with youth hockey teams.

"Sorry, I'm talking too much, aren't I?" he says after catching me looking at him too long.

"Not at all, I like it when you talk," I say.

"Are you sure? You know, you don't have to be polite with me. You can just tell me to shut up. I grew up with two siblings who were just as annoying as me. I learned a long time ago not to be offended when someone tells me I'm being too much," he laughs, but it's a sad one, and I can't help but think how wrong all those people were.

How dare they tell him he's too much? *He's perfect.*

"You're perfect," I tell him, just like he did back in Chicago, although I don't think he meant to say that out loud. He looks at me the same way he did that night too, soft and thoughtful. He blinks at me a few times and I can see how tired he is after a long weekend.

"I think it's time to go to bed," I smile and get up. I move to the linen closet by the bathroom and grab two pillows, sheets, and a big fluffy blanket for him. When I turn, I see he's standing as well, cleaning up the pizza plates and glasses we used earlier. "I can do that, you don't have to."

"I want to help," he says and heads to the small kitchen. I take the pillows and blanket to the spare room and make up his bed. I can't help but think he doesn't belong in this place. Not because I think he has high standards and would never live in a crappy house, but because he's just too beautiful, he deserves better.

I could see him taking in the small living room when he

first walked in, with the old, worn out furniture, and carpet stains that have been there for years because I couldn't afford to replace it. I expected him to look disappointed or to pity me, like Weston did when I first brought him to my house. But instead, Robbie smiled as he looked down at me and asked "Where do you keep all your hockey memorabilia? I need to see it."

I hear his footsteps down the hall and when I turn back I see him leaning sideways on the door frame watching me. He crosses his arms and part of his shirt rides up, giving me a glimpse of well-defined muscle. He looks so good in his athleisure black pants and T-shirt.

Did I imagine him? Make him up in my mind after reading too many romance novels?

"You didn't have to do that for me, I could have made the bed," he says and covers up a yawn.

"You're my guest. Deal with it."

"Well, you are an incredible hostess, Miss Wilson," he smiles and moves into the room, plopping down on the mattress. As soon as his head hits the pillow he closes his eyes and lets out a satisfied sigh. I can't help but stand there on the side of the bed watching him. My fingers itch to reach out and touch him. Anywhere. *Everywhere.* I want to push the long strands of hair off of his forehead and run my hands over his jaw the way he did to me earlier in the parking lot. I want to feel how soft his lips are. I want...

"What did you plan for us tomorrow?" he says, and I realize his eyes are now open and watching me. That soft smile is back on his face as he pats the bed next to him for me to sit.

I slowly perch on the side of the bed facing him and say, "Well, I'll need to skip my league game, but I am taking you to a really delicious diner for brunch, then we'll be mini golfing. Indoors, and glow in the dark," I whisper that last part and notice a dip in his eyebrows.

"Why would you skip your league game?" he asks tiredly.

"Well, you're my guest. I'm not going to ditch you and go play where you can't join. But it's fine, we can do something else instead. There is a museum of illusions around here, that could be fun—"

"No," he says, suddenly sitting up.

"You hate museums or something?" I try to joke.

"Olivia. Are you kidding me? You cannot deprive me of seeing you play hockey. That's not fair. How many times did you see me play?"

"Robbie, it doesn't count as watching you play if I'm there reffing," I say on a laugh.

"Okay, what about yesterday?" he counters.

Well, he's got me there.

"Fine, I've seen you play once," I roll my eyes at him.

"And now it's my turn. You're going to that league game, and you're going to win."

I smile and shake my head at his insistence. "And if I don't?"

"Then we can't be friends anymore," he says with mock seriousness.

"Shut up," I lightly shove him back and he goes without a fight. I stand up and grab the king size fluffy blanket. It gets cold at night and I usually keep the temperature at 65 year round, so I want to make sure he's comfortable. I fluff it up and throw it over him as he turns on his side and burrows in the pillows. I tuck him in lightly and he chuckles.

As I crouch down by his face I notice his eyes are closed, and I finally get my chance. My fingers reach out and gently brush his hair up and to the side. Robbie lets out a content sigh again and the corners of his mouth tug up. He opens one eye to peek at me and I run my hand over it and close it back, "Go to sleep, Robbie. Have a good night."

"Goodnight, Olivia."

I stand up and slowly move to the door, but before I can close it, Robbie says, "Olivia?"

"Yeah?"

"Thank you."

"For what?"

"For letting me in." My heart leaps, because I know he means more than just my house.

"Only you," I whisper and close the door.

SEVENTEEN

Robbie

I WAKE up to the smell of clean, unfamiliar sheets and—is that coffee? I must have slept like the dead because I haven't heard Olivia make any noise in the hallway or the kitchen. I reach for the nightstand where I left my phone but something is stopping me from reaching all the way. I look down and realize I am completely tangled in the big fluffy blanket she tucked me in last night.

I hope last night really happened and that I didn't just dream it. The way she let me in, I could tell it was hard for her, but I am so damn happy she trusted me enough to bring me into her home and tell me stories of her childhood. And the way she took care of me and brushed the hair out of my face as she was saying goodnight made my heart leap. I wanted to tell her to stay, to join me and cuddle me to sleep, but I know we're not there yet.

Once I'm disentangled from the blanket, I reach once more for the nightstand, but instead of my phone, my hand brushes against a framed picture. I realize it's a photo of young Olivia and a tall man with an impressive beard and mustache. He's proudly got an arm around her narrow shoulders while she holds up a trophy that says, 'Little Olive'. Smiling to myself, I place it back on the nightstand.

I grab my phone and look at the time. Shit, it's eleven already. I never sleep in like this, and while I was exhausted and clearly needed the sleep, I am kicking myself for not setting an alarm. The whole point of me staying an extra day was to spend it with Olivia not sleep the day away. I quickly get up and rummage through my overnight bag for some fresh clothes and toiletries, then head out to the bathroom.

My hair is a bit messy from sleep but at least I don't need a shower so Olivia and I can get on with our plans for the day. I find her in the kitchen scrolling on her phone, a cup of fresh coffee nearby. She looks beautiful. The light coming from the kitchen window makes her brown hair shine brighter. She's wearing black jeans and another cable-knit sweater, this one not brown, but dark green. She even has some makeup on, which is surprising because she usually doesn't wear any. Not during games at least.

"Good morning," I say while slowly moving into the small kitchen.

"Hey, how did you sleep?" she says with a smile and stands up from the table.

I rub the back of my neck and admit, "Really good, but you shouldn't have let me sleep in so late."

"Why?"

"Because, now I have even less time to spend with you," I say as I look at the collar of her sweater. There's a small hole there that draws my gaze. So I take in the rest of her sweater and notice it's seen better days. The cuffs are a bit frayed and the color is a little faded. I wonder if she keeps wearing it because she likes it or if she simply can't afford new clothes. I knew she was being frugal, but I thought that was because eating out all the time is expensive. Now I wonder if there is more to it.

"I'd rather have you well rested than exhausted," she says, breaking me out of my thoughts. I notice she moved to the coffee pot and is now holding out a cup for me.

"Thanks," I take a few sips and turn towards her, each of us leaning into opposite counters. With how narrow the kitchen corridor is, I can extend one foot and tap hers with it, which I do. "So, what's the first thing we are doing?"

"Well, I was going to take us to one of my favorite diners, but they get really busy around this time. So, I was thinking," she says, tucking her hair behind her ears with both hands, "my grandma called me earlier and said she is making French toast casserole with bacon and eggs. So if you'd be okay meeting her, she invited us over." She nervously peeks up at me.

A big smile takes over my face. Aw, hell. She wants me to meet her grandma? "That sounds delicious. What are we waiting for?" I say, patting my stomach.

She laughs and says, "Finish your coffee, then we'll go."

FORTY-FIVE MINUTES later we are in front of a small townhouse knocking on a bright pink door. After telling me that Sunday brunches are tradition whenever she has the day off, I insisted she stop at the nearest grocery store. My mother would kill me if I showed up to someone's house for the first time without a gift.

So here I am, with a bouquet of flowers and a box of

donuts that Olivia assured me were her grandma's favorite. My fingers drum on the side of the donut box as we wait for her grandma to open the door. Olivia notices and looks up at me as she says, "Don't worry, I promise she doesn't bite."

I groan inwardly. Great, now she knows I'm nervous. *But does she know why?* Does she realize that every time I look at her, my breath catches and it doesn't release until her eyes are on me too? Does she feel this pull between us? Does she also wonder what our kisses would be like?

Before I can respond with a joke and make this moment more lighthearted, the door swings wide open and there's a petite woman with white hair and a bright pink apron with donuts on it that greets us.

"Oliviaaaa," she says brightly and squeezes her granddaughter in a bone crushing hug. She then peeks up at me over Olivia's shoulder and gives me a mischievous look. Once they break apart, Olivia moves to my side and touches my arm, the one holding the box of donuts and says, "Grams, this is Robbie."

My mouth is dry and I swear I am sweating, but I manage to clear my throat and stick out the arm with the bouquet of flowers. "For you, Miss Elizabeth," I say and give her one of my brightest, more sincere smiles. But my whole body is tense, because holy shit. This is Olivia's only living family, and here I am being introduced to her. What if she hates me?

Elizabeth, AKA Grams, as Olivia calls her, has both hands on her hips and her eyes narrowed at me. She doesn't take the flowers and doesn't say anything, so I nervously look at Olivia with a look of *oh shit, what did I do wrong* and *dear God please help me out of it*. Olivia's eyes widen and she gives me a small shrug all but saying, *I don't know either.*

But then, Grams starts laughing. Uncontrollably. And there are tears in her eyes as she wheezes, "I'm just messing with you, honey."

We both laugh along, but I'm still a little worried. My shoulders relax more when she takes the flowers from my hands and pats my chest affectionately. "Olivia said you like to joke around so I wanted to see what you're all about."

"Did I pass the test?" I say.

"We'll see," she hums as she turns and leads us inside. The townhouse is just as bright on the inside as it is on the outside. Grams must be a huge fan of the color pink, because it's everywhere. The walls are pink, the flowers on the entry table are also a dark shade of pink, and even the fridge is a pastel pink.

"These are for you as well," I say and place the donuts on the kitchen island.

She saunters over and opens the box and her eyes light up again when she realizes they're her favorite donuts. "Mmm, yes. Definitely passed the test now," she says and reaches for a sprinkle donut and takes a big bite of it.

"Grams, can you please not start with the dessert?" Olivia chides her and Grams rolls her eyes.

She elbows me in the side to grab my attention and says, "Will you get my granddaughter to stop being such a hardass? I swear sometimes she doesn't know how to have fun."

Olivia doesn't hear this as she takes it upon herself to look through cupboards and pull out plates and silverware to set the table. I keep my eyes on her the whole time but tell Grams, "I don't think she's a hardass. I think she's perseverant, and smart, and I think she knows how to have fun with the people that matter to her."

When I don't get a reply, I look down at the adorable

old lady, with chocolate and sprinkles on her face. I try my best to smother a smile at her appearance, but she takes me by surprise as she says, "Take care of her, will you? Lord knows she's been through so much, and not many people have cared for her like they should have."

My heart constricts and for a moment I am angry again, because how could anyone not love her like she deserves to be loved? Fiercely and unconditionally.

I swallow down and say, "I will, I promise." She searches my face for a moment, then nods and springs away to check on the casserole.

I feel Olivia coming up behind me and I give her a smile, telling her I'm doing great so she doesn't worry. I help Grams with the bacon and eggs and the three of us have brunch together. Grams of course pulled out orange juice and champagne to make mimosas. While Olivia stopped after one since she's driving, Grams and I are now on our third.

She's been telling lots of stories of Olivia as a kid and I've been absorbing it all with rapt interest. "Would you like to see some baby pictures?" Grams says excitedly.

"Grams, noo," Olivia groans as I say, "I am not leaving here until I do."

"Robbie, why?" she says as Grams heads to another room to look for the album.

"I need to see them, *Olive*. It's a must," I say, leaning into her a bit. When I look at her face, I realize she's not smiling. She seems detached. "Hey, where'd you go just now?"

She looks at me and blinks away some tears. Shit. What did I say? "Sorry, nothing. Nowhere, I'm good."

She's not good. My hand touches her right knee to stall her bouncing and this time I ask more gently. "Did I say something wrong? Is it the pictures? We don't have to look at them if you don't want to."

"No, it's not that," she says softly, "It's just—my dad was the only one to call me Olive. I don't really like nicknames, but I loved it when he called me that." Her shoulders slump and this time a tear escapes her and rolls down her cheek. Before I can second guess myself, I cup her face and wipe her tear away, then give her a bear hug. She sighs in the crook of my neck and I hug her even tighter.

"I'm sorry, I didn't know. I won't do it again," I say.

She shrugs in my arms and bunches my sweater in her fists. "I didn't hate it, I was just caught by surprise. You can call me that, if you want."

"Are you sure? I don't want to make you cry any more than I have," I say with a smile.

She chuckles lightly, "I'm sure. But this just means I get to come up with a nickname for you."

I groan. "Oh, please no. I've had so many over the years and they are all terrible."

"That's the deal. Take it or leave it," she says pausing for effect, "Bob."

"Ugh, no."

"Bobby?"

"No."

"Rob?"

"Gross. No," I say, giving her a mock glare.

"I know the perfect one," she says and pulls out of my arms.

I narrow my eyes at her, "What is it?"

Her eyes are glinting as she says, "*Bobbert*."

I choke on a laugh and shake my head, "We can't be friends anymore."

After half an hour of looking through so many adorable

pictures of Olivia, she finally manages to get Grams to put them away.

"I wanted to see more though," I say with a pout, reluctantly letting go of an adorable picture of her in hockey gear. She must have been around fourteen and she was standing next to her dad after one of her games.

"That's okay, I think you've seen enough," she huffs, but gives me a small smile. She takes the picture and looks down at it mournfully. "I miss him," she admits softly.

I nod and slide my hand from the back of her chair to her shoulder blades where I rub soothing circles. I don't know what to say to make her feel better. I've never had to deal with this kind of grief.

Grams gathers up the album and some of the wayward pictures that are strewn all over the table and puts them away. When she comes back, we are getting ready to leave.

"It was a pleasure meeting you, Miss Elizabeth," I say, taking her hand and bending down to kiss it. The old lady blushes and grabs my shoulders for a swift hug.

"If you so much as hurt her, I will hunt you down all the way to Michigan and make you pay," she whispers in my ear then gives me a pat on the back and lets me go.

Noted.

"I would expect nothing less," I reply, meaning it, too. The lady may look small and frail, but she's got quite the grip.

She winks at me as she gives Olivia a hug and we head to the car.

"What was that all about?" Olivia asks once we're in her car.

I laugh and shake my head. "Nothing. Your Grams is a sweetheart." I smirk to myself.

She nods along and pulls out of the driveway. "You ready for some mini golf?"

I APPARENTLY SUCK at mini golf. Olivia absolutely destroyed me and has been soaking in the victory for the whole drive to the arena.

"Okay, alright. I admit, you are better at mini golf than I am. Happy now?" I groan.

"Yes, thank you, Bobbert," she says playfully and I roll my eyes. She has not stopped calling me that stupid nickname since brunch.

Once we arrive, I notice that the arena is much smaller than the venues we play our professional games at. There is only one rink and one of the logos outside shows the name of a high school hockey team.

I offer to carry Olivia's bag and stick but she just gives me a glare telling me to mind my own business. Okay, point taken. As she was packing it earlier in the morning, I noticed how frayed and outdated her gear was. I think I even saw some holes in her gloves. I wanted to ask her more about her financial situation, but didn't want to make things weird.

We see a few other people heading inside and one of them is a guy with dark hair and an obnoxiously loud voice. He glances over at us and snickers "Look who decided she's good enough to grace us with her presence all of a sudden."

I can see Olivia tense next to me but she doesn't respond. She mentioned she missed a few league games, but this guy doesn't need to be a dick about it. I must not be the only one thinking that because the blonde girl next to him jabs him in the ribs and says, "Don't be a dick, Mark. Glad you could make it today, Liv."

My eyebrows go up and I look over at Olivia and mouth *Liv?* She rolls her eyes and addresses the blonde, "Hey Amelia, thanks. And—" she falters for a moment but after noticing me looking at her she straightens up and continues, "I actually don't like nicknames. I'd prefer it if you just called me Olivia."

The blonde, Amelia, is shocked for just a moment, then she gives Olivia a big smile and says, "Sure thing. Who's your friend?"

"This is Robbie. He's my biggest fan, and he's here to watch me play," she jokes. She's not wrong though. I am so gone for this girl, I would watch her do even the most trivial tasks, as long as I get to be near her.

I've realized this weekend that she doesn't have a lot of people in her life, and the fact that she's let me in makes my heart happy. I want to support her in every way, help her overcome her fears, and make her see that I'm smitten with her.

Mark's comment brings me out of my thoughts as he says, "What, you're not good enough to play?"

I turn my head toward him and slowly look him up and down. He's pretty skinny to be a hockey player and he's about four inches shorter than me. I take my time replying and out of the corner of my eye, I can see Olivia suppressing a smile. "Unfortunately, I didn't come prepared, but I'll make sure to bring my gear next time," I say with a wink at him.

"Alright, we better head in before we're late," Amelia says.

As we head inside, Olivia falls back to walk by my side, so I take a moment to ask what's on my mind "Everything okay? There seemed to be some tension with that Mark guy."

She sighs and quietly says "He's been kind of an asshole the last few times I've seen him. I guess he can't handle a woman saying no to him." Her face is set in a frown and I hate seeing it there after all the happy, smiling moments we had today. So I reach out with both my hands and poke her cheeks up in a smile. Her eyebrows go up as she looks at me but there's a glimmer in her eyes.

"Do me a favor and kick his ass on the ice, yeah?"

"It's a no-checking kind of league, and he's usually on my team," she says dejectedly.

"Switch with someone else. You have a reversible jersey, right?"

"I do. I guess that could be arranged," she lets out a slow smile that makes my breath hitch.

"I'll be out there cheering. Your number one fan, remember?" I smile back.

As I wait for the game to start, I grab some popcorn and a fountain drink from the small concession stand and find a good spot on the metal benches that overlook the rink.

I wave and take pictures as Olivia gets on the ice and skates to my end of the glass. I notice she's playing on white while Mark is on the black team; I smile and give her a thumbs up.

While she says she's out of practice, it's easy to see that she's by far the best skater here. While her puck control could use a bit of improvement, she manages to steal the puck away from Mark and score within the first shift. My girl is determined.

My girl.

When did I start thinking of her as mine?

I close my eyes and let my head drop between my shoulders. I am hopeless. I think I might be in love. And the worst part is, I don't know if she would even want me. While she may accept me as a friend, would she want me as more? What would our relationship even look like? Both of our lives are so hectic.

An hour goes by as I am lost in my own thoughts. I watch Olivia every time she takes on a shift and make sure to stand up and cheer every time she makes an assist or a goal, which is often. Meanwhile, I keep thinking of ways to see her again, and I come up with a plan.

By the time she is showered and changed, I am waiting in the lobby, scrolling through all the pictures I have of her in my phone. There is a perfect one of her skating at the ribbon in Chicago. The skyscrapers are lit up behind her and there are twinkle lights above her as she's mid-turn. Her movement looks graceful but a bit blurry, but the look on her face is my favorite part. It's pure happiness. Her green eyes are bright, her hair is let down and falling softly around her face. And her smile is wide and perfect.

I'm so fucked.

EIGHTEEN

Olivia

I MAY NOT HAVE CHECKED Mark into the boards, but I did metaphorically wipe the ice with him. I probably pushed myself harder than usual and I'll definitely regret the burnout in the next few days, but it was worth it. Because Robbie was there in the stands, cheering for me. I haven't had anyone cheer for me since my dad. While Grams wanted to come to my college games, I always told her not to, making up the excuse that it was too far away for her to drive. And Weston said the fans were too intense for him and he didn't want to stand in the cold just to watch some college team. Why the hell did I date that loser?

After I shower and pack up, I head out and find Robbie in the lobby, looking at his phone with a sad smile on his face. "What's got you down, Bobbert?" I ask, nudging his foot with mine.

He shakes his head, standing up to give me a hug.

"Nothing. You were amazing out there." Is it just me or is he hanging on a bit longer than usual?

"Thanks, it was all for my number one fan," I joke as we break apart but he doesn't take a step away. I look up at him and find that he's not smiling. His expression looks almost like longing. And it feels like his eyes are pinning me to the spot and looking straight into my soul.

"Are you hungry?" he asks, breaking the moment.

"A little. Do you think we have time to get something before heading to the airport?"

Please say yes, I want to spend more time with you.

"We have about an hour, so maybe someplace that is quick," he says in a tone I can't quite make out. He seems sad for some reason. Is it because he's leaving? *I'm sad about that too.*

"I know just the place."

Robbie is quiet the whole car ride to one of my favorite delis. After my two failed attempts at making conversation, I am quiet too. I want to know what is going on in that beautiful head of his. He's quiet as we eat and now I'm starting to get worried.

"So, did you have a fun weekend? I know it doesn't compare to Chicago," I say, attempting to break him out of this funk one last time.

He finishes his last bite of sandwich and gives me another intense look as he says "I had the best time. I'm so happy I got to know you better. That you let me in."

I nod and say, "Yeah, same here." I expect him to say more, but he doesn't. He gives me a half smile and throws away our trash. Okay then, I guess that's that.

I can't help thinking this is going to be an awkward car ride again. And I'm right.

Robbie looks out the window the entire drive to the airport as we just listen to the 80s radio station. Every now and then I see him tap his foot or his fingers and can't help but wonder what he is possibly anxious about.

We approach the airport and I finally break the silence, "Should I go to the drop-off or park?" My heart is in my throat. If he says drop-off, that means something is wrong and he doesn't even want to say a proper goodbye, right? But if he tells me to park, maybe that means he wants me there until the last moment when he has to go through security.

Before I can panic more, he says, "Park."

I bring the car to a stop in one of the empty spots and get out. Robbie does too and grabs his overnight bag from the backseat. He checks that he has everything he needs and we head inside.

"I checked in on my phone earlier at the arena, so I don't need to do that here," he says softly, peeking a glance at me. I try to keep all the emotions off of my face as I walk alongside him to the security area.

Robbie fidgets with the strap of his bag and then abruptly turns to face me, bringing me to a stop. This is it. He's leaving and I won't see him again until the day after Thanksgiving when I am back in Grand Marquee. And by his demeanor this afternoon, he didn't have as much fun as he said he did.

Is he about to tell me that we can't hang out again?

Is it because of me? Was I not enough? Was I too much?

I feel the pressure behind my eyes and bite my lip to not let the tears out. I look everywhere but at Robbie's face. If he's about to let me down gently, I might actually run and hide in a hole for the rest of my life.

"I was thinking—" he says, but pauses like he needs to collect his thoughts. This is it. I close my eyes and take a deep breath as I prepare myself for his next words. "You should come spend Thanksgiving with me."

My eyes fly open and move to his face. He looks nervous as hell. And what did he just say? "What?" I ask, dumbfounded.

He swallows and says "Well, I know you have your Grams here, but I'd like you to come spend Thanksgiving with me and my family. I met the most important person in your life, it's only fair you get to do the same."

I furrow my brow and ask, "Is this a pity ask?"

His eyes widen and then flare. "I would never pity you. You are one of the strongest people I've ever met. I admire the shit out of you. You let me in this weekend and it made me see how truly incredible you are. So no, I am not asking because I pity you. I am asking because I want to let you in as well."

A stupid tear escapes me but Robbie's thumb is there to catch it. Again. "Olive," he whispers, and the way he says it is enough for me to break. I step into his arms and hug him as tightly as I can. He squeezes me back just as hard and we just stand there in each other's embrace for a few minutes. Neither of us willing to let go.

"I would love to spend the holiday with you," I mumble against his neck and I can feel him relax in relief. Was he really worried I would say no? Does he not know how much I crave his presence? "Is this why you were so quiet the whole ride here?"

He pulls back a bit so we can see each other and he nods. "I didn't want to overstep any boundaries. Wasn't sure if it was too much, too soon."

"It's not."

He gives me a full smile this time and I can't help but mirror it. "Good. I was thinking you could fly in on Wednesday night, we can spend Thanksgiving with my family. Then Friday it lines up perfectly with you officiating our game. And if you are open to it, you can stay until Sunday. I have those next two days off. There are some other family traditions we have, like cutting down our own Christmas tree from the farm and watching holiday movies. Plus, I can show you around Grand Marquee," he's getting so excited but I need to tamp it down.

"I'll have to check hotel prices... I'm not sure I could afford staying that long. And I might have to take a bus if flights are expensive," I say in a rush.

"Are you kidding? You're not paying for any hotels. You'll stay at my house. And I know you'll probably say no, but I do want to help pay for your ticket. After all, this was all my last minute idea. Let me help. I'd rather spend more time with you than wait around for the bus to bring you," he smiles hopefully.

I shake my head but smile back and say, "I'll take you up on the offer to stay with you, but I can figure out the plane ticket."

"Just, promise me you'll ask for help if you want it? Please don't bail," he asks. And it's that last plea that does it. *Please don't bail.*

"I would never. I'll be there," I hold his gaze as I say this and he nods. Then he wraps me up in another big hug.

Holy shit, I might be addicted to this man's hugs. They are everything. He makes me feel safe and cherished and I haven't felt that in over a decade.

"I'll miss you," he says, but reluctantly pulls away and starts moving backward toward security.

"I'll miss you too, Bobbert," I say with a wave and watch him walk away until he's all the way past security. Right before he can get out of sight he turns toward me one more time and gives me that perfectly dimpled smile.

And as for me, my hands grip the wheel and I smile stupid the whole way home.

POND HOCKEY

Olivia

What should I wear to Thanksgiving dinner?

Robbie

You're overthinking this, Olive. Whatever you want. Jeans, sweater, sweatshirt...as long as you don't show up in your hockey uniform, you're fine.

Why do I feel like there's a story there?

One year, the lake behind my parent's house was frozen solid so all of us brought our gear and played pond hockey. My mom was mad that we were all sweaty at the dinner table. We've learned our lesson since.

Bobbert, you rascal.

You know it ;)

Can I admit I'm kind of nervous to meet your family?

> I promise you, there's no reason to be nervous.

I just hope they like me.

NINETEEN

Robbie

I GOT out of practice not too long ago and found a text from Olivia.

> Boarding now. Can't wait to see you.

I don't reply because the text was from an hour ago, but I do head home right away. I shower and change my clothes, feed the cats, and make sure the entire house is clean and that the spare bedroom is packed with everything Olivia would need: blankets, extra pillows, toiletries. I even had my sister, Alice, pick out some candles and nice decorations. Let's just say that room only had minimal furniture before I gave Alice my credit card and free reign on decorating.

Speaking of my sister, I see her name flashing on my screen and pick up the phone as I look around the house.

"Hey, Al."

"Hey, Roro," she uses my childhood nickname to annoy

me, but little does she know, it's actually one of the few I like. When Alice was little, she couldn't pronounce Robbie so she always called me Roro. I'll never tell her how much I like it though, she would be insufferable.

I give her an over-the-top sigh and groan and say, "What's up? Why are you calling? I'm about to head to the airport."

"Don't worry, I'm not going to keep you away from this mysterious girl that has you completely smitten." Alice is the only one I told about my feelings for Olivia. The rest of my family just knows I'm bringing an extra friend over for the holiday. "Did you like the stuff I bought?"

"Yeah, the place looks very homey. You did awesome, Al," I say proudly.

"Yes, well, I would have liked to know some more details about her, but you were holding out on me."

"I was not!"

"You didn't tell me what kind of books she likes—I would have gotten her a couple and left them on the nightstand. OMG, I hope she's a romance girlie so I can talk to her about all my favorite books!" Oh no, time to tamp down the excitement.

"Al, I know you're excited, but please try not to overwhelm her, okay? I have the feeling she's already going to be skittish." Olivia and I spent the last week and a half chatting about the holiday and plans, and she mentioned she was nervous to meet my crazy family. I don't blame her, she's probably not used to our level of insanity. Between my parents, my two siblings, my sister-in-law and two nieces, and Jordan, Ash and Eli—they join us every year for Thanksgiving dinner—it gets pretty rowdy in the Elliot household.

"I'm not going to accost her, Roro, don't worry. I'm just

excited, you haven't brought a woman home since Diana, and that was like a billion years ago."

"It's been six years, and that was different."

"How so?"

Well, for one, I don't think I was in love with Diana. I liked her a lot, and she was my first and only serious girlfriend, but she wanted to get married and start a family right away. I was 26 and still hoping to make it back to the NHL, so settling down at that age was the furthest thing from my mind. She all but told me she wanted me to eventually quit hockey.

We broke up amicably after having some heart-to-hearts about what we both wanted our futures to look like. And the fact that I wasn't completely, madly in love with her made it easy enough to move on from that relationship. Funny how six years can change a person. Because I think I am ready to settle down now, but the only difference is, I would *never* ask my partner to give up their dream for me.

"It just is. Olivia means a lot to me, okay?"

"Okay, I won't push. Just know I'm happy for you, big brother. You deserve to be happy, and from what you've told me, she's at least one source of that happiness. So, I'm team *Rolivia*."

"That sounds like a type of medicine you see advertised on TV," I deadpan.

"Ha! Good one."

"Alright, I gotta head out now."

"Oh, one more thing—" I wait but there's silence on her end.

"Spit it out..."

"Is Jordan going to bring anyone to Thanksgiving?" That's a weird question. Jordan isn't seeing anyone that I'm aware of, so why would he? And why is my little sister asking about it?

"Not that I know of, why?"

"No reason," she says quickly. Strange.

I sigh and say, "Okay, I'll see you tomorrow. Make sure everyone is on their best behavior, yeah?"

"Aye aye captain!" she says and hangs up and I head for the airport.

I'M WAITING by the baggage claim area, pacing back and forth in anticipation. Olivia's flight landed 15 minutes ago and with how small this airport is, she should be coming out any moment now. My phone buzzes and I quickly take it out of my jacket pocket. It's a text from Olivia.

> Nervous to see me, Bobbert? :)

If she only knew. I look up and around and I finally spot her. She's wearing leggings and one of those old, faded hockey sweatshirts that I know she loves. Her hair is down, but it looks different. Shorter. While it used to go down to the top of her breasts, it now only reaches her shoulders. She looks at me with a big smile and starts walking a bit faster, dragging her carry-on behind her. She looks breathtaking.

I start walking towards her and we end up meeting in the middle. My hands immediately reach around her to give her a hug. I know she loves them because every time I hug her, she practically melts in my arms. Her head rests in that perfect spot under my chin, and for a moment we just stand there like that. Breathing each other in. Everything is right in the world again because she's here. In my arms.

"How was your flight?" I ask, eager to hear her voice.

"It was good, a little disappointing I couldn't find one that was nonstop. I could have been here two hours sooner if I did."

"That's okay, you're here now," I say cheerfully, grabbing her carry-on and leading her to the baggage carousel. "What does your other suitcase look like?"

"It's just plain black, but it has a pink tag on it."

"Grams?" I ask at the same time she huffs out, "Grams." We both laugh, and I throw an arm around her shoulders, keeping her close to me.

After we grab her bag and make our way to the car, Olivia asks, "Do we have any plans tonight?"

"Not really, I planned on making us dinner while you unpack. Afterwards we can watch a movie if you'd like."

"Ooh, what are you making for dinner? And also, are your cats cuddly?" she asks excitedly.

"Chicken parm. And no, not really. Since I'm not home all the time, they've learned to be pretty independent. They love to play though and have lots of toys."

"Oh. Cool," she says, but I can tell she's a bit disappointed by that. If she's feeling cuddly, she can just use me.

"Feeling cuddly?" I ask, wiggling my eyebrows at her.

She shakes her head but smiles down at her lap as she says, "Maybe a little."

"Well, I'm sure we can find a solution," I look over at her again as I say it and give her a quick wink. I see her cheeks go a little pink.

We pull up to my ranch-style home that's a little ways north of Grand Marquee. Even though it's not fully dark yet, I made sure to turn on my white Christmas lights that I've had up the whole year. I pull in to the garage.

"You have two cars?" Olivia asks, eying my truck as we get out and start unloading her suitcases.

"Yeah, I use the truck a lot over the summer, it's useful for lots of things. Plus, Alice borrows it quite frequently and I can't seem to part with it."

"That's cool," she says.

"I know two cars for one guy seems a bit overkill, but trust me, it's kind of a need when I have such a big family."

She places her hand on my forearm and says with a chuckle, "Robbie, you don't have to explain yourself to me. I'm not judging you, I promise."

"I just don't want you to think I'm an entitled prick," I say, frowning. I don't want her to get the wrong impression. I want to get this right.

"You're not a prick. You're literally the nicest person I've ever met," she squeezes my arm and I give her a smile.

"C'mon, let me show you inside."

※

THE FIRST THING I show Olivia is the kitchen and living room. She's immediately impressed by the openness of the floor plan, taking a lap around the kitchen island, pausing to gawk at the large dining room table that can easily sit twelve people.

"Wow, how often do you use this?" she asks.

"Weekly," I respond with a smile and give her the space to continue her perusal. As soon as she notices the large couch, she makes a beeline for it and sprawls on it dramatically.

"If you think that couch is comfortable, let me show you

the bedroom," I say, looking down at her from behind the couch.

She sits up alarmingly quick and her eyebrows go up. Shit, I didn't mean to imply I'd be showing her my bedroom. "I mean, let me show you your bedroom, down the hall."

I can see the amusement lighting up her face as she says, "Okay."

Once we get to the spare bedroom, across the hall from my own, I place her bag down and nod for her to explore.

"Do you treat all your guests like they're in a five-star hotel?" she asks, sniffing one of the candles on the dresser.

"Just you," I reply honestly. She takes a deep breath and continues to look around. "Is it too much? I asked Alice to help me decorate the place a bit. It was hardly used before."

"No, it's perfect. I like her style," she says and I feel relieved.

"She was mad I never asked you what your favorite types of books are. Fair warning, she's a book nerd and very excited to talk to someone else about it."

"I love that. I'll make sure to bring it up tomorrow. Any other family-bonding tips you can give me?"

I shake my head and step closer to give her a hug. "Just be yourself, I promise they will love you." She nods her head against me.

We don't stay like that for long, because the next second her stomach rumbles so loud it scares Caramel, my orange tabby that was apparently circling our legs and purring. He scurries out of the room and we both look after him, amused.

"Sorry, Caramel," Olivia yells after him.

I chuckle. She's adorable. And hungry. "How about you unpack and get comfortable for the night and I'll go get started on food."

"Okay."

I move around my kitchen with ease and pull out all the ingredients I need for dinner. I already breaded the chicken, it just needs to be fried, so I get a pan ready with oil. I didn't have time to make pasta from scratch, so I am boiling a pot for dried spaghetti. While the chicken is frying, I am getting salad ingredients out and prepping the mozzarella.

"That smells delicious," Olivia says, as I am flipping over the chicken. The crust is crispy and perfectly browned.

"Hopefully, it tastes even better," I say with a smile over my shoulder. "Would you like some wine?"

"Sure."

"Any preference?"

"White, if you have it."

"Why, I do, Miss Olive. Take a seat." I gesture to the bar stools at the kitchen island. I reach into the wine cooler that's built into the kitchen island and open a bottle of Chardonnay.

"I want to help. What can I do?" Olivia says.

"Would you like to make the salad? Everything you need is right here, it just needs to be mixed up."

She squints at me, but her lips are tugging at the corners. "Are you saying I can't handle something more complex than a salad?"

"Honey, you told me you burnt pasta the last time you made it. I am not letting you anywhere near my stove." I grin at her and catch the cherry tomato she chucks at me.

"I may not know how to cook, but I want to learn." I nod along and point over to the stove for her to join me. My other cat, Beans, is circling the area, looking for bits of food and Olivia stops to pet him on her way over to me. I'm surprised he lets her. Like I said, my cats are not super friendly.

"Okay, so the chicken is fried now, so we are going to move it into this pan, then top it off with lots of sauce and mozzarella."

"Got it, I can handle that."

"Good, in the meantime I will add the pasta to the boiling water."

"Okay, that's good that you're doing that. I'd probably manage to burn myself somehow," she says, eying the pasta water like it personally offended her.

I laugh and she does too, and we work in companionable silence for a few minutes. Once the chicken is in the oven and the pasta is boiling, we take a few sips of wine and a couple bites of salad.

"How often do you cook for yourself?" Olivia asks.

"As often as I can. I really like cooking and baking, it soothes me somehow. I like having something to do with my hands I guess. I was never still as a kid, so my mom would always take me in the kitchen with her and make me help out."

"It's nice that you learned so young."

"Yeah, she taught me a lot," I say softly. "I'm actually baking some pies and focaccia tomorrow. So if you hear noises early in the morning, I promise it's not a burglar."

She laughs, "I wondered why there were earplugs left on my nightstand. I just figured you snore really loudly."

I bring my hands up to my chest in mock offense. "I do not snore...that badly."

"I'd like to help with those too, if you want company in the morning," she says looking up at me with her hopeful, bright green eyes.

"Of course I want company. That's kind of the whole reason you're here." I lightly jab her with my elbow.

After we eat dinner at the kitchen island, we fill up our

wine again and move to the couch for a movie. I'm a gentleman so I let Olivia pick and she chooses *Back to the Future*. Not even twenty minutes into the movie, Caramel jumps up on the couch and loaves up between me and Olivia. I was going to try to get closer to her, but now I can't. What a cockblock.

Olivia tentatively reaches out a hand and pets him all over and he starts purring so loud he sounds like a helicopter about to take off. Traitor. He never sits with me like this. Beans is usually around me and more likely the one to ask for pets.

Speaking of Beans, the devil appears. He jumps up on the other side of Olivia and after taking one look at Caramel and all the pets he's getting, he decides to get in on the action as well. He slowly moves to Olivia's lap and after making some very defined biscuits on the blanket covering her legs, he sits down. In her lap. Fucking hell.

I've had these cats for years and they never do this with anyone except me on occasion. It looks like I'm not the only one that's smitten with Olivia.

She turns her wide eyes at me and mouths, *Oh my god!*

"These bastards are trying to steal you from me," I whisper with a head shake.

"Trying? I'm sorry Bobbert, but they had me the moment I walked through that door," she says, grinning at me.

Fuck. She's goddamn perfect.

WE SPEND Thanksgiving morning baking the pies and the focaccia, working together seamlessly. Olivia asks me lots of questions and I have her assist me with every step.

We work so damn well together. I wonder if she notices that too. It's like we're in perfect sync.

We head out to my parent's house, which is an hour drive out of town and right on a small lake. While it's not snowing yet, the temperature has dropped to freezing, so we make sure to bring coats. I turned the car on early and preheated the seats for us which Olivia made fun of me about. Whatever, at least her butt was warm the whole drive.

As we pull into my parent's driveway, I can tell Olivia is nervous, even though I did my best to reassure her she has nothing to worry about.

"Hey," I say, and turn in my driver's seat to look at her, "you remember what you told me when I met your grandma?"

She stops fidgeting and turns to face me as well, "Not really."

"You said, *don't worry, she won't bite.*" She gives me a small smile and takes a deep breath. "They won't bite either. Except for my nieces, they might actually bite you. Just fair warning." That gets me a laugh and I'll take it as a sign that we're good to go. "Ready?" I ask.

"Yeah, let's do this."

We don't ring the doorbell because my parents always leave the door unlocked. I lead Olivia inside, both of us carrying the dishes we made. The house is already a mess. There are toys everywhere, courtesy of my nieces Lory and Katie and there is loud conversation coming from the kitchen. We pass the living room and I see my dad, Jordan, and my sister, of all people, sitting on the couch watching the football game. Jordan and my dad are watching the TV, having a conversation about how our team is making a comeback this year, and Alice is watching...Jordan.

I shake my head, astounded I've never noticed her crush before and call out, "Hey, Al. Can I get some help here?" Her head immediately turns in my direction and her cheeks are bright red from getting caught ogling one of my best friends. I give her a smirk expecting her to get mad, but she's not looking at me anymore. Her eyes are glued to Olivia.

Alice gives me a smirk right back and says, "Olivia, hi, it's so nice to meet you!" Then she all but tackles her with a hug. "I've heard so much about you!"

To her credit, Olivia accepts the hug albeit wearily and squints her eyes at me. "All good things, I hope."

"Of course! I'm so happy you're here," Alice says, and I can see the relief in Olivia's shoulders as she takes in my 5'4" sister with her dark blonde hair and blue eyes. Out of my two siblings, Alice and I look the most alike. My brother inherited my father's dark hair and my mother's brown eyes.

Speaking of my brother, he rounds the corner to the living room and pats me on the back. No *hello*, no *how've you been*, no offer to take one of the three pies I'm balancing in my arms. He does however notice Olivia and introduces himself.

"Hey, I'm Michael. You must be Olivia!" He's all smiles and politeness now. "Can I take those focaccias from you?"

"I don't see you offering to take some of these pies," I grumble.

"You're not a guest, dummy."

"Honey, be nice," Tangela says, coming out of the kitchen to see what all of the commotion is about. She grabs one of the pies from me and I give her an appreciating smile, which she returns.

"Good to see you, Robbie, and nice to meet you, Olivia! Let's get all these in the kitchen and introduce you to the rest of the family."

The kitchen is overrun with both people and food. There's barely any space to put down the bread and pies, but somehow I manage. Tangela rounds up her daughters and gets them to join their grandpa and uncle on the couch. Eli is helping my mom peel the potatoes and Ash seems to struggle arranging a charcuterie board.

"Who let Ash in the kitchen?" I quip.

"Ha-ha, just because I'm not as good as you, Grandpa, doesn't mean I can't help out," he says, shoving a handful of cheese in his mouth.

"Classy," I say, rolling my eyes.

"Olivia, is that you?" he says with a mouthful. Everyone's gaze turns to the woman that's half hiding behind me and she gives a shy wave and a nod.

I clear my throat and move my arm around her, letting my hand rest on the small of her back and bringing her forward. "Everyone, this is Olivia." I keep my eyes trained on her face and notice the slight pink there.

"Nice to meet you all." She barely gets the words out before my mother comes over and wraps her in a big hug. If it catches her by surprise, she doesn't show it. Olivia immediately returns it and gives me a small smile.

"We're so glad you're here," my mother says. "Any friend of Robbie's is practically part of the family." She lets Olivia go and returns back to her pot of gravy.

Olivia is quiet and when I look over at her again I see her eyes are a bit misty. I move in front of her and use my fingers to bring her chin up. There's a vulnerability in her eyes that makes me pause. I can tell she's overwhelmed right now and my mom's comment about being part of the family is probably what caused it. I ask her in a whisper so no one else hears, "Are you okay?"

She takes a deep inhale and nods. Her smile is small,

but it's there. But I need more, I need to make sure she's fine.

"Let me show you where the bathroom is," I say loud enough for everyone to hear so they don't follow us around. Alice especially. I look over my shoulder and see Alice watching us in that assessing way of hers. She mouths, *All good?* and I nod.

"You didn't have to rescue me like that. I promise, I'm okay," she says as we reach the end of the hall where the bathroom is.

I search her face to make sure then say, "Okay. I believe you. And even if you're not, that's okay too. I know my family can be a lot—"

"No, that's not it. I just didn't expect them to be so nice to a complete stranger. I should have realized it though, you must take after them," she says.

"I told you they won't bite." I smile at her and give her another hug for good measure. I have a feeling she'll fit in just fine.

TWENTY

Olivia

ROBBIE'S FAMILY is the nicest. Ever. I don't know why I was so nervous. His sister immediately started talking to me about books and music and we found that we have so much in common. His nieces are adorable and were very curious about me. They've asked me every possible question in existence. I feel like the whole family knows every detail about me now.

Eli, Jordan, and Ash asked me lots of questions too, mostly about hockey since that's the main thing we all have in common. Robbie told everyone how amazing I was on the ice in my beer league game, and the way he said it, like he was proud of me, made me so happy. I try to control my facial expressions, but on the inside I am an emotional mess. I don't know how to respond to all this praise and tenderness. No one's ever made me feel the way Robbie does.

My emotions must show on my face every time I look at Robbie though, because I catch Alice smiling at me multiple times during dinner. She has a knowing gleam in her eyes. Can she see how gone I am for him? How much I adore him?

The rest of the day passes too quickly in a happy blur. We have dinner together at a long table that fits all twelve of us. While earlier in the day it was beautifully decorated with ornaments and flowers, during dinner it was all replaced with lots and lots of dishes. The food was amazing and I can't remember the last time I had such a feast for Thanksgiving. While my grandma and her roommates host one every year, they're not as spry as they used to be and I am terrible at cooking. So our Thanksgivings usually involve some store-bought sides and desserts alongside a small turkey.

I will definitely regret eating all of this food tomorrow, especially since I have to work in the evening. At least I can sleep in and recharge a bit while Robbie goes to practice in the morning. The two of us, alongside Jordan, Ash, and Eli, left early so the guys could get a good night's rest.

As we get inside the house we head straight to the bedrooms that are across from each other. I turn to tell him goodnight, but Robbie is already turned toward me lips parted like he's about to say something. My eyes jump to his lips and I swallow. God, I want to know what he tastes like.

"Did you have a good day?" he asks in a low voice that sounds too sexy for the simple question he just asked.

"The best," I say in a whisper and bring my eyes up to his. They are so full of longing and softness that for a moment I am stunned.

He takes a step towards me and reaches up to tuck a strand of my hair behind my ear. His hand lingers there, his thumb brushing my earlobe. I close my eyes and lean into his touch and he fully cups my cheek with his hand. As he starts stroking my cheekbone, I open my eyes and see him staring at my lips. *Kiss me. Please.*

"Goodnight, Olive," he says softly and leans in. I hold my breath as he kisses my cheek, right where his thumb was caressing me earlier. He lingers for a beat, then steps back. I want to tell him to give me more. To kiss me for real. I want to grab him by his shirt and push him against the wall. I want to see if I can unravel him the way I *know* he could unravel me. Piece by piece.

But I don't. Because I'm scared to make the first move. I don't want to lose whatever friendship we've built so far if it turns out I've misread this whole thing. So I say, "Goodnight, Robbie." Then we both go to our separate bedrooms.

That night, I dream of a kiss that could have been. Perfect. Needy. Explosive.

WHILE ROBBIE IS AT PRACTICE, I expect to be alone with the cats, but I am pleasantly surprised when I get a text from Alice. We exchanged phone numbers the night before and she promised she would check in on me so I don't get bored. I told her it would be fine, but she didn't listen and I am glad for it. She shows up at the front door with pastries and coffee for us both and we spend hours chatting about books and, surprisingly, Robbie.

"So, Olivia. What are your intentions with my brother?" Alice asks out of nowhere.

"What do you mean?" I ask nervously.

She rolls her eyes and gives me a knowing smile. "Come on. I could see it written all over your face last night. The way you looked at him like he was the moon and the stars," she sing-songs. "You like him."

My cheeks burn and I look down at my lap as I give Beans some head scratches. I don't know how to reply. I debate lying and saying we're just friends. But what if she tells him that? That's the last thing I want. My eyes get misty just thinking about the possibility of losing him.

Alice is quiet and lets me process my thoughts without prodding for a quick answer which I appreciate. When I look back up at her she's not smiling smugly at me anymore. Her eyes are wide and concerned. "Olivia, I'm sorry. I—I didn't mean to push. You don't have to tell me anything—"

"I think I might be in love with him," I whisper on a shaky breath.

Alice looks at me for a moment but doesn't say anything. Then her face breaks into a smile that resembles Robbie's. "That's amazing news."

"Is it?" I say, and my voice breaks.

"Of course," she says, pulling me into a fierce hug, "why wouldn't it be? You two are perfect for each other."

I can't stop crying for some reason and while I feel bad for getting tears and snot all over Alice's nice cashmere sweater, she started this. I blame her for my meltdown.

"I'm scared."

"Of what?"

"Losing him. If he knows how I feel but doesn't feel the same, that might destroy everything we've built so far. I know we only met a month and a half ago, but we talk every single day. Is it pathetic that he's the best part of my day?"

Alice pulls back and holds me by my shoulders. "Olivia, listen to me," she says in a stern voice I haven't heard her use before now. "Robbie is my best friend, he's the person I always go to for sound advice. And you know what he always does when I'm in a predicament? He lists the facts. So that's what I'm going to do for you. Okay?"

I nod, but my tears keep falling. What have I done to deserve the kindness and friendship of these amazing people?

"*One*, Robbie doesn't bring dates to family events and holidays. Ever. Unless he's serious about them. And this year, he brought *you*.

"*Two*, the night you two met, he couldn't shut up about you."

I snort. "Yeah, probably because I was a bitch to him on the ice."

"That's not the night I'm talking about. The one before. After the dinner at the brewery, he said he saw Ash talking to the most beautiful girl he had ever seen. And after he realized who you were, he was even more intrigued."

He remembers me from that night at the brewery? I must have looked like such an idiot, with ketchup stains on my sweatshirt, ogling his big family.

"*Three*, he spent all of last weekend buying all your favorite snacks, and looking up decorations for the spare bedroom to make it more homey. If he had the time, he would have picked everything out and decorated it himself. I know my brother, and trust me, he feels the same about you."

I'm quiet for a beat because I know she's right. I can see the longing and want on his face every time he looks at me. I can also see how attuned he is to me and my feelings. He always makes sure I'm included in the conversation when we're in a group, and he always listens to what I have to say, even if it's something trivial.

"Why hasn't he said anything?" I ask helplessly.

She sighs and pulls me in another hug. "I think he senses that you're scared. And if I can describe my brother in one word, it's *patient*. I promise you he's either waiting for you to make the first move or biding his time until he senses some more confidence from you."

I nod and hug her some more until I hear the garage door slam closed and footsteps coming towards the living room where we are. We break apart and I hastily wipe my tears away before Robbie can notice, but it's too late.

He looks incredible. His cheeks are pink and his hair is still a bit damp from his shower. He's wearing gray joggers and a black long sleeve fleece that hugs his body just right.

"Hey Roro," Alice greets him, but he's frozen to the spot, staring at me and frowning.

"Olive, why are you crying?" he says in a low voice and I notice his fists clenching at his side.

"Oh, it's nothing." I give him the best smile I can muster. *Fuck*. He won't believe me, he never does when I say it's nothing.

"Al, what did you do?" He turns his angry gaze on his sister and I can't let her take the fall for this.

So I blurt out, "We were talking about a book. A really sad book." I look at Alice and widen my eyes. *Go along, please.* She catches my eye and gives me a small nod.

"That's right, we had pastries, and coffee, and delightful conversation that turned to books. One of our favorite characters dies at the end of this romance. It's tragic."

Robbie narrows his eyes at Alice and it's clear that he doesn't believe us, but he gives me a weary look. "You sure you're okay? Also, that sounds like a shitty romance."

"Yes, I promise. How was practice?" My diversion from the topic seems to work and Robbie tells us all about practice and the fan event they had to do, which is why he is back an hour later than planned.

We only have a few hours to kill until we have to head to the arena for tonight's hockey game, so the three of us spend it having a small meal and watching *Back to the Future II*. Alice moves over to the oversized chair and lets me and Robbie share the couch with the cats, who once again join me. Robbie eyes me every few minutes but I try not to give anything away. I also don't cry any more.

Because I have a plan.

TWENTY-ONE

Robbie

SOMETHING IS OFF WITH OLIVIA. Ever since yesterday when I caught her crying and hugging my sister on the couch, something has been off. I also haven't had a lot of time to talk to her. As soon as our movie ended, we packed up the car and headed to the arena to get ready for the game.

I love our home games during the holidays. We always have something fun for the fans. Every year during our first game after Thanksgiving we ask fans to bring plush toys and throw them on the ice after our team scores the first goal. Then all the players, referees, and ice crew members skate around collecting them in giant bags and they all get donated at the end of the night to the Children's Hospital. It's one of my favorite traditions.

We won the game last night, although it wasn't an easy one. Ashton started a fight with one of the Quebec Loonies and got himself two penalties. We got scored on during that penalty kill. Then we got scored on again when I high sticked another guy and Olivia sent me to the penalty box. I wanted to talk to her, but out there on the ice, she's all professional. She barely said anything to me or the rest of the guys. I couldn't tell if whatever was bothering her earlier in the day was making her keep her distance from me.

The drive back to my house was filled with silence, but it didn't feel awkward. We were both tired, and at some point I turned on the radio so we listened in comfortable silence. Once back at my house, we had some leftovers, made some small talk, and then we both went to bed. She didn't suggest we watch a movie and I didn't suggest we have a drink together.

This morning, I woke up early and made pancakes from scratch, as well as a breakfast casserole. I brewed coffee and prepared the table for us to have breakfast at. When I went to wake up Olivia, I found that she had left her door open a crack overnight and both cats slithered in at some point. The three of them looked so cozy sleeping together, I couldn't help myself—I snapped a picture and set it as her contact picture. And maybe my background too. *Okay, definitely my background.*

I had a couple bites of pancake but put the rest away to warm up later when Olivia woke up. I then went to the basement to dig up all my Christmas decorations.

I've been deep in boxes for the last hour, when I hear footsteps upstairs and muffled noises. As she draws closer, I can hear Olivia calling out my name.

"I'm in the basement," I yell up the stairs. After a few minutes, I see her rounding the steps, both cats in tow. She's still in her pajamas and her hair is mussed from sleep, but damn if the sight of her doesn't make my heart stop. She's holding a blanket around her for warmth. "Are you cold? I can turn up the heat."

She looks down at herself and realizes she's holding the blanket. "Oh, no. I'm comfortable. Sorry, I didn't mean to disturb you, I just heard some noises and wasn't sure what was going on." She looks around, taking in the basement.

"You're not disturbing me," I say with a smile. "I tried to wake you up for breakfast, but you were trapped by two cats. And you were snoring, so I figured you were tired and wanted to sleep in."

She narrows her eyes at me and says, "I do not snore. Do I?"

I give her a pat on the shoulder and say, "Like a freight train."

She laughs but it's not her normal *shut up* laugh, it's a nervous laugh. Why is she nervous again? It's just the two of us here. Do I make her nervous? I take a few steps away and put some distance between us. Maybe I'm creeping her out. After all, this basement is not finished. It's all concrete floor and walls, basically just a glorified storage unit.

"Are you hungry?" I ask at the same time as she says, "What are you doing down here?"

"I'm getting out my Christmas decorations. We're going to meet my family at the tree farm and pick out some nice blue spruces to bring home. I want to have everything ready afterwards so we can decorate it." I take a peek at her face and see her brows pulled together. "What's wrong?" I say.

She immediately smooths her features and responds "It's nothing. I didn't realize your whole family was going to the farm."

"Yeah, it's kind of our tradition. I'm sure I told you we were going."

"I thought you meant just us—but this makes more

sense." She shakes her head and then gives me a smile that seems genuine. "I'm going to shower then. Don't want to make us late."

"We have plenty of time. We should probably finish breakfast before we leave as well."

"Okay, I'll meet you in the kitchen in a bit," she says and runs upstairs.

"O—kay," I say, dumbfounded. Yeah, something is definitely off with her.

TWENTY-TWO

Olivia

I'VE BEEN TRYING to play it cool around Robbie but I don't think it's working. Ever since I admitted to Alice that I have feelings for him it's like a cloud lifted and made everything clearer. And yet, my nerves have been through the roof. *I had a plan, damn it.* Which then promptly got derailed when Robbie mentioned his whole family is going to the farm with us to pick a tree.

Not that I am not ecstatic to spend more time with the Elliots, but my plan involved a very romantic confession from me among the Christmas trees. And provided it all went well and he reciprocated said feelings, my plan also involved some immediate make out sessions in his truck. My plan also included me taking him to a nice restaurant for a date right after we were done taking the tree back to his house.

Now I have to pivot. This is why I am not a planner. Things never work out in my favor.

I've showered and I'm pacing the kitchen after warming up the delicious food that Robbie no doubt woke up early and made. Why didn't he want my help with it? I guess I can't fault him for letting me sleep in when I did the same for him weeks ago.

"Hey," Robbie's deep voice startles me and makes me jump. I turn around to face him and see he's holding a bunch of boxes on top of each other so I step in and help.

"Hey yourself. Let me help with those."

"Thanks. We can put them on the living room floor."

"I warmed up the breakfast you made. Thanks, by the way. For making it. And for letting me sleep in." I give him a shy smile.

"Of course. Hey," he starts, looking like he might come closer to me, but he stops himself, "are you sure you're okay? You've been a little jumpy."

"Fine. It's fine," I say, my voice more high pitched than usual. I cough and then try again, "Seriously, Bobbert. I've just had a lot on my mind I guess, but I'm okay."

He searches my face and I must placate him somehow because he drops the subject. We have breakfast together, feed the cats, and then we leave for the tree farm.

※

WE PICKED up Alice and both of Robbie's parents on the way, while his brother Michael with his wife and kids are driving separately. We somehow need to fit three Christmas trees in Robbie's truck and he's convinced it's possible. Even though his mom keeps saying she wants an 11-foot tree.

As soon as we park and get out of the car, Alice immediately pulls me up ahead to chat under the excuse of getting hot cocoa.

"So, did you tell him?" She and I have been texting since last night and I may have mentioned my plan to her. I also mentioned how I am bailing on said plan because there's no way in hell I'm confessing my feelings in front of his whole family.

I groan, "No."

"Why? Just tell him. Trust me, he won't care if anyone else is around."

No, but I do. If he rejects me, which I have thought about plenty last night while wide awake, I will take it in stride. I will tell him I understand—even if I won't—and ask if he'd be willing to stay friends—which might actually be the death of me—but I won't do all that in front of his family. Because seeing just a glimpse of what they have, it's made me crave that connection so much more. And if I have to say goodbye to them too, it will break my heart.

"He's planned so many wonderful things, I just want to do the same for him. I want to plan the perfect confession and date and surprise him with it. So please, Alice, please keep this to yourself," I beg her in hushed tones.

She squeezes my arm and throws her head back on a sigh but says, "Fine, but you better do it soon. I want you both to be happy. And for the record, you could confess your feelings in a Taco Bell while you're chewing on a burrito, with cheese all over your face and Robbie would still think the world of you."

That gets a laugh out of me. She really is Robbie's sister.

Once we get hot cocoa for everyone, and the men each select a handsaw, we get in line to wait for the tractor. I've never been to a tree farm before so I don't know what to expect, but Robbie gently pulls me to his side and says, "Once the tractor gets here, we all get on it. Then they take us out to separate sections where they grow all different kinds of trees: pines, firs, spruces. They yell out the areas as we go and we request to get off. Once we're done cutting our trees, we pull it to the road and wait for the tractor to pick us back up."

"This is all seriously cool," I say, admiring the scene around us. There are so many families of all sizes, couples with kids, couples with dogs, everyone gathered to pick out their perfect tree for the holiday.

Robbie brings his gloved hand to mine and holds it. I wish it wasn't cold enough already to have to wear gloves so I could feel his skin on mine. *I'll take what I can get.* I look up from our hands at him and give him a big smile. *He makes me so happy.*

"Ready to help me find the most perfect tree so we can decorate it when we get home?"

I nod.

Home.

Why is it starting to feel like he could be my home?

⚔

AFTER A BUMPY TRACTOR RIDE, we hop off in the blue spruce section and we all start walking around, looking for the best looking trees. I can't say any of these trees are in bad shape. They're all perfectly full, although they are different shapes and sizes. Mr. Elliot says to look for the way the tree leans as well when picking out the perfect one.

Alice splits off with her parents, and Michael, Tangela, and the girls split off as well, which leaves me and Robbie.

Alone.

As we walk through the rows of trees, I notice there are not as many people around. It's blissfully silent. "I thought there would be more people here."

"Blue spruce is not as popular because it's so prickly. Most people like the firs, which have softer needles. They're missing out though, I think."

"Oh yeah?" I ask, bemused.

He shrugs but says, "I think even though something is prickly on the surface, it doesn't mean it can't bring joy to someone." He gives me an innocent look with wide eyes. He's messing with me.

I gently push him to the side and shake my head. "Ugh, you're the worst, Bobbert. And I'm not *that* prickly."

"Not anymore. Not since I've cracked the surface," he says in a chuckle, and I can't help but join in. Hell, he's right. I've always been too guarded and afraid to let people in.

I'm glad we're back to a point where we can laugh together and banter over nothing. I was worried I made things too awkward with my silence and that he'd start to pull away. But he doesn't. So I loop my hand around his free arm and say, "Let's go find that perfect tree. Do you think Caramel will try to climb it?"

"Ha, no. He's learned his lesson in the past, it hurts his fragile little paws."

We walk some more and look at the trees when all of a sudden, I feel Robbie stop in his tracks and pull his arm away. Before I can retract my hand, he grabs hold of it and points with our joined hands. "I think that may be the perfect one." Then he takes off running, dragging me along with him. I can't help but laugh at his excitement and giddiness over finding the right tree.

"What makes this the perfect one?" I say, to humor him.

"Well, you see, it doesn't lean any which way, it's pretty straight. That's a big thing. Also, it's full all the way around, so I don't have to hide the naked part and face it towards the wall when I get home. And then to top it off, it's the perfect height for my living room. I'd say this tree is about seven feet tall."

"Hmm. Okay then. I'll admit, it's a pretty good tree."

While Robbie gets down on the ground and starts sawing away at the tree, I hold it steady, making sure it doesn't fall. It doesn't take him long to finish sawing, all while managing to hum *It's Beginning to Look a Lot Like Christmas*.

It's almost like he's conjured the spirit of Christmas because as soon as he finishes with the tree, it starts to snow. The flakes are small, but they are quite noticeable in only a few minutes.

As Robbie starts to get up off the ground, I do my best to hold the tree steady, but the thing is heavy as hell. I feel something pulling the tree to the opposite side and before I know it, it is out of my hands and falling backwards. Towards Robbie. I hear him shuffle and curse. *Shit, shit, shit.*

I quickly fling myself at the tree and try to grab it, but my foot trips on a root and the next thing I know, I am also falling along with the tree. I shove it to the side and expect to eat dirt, but I end up falling right on top of Robbie.

It takes me a second to collect myself and when I open my eyes I see Robbie looking right at me. Our faces are so close together, we're basically sharing the same breath. I am fully on top of him, my legs mingling with his, our chests aligned. I frantically look around and pat him down for any injuries. Only when I bring my hand to cup his face does he say, "I'm okay, Olive."

Now that I can breathe easy, I sigh and drop my head down in the crook of his neck. "I'm sorry, I don't know what happened. One second I had a hold of it and the next it was falling."

His right arm hooks around me and he holds me tight as he says, "It wasn't your fault, my jacket got stuck on a branch and it pulled the tree. If anything, you saved me by pushing it out of the way."

I look back at him. "I could have really hurt you though."

Robbie pulls my forehead against his and whispers, "You could never."

I take in a breath and really look at him. He's giving me his full attention as always. It's just us down here on the cold, hard ground, and we're so close.

I could tell him now.

I could kiss him.

My heart must have a mind of its own because before I know what I'm doing, I lean further in. There's not much distance left between our lips and from the look on Robbie's face, he *really* wants me to kiss him. His head tilts a bit so our lips are millimeters apart. I get closer and our lips faintly brush and—

"Olivia! Roro! You two out here?"

Both our heads whip to the side to see Alice as she rounds one of the blue spruces and stops in her tracks at the sight of us both tangled on the ground.

Robbie sighs and lets his head drop to the ground, his eyes closed in frustration. I feel it too. We were so close. I reluctantly get off of him and reach back down to give him a hand which he takes. By the time we're both fully standing, his nieces show up to let us know everyone else got their trees and are waiting for the *tactor,* as the youngest, Lory so nicely put it. Alice gives me an apologetic look and mouths, *Sorry.*

Robbie claps his hands and says, "Alright, let me grab this tree and we can be on our way. I have something very important I need to do when I get home." He looks over at me as I grab one end of the tree and he grabs the other.

"Is it to decorate the tree?" his eldest niece Katie asks.

"It sure is," he says cheerfully. Then, he looks over at me, smiles wide, and winks.

TWENTY-THREE

Robbie

OLIVIA WAS GOING to kiss me. There's no doubt about it. After my sister so rudely interrupted us, we all carried our trees and rode the tractor back to the main area where our trees got shaken, drilled and tied up. Once all of them were in the back of my truck, we had to make a detour to drop them all off at both my parents' and Michael's house.

Two hours later, we're finally back at my house and we just brought the tree inside. While I grab some water to fill the tree stand, I see Olivia fidgeting with one of the couch pillows. We haven't said much since our almost-kiss, mostly just working together to get the tree situated.

I want to kiss her so badly, but if I start, I don't think I'll be able to stop.

"Ready to decorate?" I say once I finish filling up the tree stand.

"Yeah, let's do it." She perks up. "Any specific way you like to decorate it?"

"I usually start with the lights and garland, and then go from there. Let the vibes take over."

She feigns surprise. "I'm sorry, you don't have a twelve-step plan on how to decorate this tree? I'm disappointed in you, Bobbert."

I straighten and point at her with the tree topper. "I had a twenty-four-step plan, but I'm trying not to scare you away."

She laughs and shakes her head. "Impossible. You're stuck with me, Bobbert." She holds my gaze for a beat longer and I can see the soft smile that is tugging at her lips.

Stop focusing on her lips. For now.

We spend the rest of the afternoon listening to Christmas songs and decorating not only the tree, but also the rest of the house. My Christmas lights were already up and once it got dark we went outside and turned them on. I opted for no color this year, so the lights are a mix of soft and bright white and they range from icicles dangling from the porch, to snowflakes wrapped around the pillars.

It's been snowing all day, and there's a thin layer of snow on the ground. It makes the house look like a picture-perfect holiday card. The giant blue spruce wreath on the front door is decorated with a single red bow, and there is more greenery we placed around the window sills.

"It's beautiful," she says as she takes it in.

"I couldn't have done it without you," I say and wrap an arm around her shoulder, giving her temple a soft kiss. "Thank you. For being here. You've made this holiday extra special."

Olivia wraps her arm closest to me around my waist and rests her head on my shoulder. I squeeze her tight against my side and rest my own head on top of hers. We stand there like that for a minute until I feel her shiver.

"Come on, let's go inside and make some hot cocoa," I say, letting go for a second before reaching down and grabbing her hand. We walk to the front door, but after climbing the few steps to the porch, I tug on her hand so she stops with me.

"Olive," I say to get her attention. Once she turns her beautiful green eyes on me, I smile and look up at the mistletoe. She follows and I immediately see the confusion on her face turn into excitement. Her eyes go wide and she looks back at me with a smile.

"When did you do this?"

I give her a grin. "When I sent you to the truck for the wreath. I was very quick and sneaky about it," I whisper.

Her smile is infectious and I can't help but return it. So we stand there, under the mistletoe, grinning at each other. I'm still holding her hand, so I tug on it again and pull her into me. As soon as our bodies collide, everything around us goes still.

She is everything.

From the moment I saw her, she's been a beacon of light. When I'm away from her, I'm glued to my phone, waiting for the next text or call. Waiting for her to complain about her job or to tell me about her day. The fact that I get to be the person she confides in makes my heart soar. I've always craved that kind of connection with someone in a relationship.

We're so close our foreheads are touching and I bring my other hand up to her face. My fingers are cold, but so is her cheek as I gently caress it. She leans into me more and our noses brush. This is it.

As I bring my lips to hers, I hear gravel crunching and a set of bright lights blinding us from the driveway. We both break apart a few inches and look to the side.

A car stops and I can't make out who it is until they turn off their headlights. Ash jumps out of the driver's side and Elias, Jordan, and Alice follow. Why are they all here?

I groan and drop my head between Olivia's head and shoulder. She lets go of my hand and pats me on the back. I give her neck a quick kiss and quietly say, "I can't believe this happened again." Then I pull back and glare at my so-called friends and sister.

"What are you all doing here?" I say, sulking.

"Oh, cheer up, Grandpa," Ash says. "We came to see how you decorated. Plus, it's Olivia's last night in town, we wanted to hang out. You can't just keep her all to yourself," he says with a damn smile on his face. *Asshole.*

"I sure can. Don't you know it's rude to show up uninvited?" I say back with more bark than bite.

"I tried to tell him we should just leave you be, but he won't listen," Eli says, hands in his coat pocket.

"I also tried to stop him, for the record," Alice supplies, as she comes up to give me a quick hug before doing the same with Olivia.

"I was enjoying a game of *Overwatch* when he kidnapped me," Jordan offers.

Great. I guess it's "friends' night" in. I contemplate telling them to hit the road so I sigh and give Olivia a longing look and a pout, but she's smiling and giving everyone hugs. As we all head inside, I realize how important this might be for her. She doesn't have many friends, and the fact that mine accepted her so quickly and made her part of our group must make her happy. How can I deny her that?

WE SPEND the whole night playing board games, drinking mulled wine, and talking about anything and everything. Elias shares stories from his hometown in Finland and Olivia asks him lots of questions about his family and how he got interested in playing goalie.

Alice and Jordan seem to be in their own little bubble for most of the time, chatting and laughing. I'll have to find out what's going on with them. Is he interested in my sister?

Ash is unabashedly loud and flirtatious, asking Olivia lots of questions as well. I don't know if he's doing it to rile me up or if it's just his way of being friendly, but he keeps finding ways to touch Olivia. Whether it's to grab her arm to get her attention, or take her hand to "admire" her rings. My fingers are aching from clenching them so tight the whole night.

Olivia must notice my change in demeanor because once we finish the board game we were playing, her hand finds mine under the table and she laces our fingers together. That one small touch makes me swallow the tight knot in my throat.

Somehow, she knows exactly what I need to make me feel better. I squeeze her hand to let her know I'm okay and when I look up, I see Ash giving me a smirk and a wink. Bastard.

Once we're all thoroughly buzzed, we move to the couches in the living room and put on a Christmas movie. We're all laughing at Clark Griswold's shenanigans and by the time the movie ends, both Olivia and Alice are asleep on the couch the three of us are sitting on. Beans is curled in Olivia's lap next to me and Caramel is napping in his cat tree. Ash is passed out on the loveseat he's sharing with Elias, who is shaking his head at him. Jordan is almost asleep on the oversized chair, one leg dangling off the side.

I guess we're having a sleepover. "Hey Jordan, can you pick Alice up and bring her to the spare bedroom?" He jolts at my question and stands up, hesitating for a second before leaning down and gently picking up my sister.

I pick up Beans and give him a few pets even though he's clearly mad at me and giving me a death glare. I deposit him on the cat tree below his brother. Then I move back to the couch to get Olive. Her lips are partly open and she's sound asleep. One strand of hair is covering her right eye so I gently tuck it behind her ear.

I put one hand around her back and the other under the back of her knees and gently lift her off the couch. Her head immediately finds my shoulder to rest on and I start walking down the hall. I think about letting her share a bed with Alice, but I don't know if she would appreciate that. While she enjoys physical touch, at least with me, Alice sleeps like a star fish and is a big cuddler. So, I take her to my bedroom instead.

I set her down and she immediately burrows into my bed. *Fuck*. The sight of her here, in my space, makes my heart constrict. What I wouldn't give for this night to have gone differently. While I love my friends, I would have liked nothing more than to kiss Olivia and for us to spend the night alone, preferably together in this bed.

Instead, I give her temple a soft kiss, tuck her in and go back to the living room.

Jordan is back as well and I give him a nod in thanks but he's avoiding my eyes for some reason. Is he afraid to tell me he has a crush on my sister? If he's trying to hide it, he's doing a very poor job, and frankly, I'm offended that he wouldn't tell me. While I am protective of my sister, I've known Jordan for years. He's family, and I know in my bones that he's a good guy and would be perfect for Alice. But it's not my place to say anything or intervene.

"I'll go grab some pillows and blankets. Can one of you open the sleeper sofa?" I say and move to the linen closet in the hallway. When I come back, Ash is sprawled out on the loveseat and Elias is placing a bottle of water on the floor next to him. Elias, ever the caretaker. He seems to have a soft spot for Ash, but I've never been able to figure out if it's more than friendly. Outside of telling me he went through a breakup two years ago, right before moving to the states, Elias doesn't talk about his dating life. Or his sexuality. While Ash will proudly tell us about his recent sexcapades, Eli is more private and keeps to himself.

"It'll be a tight fit, but the three of us can share the sleeper sofa," I say.

"The chair was actually pretty comfortable," Jordan says and grabs a blanket and a pillow and folds in the oversized chair.

I turn off all the lights and after Elias puts a blanket over Ash, he joins me on the sofa bed. "I'm sorry we ruined your night with Olivia," he says.

"It wasn't ruined. I think she really needed it and seemed to have a lot of fun," I say in a whisper.

"Have you thought about any potential consequences if you two start dating?"

"What do you mean?"

"I know there are no clear fraternization rules, but it could be frowned upon to have a relationship with a referee. Especially one that officiates so many of our games."

I'm quiet for a moment. I haven't thought about that, no. Elias continues. "I'm just saying, while you might be ready to retire, this is just the beginning of her career. If someone were to be punished for fraternizing, it wouldn't be you."

"Are you telling me not to pursue anything with her?" I ask with a bit of an edge in my voice.

"I'm telling you to think it through. Make sure it's what she really wants. Communicate. Trust me, it's better to be honest about your expectations ahead of time," Elias says with sadness in his voice.

"Are you speaking from experience?"

He pauses, then says, "Yes." The conversation is over once he turns on his side, away from me.

I hate that he's right. If I pursue anything with Olivia, we both need to be on the same page about what we want.

TWENTY-FOUR

Olivia

I WAKE up in an unfamiliar room. Beans is curled up next to me, so I know I'm at Robbie's house, but this is not the room I've been sleeping in the past four nights. As I slowly wake up and take in my surroundings I realize this must be Robbie's bedroom. While he briefly gave me a tour of the whole house, we didn't linger much here. Now that I take in the space I realize it's exactly what I expected from him. Unlike the spare bedroom, which has a pile of clothes inside my suitcase and toiletries spread out haphazardly around the bathroom counter, Robbie's room is neatly organized.

The door to his walk-in closet is open and I see a hamper with dirty laundry, a wall of shoes and neatly hung clothes. The king size bed has a large upholstered headboard and two nightstands, one of which has my phone and a bottle of water. I take a sip and continue my perusal. On the opposite side of the bed there is a small desk with a tablet on it and some notebooks. Next to it there are two bookcases, both full to the brim with a variety of novels, from fantasy to sci-fi, to mystery and even a couple romances.

I place the bottle of water back on the nightstand and notice a pair of reading glasses with wide, dark frames. *Holy shit.* Robbie probably looks so sexy wearing those, reading in bed. Just thinking about Robbie and this bed makes a memory surge up from last night of him carrying me in and kissing my forehead good night. The other side of the bed is empty and doesn't seem to have been slept in, which means he didn't spend the night here with me. Did he not want to or was he just trying to be nice? I would have liked nothing more than to wake up next to him. I stand up and use the bathroom before heading out to the living room to see where Robbie might be.

My phone shows that it's only eight in the morning, which is unusually early for me to be up. By my calculations, it must have been two in the morning when I fell asleep. When I get out to the living room, I stop and grin at the sight in front of me. Ash is asleep on the loveseat, snuggling a pillow and snoring softly. Jordan is passed out in the chair, his mouth open and snoring much louder than Ash. And on the sofa, which I had no idea was a pull-out, Elias is cuddling Robbie.

I keep smiling and snap a picture to tease them later on. Their friendship is incredible. While I've never encountered anything like it before, Robbie seems to have found himself a family in these guys. They mess around and make fun of each other, but they are also loyal and fiercely protective of one another. I see it on the ice as much as I see it off the ice as well.

I move to the kitchen to get a snack and maybe make a

coffee if I can be quiet, but not even five minutes later, I hear someone getting up and spin around to see who.

Robbie looks devastatingly handsome in the morning. His dark blond locks are wild and he's rubbing his eyes with his knuckles while sluggishly moving away from the couch. He then stretches his arms which makes his shirt ride up so I can see his defined muscles. He doesn't see me standing by the kitchen island yet, drooling over him, so I indulge myself another moment to unabashedly stare at him. He's gorgeous.

His eyes meet mine and for a moment we don't move. We just look at each other. His gaze is contemplative, like he wants to do something but he's unsure of the results. He starts to slowly move towards me and I notice he's wearing light gray sweatpants and he's barefoot. I don't think there's anything more attractive than a man in a dark shirt and light gray sweatpants.

Robbie gets so close to me that I have to tilt my head up a bit to look him in the eye. He gives me a soft smile and says, "Good morning. How come you're up so early?"

I poke the dimple in his cheek and he smiles bigger for me. "Dunno, I couldn't sleep any longer, I guess."

He frowns. "But you always like to sleep in."

I shrug but give him a smile back. "I was trying to make some coffee but I didn't want to wake anyone. Although, I don't really know how to use your fancy espresso machine."

He laughs softly. "I can show you later. I wouldn't use it now since it can get pretty noisy. But if you still want some caffeine I have cold brew in the fridge."

"I can wait until later." I fidget a bit since I don't know what to do now. I want to go change and maybe take a walk, but I also want to go burrow in his bed some more. But I don't want to do those things alone. I could go pack. "How come you had me sleep in your room last night?" I ask before I even think it through.

"Oh, um. Sorry about that," he says, rubbing the back of his head nervously. "I initially thought you and Alice could share the room, but then remembered she likes to sprawl out and would definitely kick you in the face at some point during the night."

That makes me chuckle. "Thanks for looking out for me then."

"Always," he says with more seriousness than the moment warrants.

"How come you didn't join me?" I ask and then realize what I just implied with that question. So I look away and talk some more in the hopes he doesn't take it the wrong way. "I just mean, it's a big bed, I'm sure we could've both fit. You didn't have to cuddle Elias for my sake."

He's silent, and when I look back at him I realize he's staring at my mouth. He clears his throat and quietly says, "If it were up to me, none of my friends would be here this morning." He takes a slow step towards me and leans down to whisper in my ear as one of his hands rests on the counter next to us, and the other finds my waist, "If it were up to me, I would have kissed you senseless under the mistletoe, fed you dinner I made from scratch instead of takeout pizza, and spent the rest of the night doing whatever you wanted to do."

He pauses and I bring a hand up to his chest because, *holy fuck*, I need to steady myself. I feel his hand flex on my waist, his fingers digging in. My palm lands right on top of his heart and I can feel how fast it's beating. His mouth is still close to my ear and I can hear him swallow before he continues, "If it were up to me, I would have made sure you didn't wake up alone, because I would've been right there next to you the whole night."

He pulls back and slowly watches my face for a reaction, but I already know what he sees written all over my face. Pure desire that is also reflected in his blue eyes. He takes a deep inhale and I fist his shirt where I am holding it right above his heart. The sound of a door closing breaks us out of our moment and we both look to see who it is. But we don't completely break apart. Robbie moves away so I can better see the hallway but he keeps his hand on my waist.

Alice stops dead in her tracks when she sees us, facepalms herself, and turns right back around and disappears into the guest bedroom.

"I should probably go and change," I say with a sigh.

"Okay," Robbie says and lets go of my waist.

I take a step away from him, but before I can leave, I turn back and say, "For the record, if it were up to me, I would've wanted the same."

THE REST of the morning goes by too quickly. I change and pack while Alice helps me. She apologizes a million times, and I assure her it's okay. It's not like we were going to make out in the kitchen with all his friends sleeping a few feet away. When we emerge from the spare bedroom, Robbie has coffee ready for everyone and even makes breakfast. They must have these hangouts often because his fridge is always stocked like he's feeding a family of six.

By the time we finish eating and everyone else leaves, Robbie and I need to head to the airport. Our drive is not silent as Robbie tells me about ideas he has for our next hangout in a few weeks. However, we don't talk about the elephant in the car. We both know there's something between us and at some point it will give. Whether it's attraction or more on his part, I'm not sure. What I am sure of, without a doubt, is how much I care about him and admire him.

Robbie parks the car and helps me with my luggage. Once I get checked in, he walks me to the security area. I glance at my phone and see I still have a few minutes, so I pull him to the side so we're not blocking the area and wrap my hands around his neck, bringing him in a tight hug. His hands immediately envelop me and hold me tight.

I can feel the prickle of tears, so I squeeze my eyes shut and tell him, "I'll miss you." He lets out a big sigh and brings one of his hands to cup the back of my head. He finds the spot between my shoulder and neck and nuzzles there. Fuck, I really don't want to leave. Especially since we didn't get a chance to talk about all the missed moments we had this week.

"I'll miss you more. But I'll see you soon, and I promise it will be just us next time," he says against my neck, then drops a small kiss there before slightly pulling away. He looks about as sad as I feel, so I impulsively move and kiss him on the cheek, while my hand caresses the tiny bit of scruff he has this morning. I linger a beat longer and Robbie closes his eyes and covers my hand with his.

"Bye, Robbie," I say and turn to walk towards security.

I don't make it more than a couple of feet before I hear, "Hey, Olive?"

I turn and see him taking rushed steps towards me. Before I can figure out what is wrong, two hands cup my face and tilt my head up, his body leaning into mine. Robbie's lips slam mine with such fervor it knocks me off kilter and I stumble back a bit. One of his arms moves from my face to my lower back and holds tight. His lips are softer than I imagined and as soon as my lips part for his, I feel the softness of his tongue on mine. He tastes like maple syrup and coffee. Sweet and delicious.

I rake my fingers through his soft hair then grip the back of his neck to bring him even closer. I don't know how long we stand there and make out, and frankly, I don't care. I am finally kissing Robbie and it's everything. He slows down the kiss, but it's not any less intense than before. He tilts my head to the side, taking the kiss deeper, exploring every inch of my mouth. I get bolder too and scrape my teeth on his lower lip, giving him a gentle nibble.

Robbie loudly groans against my lips and grips my sweater so hard I fear it might tear. That alone makes me stop and realize we're in public. I can hear some people hollering nearby, no doubt about the show we're putting on.

We're both breathing hard, chests heaving, standing there trying to recover. I can't help but grin up at Robbie and the smile he gives me back is so adoring, it might make me melt. We stop gripping each other like it's the end of the world, but we don't let go. His movements are soft as he tucks a strand of hair behind my ear and gives me another kiss. This one is chaste and sweet, a lingering press of his swollen lips to mine.

"We really should have done this sooner. Now I don't want to let you go," he says as he gives me another hug.

"Two weeks is nothing," I say meekly, not quite believing it myself. While we'll both be busy the next two weeks, it won't be nothing. I am going to miss him like crazy. And now that I know what his kisses feel like, I want more of them. I'm greedy.

"Call me when you land, okay?" he says with a peck to my head, reluctantly letting me go.

"I will. Give Caramel and Beans my love, okay?"

"They got plenty this week, I'll keep it all to myself." He winks and smiles and I can't help but grin back at him.

"So selfish!" I shake my head but start walking away. The whole flight home I think about that kiss and how it's changed so much between us. And yet, I still don't know exactly where we stand.

SHARE THE CATS

Robbie

I miss you already.

Olivia

I miss you too. How are my favorite boys?

??

Beans and Caramel, obviously.

Of course, that's all you care about. I'm starting to think the whole reason you became friends with me and spent the holiday here was to get closer to my cats.

Ah, yes. You've discovered my master plan. My goal is to get you to fall in love with me, ask me to move in, just so I can steal your cats.

> Rude. You know I'm willing to just share the cats, no need to kick me to the curb.

> Where's the fun in that?

TWENTY-FIVE

Robbie
December

THE PAST TWO weeks have been torture. Olivia and I have texted and called every single day, but we haven't talked about our feelings or what that kiss meant for the both of us. I'm taking Elias' advice and laying it all on the line. If she wants to be in a relationship with me, I won't let that affect her career.

I've given the situation a lot of thought. While there are no clear rules about fraternization between a player and an official, I can't imagine the AHL would react positively if we disclosed our relationship. Out of the remaining 50 games in the regular season, Olivia is scheduled to officiate 20 of them that involve my team. That means there will be plenty of opportunities for us to see each other over the next four months.

We could keep it a secret and not let anyone know, which may not be the most ethical thing to do, but Olivia would not make calls in my favor during a game. I know this with certainty because she's honest down to her core and she wouldn't jeopardize her career over something like that.

We could disclose our relationship and hope for the best. While I have made my peace with retiring, I wouldn't do that in the middle of the season and leave the team to scramble without a captain. I would have to see the season through, but there are ways for me to sit out a few games by getting a healthy scratch designation—which I've gotten a few of this season due to us having more than 20 people on the roster.

The issue would be if the AHL deemed it to remove Olivia from all the Manticore's games and reassign her to others. Then she wouldn't be in the same cities as me at the same time.

After two weeks of small talk and flirting over the phone, I am ready to see Olivia in person and have these lengthy conversations together. We are back in Vermont for a series of back to back games against the Vortices, our least favorite team to play. We played the first game last night, which of course got heated by the end. While Ash managed to stay out of fights against Mitchell, Jordan didn't.

At some point during the third period, the game tied 2-2, Mitchell managed to check me hard into the boards. My back was turned to him as I had possession of the puck, and as soon as I passed it across to Jordan, Mitchell flattened me against the boards. The whistle went off and a penalty was called. While I was getting my bearings, Jordan decided to pick a fight against Mitchell for his hit. That got us a penalty as well and ultimately we lost the game when Mitchell came out of the box and scored a goal. We're all dreading playing against them again tonight, but after a 3 game loss streak, we badly need a win.

Spirits were down at morning skate, but at least I have some time to myself before the game tonight, and Olivia just texted me to let me know she's on the way to the hotel. While she couldn't get an earlier flight, we still have a few hours to spend together before we have to show up at the arena. I also made plans to hang out together after the game and tomorrow before both of us need to leave.

I invited her back to Grand Marquee for Christmas and offered to help with her transportation, but she said she needs to spend it with Grams. She also has other games to officiate around that time, so she wouldn't be available for as long as she was during Thanksgiving. So after tomorrow, the next time I get to see her is New Years when we are playing a home game. She extended that trip already to spend a couple of extra days with me.

All of these thoughts are heavy on my mind as I slowly pace around the hotel lobby. I don't hear her calling my name until I turn and see her walking towards me, her equipment bag rolling behind her and a backpack dangling off one shoulder. The smile she gives me is pure happiness.

I walk over to her and grab her face with both hands, giving her a lingering kiss. She's startled for a moment but she kisses me right back. It's so reminiscent of our airport kiss, that I become dizzy for a moment. *God, that kiss.* I've thought about it every night since then. How perfect we fit together, how she melted in my arms at first and then gripped me hard and pulled me in, like she never wanted to let me go.

We've learned our lesson about making out in public though, so I keep this kiss short and sweet. At least until we get somewhere more private. "Want some help with that bag?" I ask with a smile.

"Sure. I just need to check in first before we head up."

Thankfully there is no line at the check-in desk and Olivia is able to quickly get her key card. On the way up to her room I ask, "How was your flight? How is Grams?"

"The flight was good, I listened to the playlist you sent me, by the way. I expected you to be more of an '80s music fan, not modern pop."

"I like all music, there are few genres I don't listen to," I respond.

"And Grams is fine, she says hi," Olivia says as we arrive at her door. She turns to look at me and assesses me for a moment.

"Do you want to come in?" she asks a little nervously.

I swallow hard. Of course I do. I've wanted nothing more than to be alone with her for two weeks. "I don't know if that is wise," I say hesitantly. "I think we should talk, before we take things further." Her eyes widen a bit and I realize how I've made it sound.

So I quickly add, "Not that anything more than what has happened needs to happen. Not right now, anyway. I just—" Shit, I'm rambling. "I just mean—if I go in right now, I'm going to want to keep kissing you and for the first time in my life I might not want to leave and play hockey."

She's looking at me with a smile on her face and I'm blushing like a fucking teenager. "Well, I definitely won't let us miss the game if that's what you're worried about. And if we need to talk, shouldn't we do that somewhere private?"

I nod and follow her inside, mind still spinning at all the possibilities of the two of us alone in a hotel room.

Keep your hands to yourself, Robbie.

Olivia drops her backpack somewhere on a chair and I leave her equipment bag by the door and we both take a seat at the edge of the bed.

"So," Olivia says, nervously twirling one of the rings on

her right hand. I gently grab it and interlace our fingers together.

"So," I lamely add. What is wrong with me? I've been thinking about this conversation for weeks, but now that we're here, I'm speechless?

I squeeze her fingers and turn my body towards her, bringing my knee up to rest by her thigh. "Olive, I, um, wanted to talk about us."

"Okay. That's a good idea," she says softly, her thumb brushing mine back and forth. "Can I say something first, though?"

I nod and she continues, "I've had feelings for you for a while now, even though we basically only met two months ago. To be honest, I don't think I've ever met anyone like you. I admire you so much—your patience and loyalty and kindness. You're amazing, Robbie," she says tenderly and my heart soars hearing those things.

"I know I'm not the easiest person to be around sometimes—"

I interrupt her, "That's not true."

"It is, but you seem to like me despite that. You've gotten to know me really well, better than most people, actually. It's not easy for me to trust people, but I trust you, Robbie. Completely." She watches my face and lingers a bit on my mouth before saying, "So, full disclosure, I've never been into casual dating or sex. If we decide to be together, I'm all in."

Fuck, that's exactly what I've wanted to hear. I let out a relieved breath and reach up to cup Olivia's face with my free hand. "Oh *love*, I want nothing more than to be all in with you. I just want you to be sure. Because we have some decisions to make when it comes to our jobs, and the last thing I want is to pressure you into anything you don't want to do."

She nods and says, "I've thought about that too. As much as I don't like it, we'd probably want to keep our relationship a secret for a bit, until the end of the season. I can ask to be transferred to a different region next season."

"No," I say quickly. "Remember how I told you I was considering retiring? I think I'm ready to do that after this season. I would even do it now if it didn't hurt the team."

Olivia is quiet for a beat then quietly says, "I don't want you to retire for me. What if you end up resenting that decision? Resenting me?"

"Olive, I could never resent you. I already told you I want to try something different. I would have made this choice whether or not you were in the picture. And I really want you in the picture, for the record," I say, giving her a grin.

She smiles back and rests her head on my shoulder. "If you're sure about this, then I am too. We can keep it under wraps until the end of the season."

"Sounds like a plan. But now that I'm officially your boyfriend, you need to let me help you with stuff. Like plane tickets, so you can visit me more often."

She laughs and says, "We'll see about that. Both our schedules are going to be so crazy, we'll be lucky to get any time together outside of the game we're both at."

I run my fingers through her hair as I continue holding her to me. "There is the All-Star break. We could go somewhere the whole week. My friends and I usually go to my parents' cabin up north for a few days and snowboard. Do you snowboard or ski?"

She shakes her head but says, "I've only snowboarded a couple of times. I'm pretty bad at it."

"I could teach you if you wanted. Or we can skip the cabin and just stay at my house the whole week. Just you, me, and the cats. And my meddling family, of course," I say with a laugh, thinking of all the times Alice walked in on our moments.

"I like your meddling family a lot." She pulls back and gives me a smile. "We're really going to do this? Messy, long distance relationship and all? Are you sure you don't want someone who will greet you at home after every game with a homemade meal? I can't even cook." She frowns and I know this is just her insecurities and past experiences speaking, but it still breaks my heart that she would believe I wanted anyone other than her.

"The whole housewife thing is not my style, love. Besides, I prefer to do the cooking myself," I give her a smirk. "I know you didn't have the best support in the past, especially from the one person who should have been there for you. I would never make you put your dreams on hold or ask you to make sacrifices for my sake."

A tear falls on her cheek and I gently swipe it with my thumb and kiss the spot. "As for the long distance, if anyone can make it work, it's us." I press our foreheads together and after a beat of silence, Olivia nods. Decision made. We're doing this.

I tilt her head up to me with the hand that is still cupping her face and swipe my thumb across her jaw before leaning in for a sweet kiss. Olivia's lips are soft and I take my time kissing them, licking at the seam until she lets me in. Soon, our kisses turn from sweet and exploring to fervent. She runs one hand to the back of my neck, gripping the hair there.

She takes control of the kiss and I can't even fucking think straight anymore. When Olivia bites my lip and soothes the sting with a lick I have to fist the comforter because of how painfully hard it makes me. I need to slow this down otherwise we'll be late to the game, but Olivia has other plans. In one swift move, she swings her leg over my hip, straddling me. Without taking her mouth off of mine, she pushes me down so I'm pinned to the bed.

Without thinking, I move both of my hands to the back of her thighs, close to her magnificent ass, and pull her closer to me. It's only when she freezes mid kiss that I realize how thin the materials of my joggers and her leggings are, and that she probably feels how hard and throbbing I am against her.

When she pulls back to look at me, I can see the desire written all over her face. I'm breathing harder than I would after a game and focus all my will power into holding still, letting her take what she needs. She slowly pulls back more, one hand trailing down my chest and resting on my abdomen, until she's straddling me, her back straight. My hands move from the back of her thighs to the front, rubbing circles on her leggings.

Eyes locked with mine, Olivia circles her hips and shifts her weight on top of me. My eyes close and my hips snap up of their own volition, fingers digging into her legs. Olivia continues to circle her hips on top of me all while moving her hand under my sweatshirt, finding all the hard ridges of my stomach.

Her fingers are slightly cold on my skin and it makes me shiver and clench my muscles in pleasure. I'm so fucking close I might embarrass myself during our first make out session. I try to slow her down by bringing one hand to her back and holding her to me, but all that does is make her more eager. She leaves a trail of kisses from my jaw to my neck, to my collarbone where she softly bites. I groan out a husky "Fuck," which only makes Olivia move more.

I use both my arms to hold her tightly to me then flip us both around so I can be on top. The move surprises her and she lets out a little squeak and a laugh. I pull back and smile down at her. "I can't believe I'm saying this, but maybe we should slow down. We do have to leave shortly."

She looks over at the clock on the nightstand and shakes her head. "We have half an hour."

"That's not enough time for all the things I want to do to you," I say in a low voice, licking my lips as I glance down at our joint bodies. My right hand is braced above her head, the other holding tightly to her leg that's hiked around my waist. My cock is perfectly lined up with her pussy and I can't help the groan I let out just seeing us in this position.

Olivia brings both her hands to my face and pulls me in for an eager kiss. Only when we break apart for air does she say, "I don't think we should go to work when we're both so sexually pent up."

"Are you asking me to play hooky?" I smile into her neck.

"I'm asking you to make me come," she says, breathlessly.

Fuck. What have I done to deserve this girl?

I gently bite down on her ear lobe and can't help but revel in the shiver she gives me. "How do you want to come?" I whisper low in her ear. That gets me a small whine and a thrust upwards. "You gotta use your words, love. Tell me what you need."

She groans as I continue leaving a trail of kisses from behind her ear to her throat. Her fingers grip my sweatshirt tightly and she's panting against my mouth as I lean in for another kiss. "Tell me," I whisper against her lips.

"I want—"

"What do you want?"

"I want your fingers inside me." Her admission surprises me since I didn't expect her to be so blunt about it. But fuck if it doesn't turn me on more.

I slowly back away and unhook her leg from my waist before reaching back down and hooking my fingers around the waistband of her leggings. Olivia's breathing is hard and she throws her head back, eyes closed in anticipation. I can't have that, so I say, "Eyes on me, Olive."

Her eyes immediately lock with mine and I hold her gaze while I slowly pull down her leggings and underwear. Instead of asking her to lift her hips, I reach around and pull the materials down over her perfectly round ass myself, taking my time. Only when she pants in frustration, do I finally finish pulling her pants down all the way and throw them across the room.

I finally look down at her and swear at how perfect and glistening she is for me. I lean back down and hover over her, propped up on my left elbow while my right hand leaves a trail of caresses from her calf all the way to her hip. I kiss her senseless while running my knuckles over her hip bone, the neatly trimmed hair, and down to her clit. As soon as my knuckle flicks it, she arches up and moans against my lips.

Fuck. She's so wet and perfect and I want to take my time and keep her in this hotel room for days while I explore every inch of her skin. But we need to leave in twenty minutes, so I stop teasing her and slowly pump my middle finger inside her. I groan at how tight she feels with just one finger and she sucks in a gasp as I continue moving in and out. One of her hands moves to grip my shoulder while the other circles my neck and she brings me closer, her kisses becoming more erratic. "More," she whispers.

I add a second finger and curl them both inside, which makes her moan and squeeze me harder as she starts grinding her hips against my hand. I move my thumb over her clit and she shudders, but doesn't come yet. I can tell she's close by how tightly she's holding me and how heavy her breathing becomes.

I wonder if talking dirty to her would put her over the edge or if she'd prefer praise. I decide to go with praise as I move my fingers faster inside her and continue to rub her clit with my thumb. "Fuck, you're taking my fingers so well." I lean in and whisper in her ear, "Such a good girl."

She immediately starts clenching against my fingers and her leg starts shaking. The way she moans my name is almost pornographic and enough to bring me close as well. I keep my fingers still inside her but continue to slowly move my thumb until she puts her hand on top of mine to stop me. I pull them out and give her a lingering kiss, trying to keep my erection away from her so I don't just burst.

"Fuck, that was so intense," she pants out and kisses me some more, her hand trailing down to my cock. I gently stop her before she can touch me but the look she gives me is almost wounded. "You don't want me to touch you?"

I choke on a laugh, "Of course I do, but fucking hell, I need to last more than five seconds here."

"I don't care about that, I just want to make you feel good," she says, moving her hand out from under mine and palming me through my joggers. When my body almost collapses on top of her from one touch, she smiles and pushes me down on my back. With the same precision as me, she pulls my layers down to my thighs. My cock bobs against my stomach and Olivia reaches up and takes my sweatshirt off.

She bends down and leaves trails of kisses from my neck to my collarbone and down my abdomen, all the while swiping at my head and spreading the wetness around. Her touch feels so good I have to fist the sheets and control myself. She reaches over and takes one of my hands, bringing it to my cock as she says, "Show me how you like it."

God, the desire on her face makes me want to never leave this room, but we're on a schedule and I need to stop stalling. So I cover her hand with mine and guide her, showing her how much pressure to apply and how hard to squeeze. "I'm close," I manage to say before going back to fisting the sheets and throwing my head back. She continues to pump me at a fast pace, twisting at the head just how I like it, even as she moves a bit higher up my body and brings her other hand to my throat, not really squeezing but applying a bit of pressure.

Never thought I would be into that, but seeing the wild look in her eyes as she fucks me with her hand and keeps that possessive hand on my throat is enough to tip me over the edge. As soon as she feels me coming, she spreads it around her fingers and continues to stroke me, making my own body shake. Her hand at my throat lets up and she kisses me hard as I come down from the high. *Holy fuck, I've never come so hard in my life.*

TWENTY-SIX

Olivia

I DON'T THINK I've ever smiled this much in public in my whole life. The referee locker room is smaller here than most places so the four of us are packed in, getting ready. The other guys are making jokes and getting hyped up, and for once, I actually join in.

"I can't wait for New Year's. I took some time off and my wife and I are going to California for a few days," says Ben, one of the linesmen officiating tonight.

"That's cool, are you visiting anything in particular?" I find myself asking. *Look at me, making conversation with my peers.*

"We're probably going to Disneyland and the beach. Kind of winging it and finding time to relax," he says with a smile.

"That sounds awesome," I say, returning it.

I try not to think too much about why I'm in such a good mood, but my thoughts stray to Robbie even though they shouldn't right now. I'm supposed to keep it professional. I just can't forget the look on his face after we both came down from our highs, how he got a warm washcloth and cleaned us both up before cuddling me and whispering all the things he wanted to do to me later.

I would have stayed there in that moment forever if my alarm hadn't gone off letting us know it was time to head to the arena. My entire body is buzzing with excitement, and for once, I can't wait for this game to be over.

The crowd is rowdy as ever and they start booing the officials as soon as we get on the ice. I can tell there is leftover tension between the two teams from yesterday's game which means I need to stay on high alert. Especially when Mitchell is involved.

Speaking of the devil, he skates past me and gives me a look of pure disdain. I will never understand how some people can't separate their personal feelings from their work. While he's an asshole on the ice, I would never make the presumption Mitchell was an asshole in his personal life. Although, after what Robbie told me about how he picked a fight with Ash at a bar last time we were here, that makes me lose hope in his humanity.

The first period goes by quickly, uneventfully. Nobody scores, but there are a few minor penalties. Thankfully nothing to start a fight over. The second period starts out hot, with Ash scoring a goal in the first 20 seconds, and I can feel the shift in tension. The Vortices start to hit harder, one of them even checking a Manticores hard on the open ice. The Manticores player stays down so I blow the whistle to stop play, but I'm not calling out a penalty. While the hit was hard, it was a legal move. There was no tripping or holding, just good old fashioned checking.

The Manticores player manages to stand up by himself

and I escort him to the bench, but when I turn around I see an angry Ash in my face.

"What the hell was that, Olivia? You're not going to call a penalty?"

I take a deep breath and say, "The hit was legal. We're moving on now."

He takes a step closer to me like he wants to argue further, but I am not going to indulge his tantrum.

"The hell it was, our guy was hurt, he's literally walking out the tunnel and probably has a concussion!" I start skating away from him but he follows. "Olivia, come on!"

I round on him so fast he draws up short, "That's *ref* to you, in case you've forgotten yourself. And if you don't drop it, I will put you in the box." I know he's just frustrated with the situation and not really lashing out at me, but the more he continues with his tantrum, the more he's undermining my authority.

He doesn't learn his lesson though because as soon as the face-off ends, Ashton trips up the Vortices player that checked his friend earlier. I immediately blow the whistle but before Ben, the linesmen, can intervene, both Ashton and the other guy drop their gloves and start fighting. They both manage to get a few punches to the face and it takes all four of us officials to break them up. I place myself right in front of Ash and start leading him backwards to the box. He's still yelling profanities at the other guy and promises to kick his ass.

I roll my eyes and push him a bit harder muttering under my breath "Cavemen." Ash takes a deep breath and looks down at me and I draw up for another verbal attack but the corners of his lips are tugging up and his eyes are amused.

"Sorry, ref," he says and enters the penalty box. I shake

my head and see Robbie skating up to us, carrying Ash's stick and gloves.

Robbie shakes his head in disappointment and says, "I thought you were going to stay out of the box."

Ash looks away and shrugs "Whatever, leopard can't change his spots and all that." Robbie sighs in defeat and skates away but he doesn't see the look of self-loathing on Ash's face.

"You wanna know something about leopards?" Ash looks at me with curiosity and a little bit of doubt. "They're magnificent and fight to win," I say before skating away and sorting out all the penalties. Both Ash and the Vortices player get five minutes for fighting and Ash gets another two minutes for tripping, which means the Vortices are at an advantage, which Mitchell capitalizes on immediately and scores.

Ash must have heard my subtle advice, that he needs to focus on winning the game instead of fighting, because he scores his second goal of the night with a minute left in the period. On his way to the bench he gives me a wink and Robbie raises his eyebrows at the exchange. I just smile and shake my head. That boy is something else. He's cocky and boisterous, but he's damn good at what he does and he just needs someone to believe in him.

The third period is just as crazy as the second, except it's the Vortices that spend the majority of the time in the penalty box. More fights break out and penalties get called, but both teams also score. The Manticores lead 3-2 with 5 minutes remaining in the game when Robbie scores on a breakaway. I smile to myself as we reset because that was a damn good goal, but Mitchell catches me and glares at me.

"Playing favorites, I see," he says and spits at my feet. What a fucking asshole. I know I shouldn't let his words bother me, but I can't help it. I also can't help the anger I feel every time he comes near me, which is why I say, "I can appreciate a good goal when I see one. Can't say the same for you, though." His face is beet red and he's seething. I'm sure he'd like nothing more than to throw me down on the ice right now, but he knows he can't. So I just skate away.

I expect him to retaliate somehow, but the next couple minutes are surprisingly docile on both ends. That is, until Mitchell hip checks Robbie so hard he goes flying and lands hard on his left side. The other referee calls the penalty as clipping since that was clearly a dirty hit. Robbie gets up on his own but he's clearly in pain and Jordan helps him down to the tunnel.

My heart is beating so fast, and I can't stop thinking about that hit. Mitchell is bitching about that not being a penalty when we all know he did it on purpose. The other referee gives him a major penalty as well and has him leave the game completely since there is not much left on the clock.

With Mitchell gone, the Vortices pull their goalie in an attempt to make a play, but all that leads to is the Manticores scoring an empty net goal. Ash is the one to score, which means he gets a hat trick. Too bad it's not a home game where fans would actually throw their hats on the ice for him. We skate to the tunnel together and he says, "Thanks, for earlier. I appreciate you looking out for me."

I nod but don't quite know what else to say. My head is spinning about Robbie. I hope he's not seriously injured. Ash must see the worry on my face because he adds, "Don't worry, I'll check on him and text you an update, okay?" I nod and then hurry to the locker room to get changed and wait in the lobby with my phone in hand. Hoping for good news.

A WHILE LATER, a bunch of Manticores players and staff leave the arena, but I still haven't caught sight of Robbie and his group. I'm pacing around the lobby when I finally hear them.

"That Mitchell guy needs to get suspended for that hip check. That was bullshit. You could have gotten seriously injured," Jordan says hotly.

"He is seriously injured," Elias says with a somber face. That makes me start to move in their direction and see Robbie for myself. How hurt is he?

As soon as I approach them, Elias and Jordan move out of the way and I come face to face with Robbie. His head is down, but when he looks up our eyes lock and I can see the exhaustion and sadness in them. Fuck, it makes me devastated to see him like this. I want to run and wrap my hands around him but I don't know where we stand in front of his friends. So I lamely say, "Hey. How are you?"

Robbie doesn't hesitate and walks up to me for a hug. His left arm is in a sling and my heart drops. I do my best to hug him back without hurting him. As soon as he drops his head in the crook of my neck he sighs and says "I'm much better now. Can we please get out of here?"

"Of course, but I need to know how bad it is," I say, brushing his dark blonde hair away from his forehead.

"Nothing is broken or too serious. It's just a sprain, but the team physician recommended I sit out for a couple of games," he says miserably. I link my fingers together with his uninjured hand and we all walk outside where a van Jordan requested is waiting to take us to the hotel.

Once we get there, we all head to the bar and get a drink, the guys brooding about the game. I feel so bad for them, it seems like every time they play the Vortices, something bad happens and they can't even enjoy the win they worked so hard for.

"So, you two made things official?" Ashton asks with a smirk as he sips his old fashioned. I blush and take a sip of my own drink as Robbie turns his tired eyes on me. He's giving me the smile I love most on him, the soft one reserved just for me. His eyes trace my face, lingering on my lips and that's my cue to get us out of here and into the same bed together.

Even if we can't do all the sexy stuff we had planned since his arm is in a sling, I still want to spend the night curled up against him. I down the rest of my drink and stand up, offering a hand to Robbie, which he eagerly takes.

"Guys, if you'll excuse us, I think this couple is going to head to bed," I say with a grin on my face. Elias and Jordan give us smiles and mumbles of good night and Ash winks at us as we make our way out of the bar.

Robbie puts his good arm around my shoulder and drops his head on top of mine. We stand like that the whole elevator ride up to my room. Robbie brought his bag in here earlier since he planned on spending the night so I ask him, "Do you need help getting pajamas out, or washing up?" I ask that last part nervously.

"I usually sleep in my underwear. Is that okay?"

"Yeah, of course." Like I would complain ever seeing him mostly naked.

"I probably should wash up a bit, I didn't get a chance to shower at the arena," he says on a yawn. "You don't have to assist me if you feel uncomfortable."

"Why would I feel uncomfortable?"

He shrugs but points at my right hand where I am fidgeting with my ring. Stupid habit. "You play with that a lot when you get nervous." His face settles into a frown and he sighs, "I don't want to make you nervous."

"You're not the reason I am nervous." One corner of his mouth hitches up like he doesn't believe me. "I promise," I say, inching closer to him and untying his sling, "I'm nervous because I was thinking of the logistics of helping you. Like, I'd probably have to get in the shower with you."

I take a breath and dare to look up at his confused face. "I'm nervous about you seeing me completely naked. I know we did stuff earlier, but it's just different, I guess." Now it's my turn to frown. I'm not sure where this insecurity is coming from, but I don't want to disappoint him. Earlier the curtains were drawn and the lights were dim when we got intimate. But in the harsh bathroom light, I'm not so sure I measure up to his imagination.

"Olive," he whispers and takes my hand in his, bringing it up to his heart. "We all have insecurities, but you know what? Whatever imperfections you think you may have don't matter to me. I care about *you*, your beautiful heart and soul. Your body will change with time, as will mine, but that won't make me see you any differently. You'll always be perfect to me." He lets go of my hand to wipe the tear that escapes me and bends down to give me a sweet kiss.

He straightens out his arm a few times and winces a bit, so I gently bring it back in the position he had it in before I took the sling off. "Don't make it worse, please."

"You don't have to take care of me, you know. I've gotten hurt before and kept myself alive." The smile he gives me is tender but a little sad. Something in the way he says that bothers me. *I've kept myself alive.* I can't imagine his family not caring for him when he was hurt before. Unless he didn't tell them because he didn't want them to worry. Now that sounds like something he would do.

I swallow hard and shake my head at him. "As if you could get rid of me that easily. You will let me take care of you and dote on you like a mother hen, and you will not complain about it. Understand me?"

I give him my most stern expression and he sighs and says, "Yes, ma'am." I catch his satisfied smile as we walk into the bathroom.

I turn the water on and wait for it to get hot, then help Robbie out of his sweatshirt, making sure not to bump his left arm. He takes off the rest of his clothes and I do too. I'm trying hard to fight the urge to cover myself as we stand there completely naked, staring at each other. He's trying hard not to look at my breasts. I give him a delighted smirk and his nostrils flare with desire. I walk up to him and wind my arms around his waist, stepping closer and then pressing a kiss right above his heart. I can feel him growing hard against me but before I lose all sense, I grab his good hand and guide him to the shower.

As promised, I dote on him and smack his hand when he tries to reach for the washcloth. I make him stand there under the hot water as I lather it up with soap and run it across his perfect collarbones and chest, down his defined abs and back up the sides. I turn him around and do the same with his broad back and narrow waist, pressing myself against him in a hug when I am done. He turns back around and kisses me slowly but intently. His tongue is eager and hot against mine and he pulls me in closer so I can feel his erection against my stomach.

I slowly run my hand down his chest and tease him before taking him in my hand. He groans in my mouth and bites my lower lip, soothing it with a lick almost immediately. He's panting as he pulls back and says, "You don't have to do that."

"Shh. Let me take care of you. Please," I say and nip at his jaw. Robbie's blue eyes are mostly black as his pupils dilate in pleasure. He gives me a nod and that's all I need to drop down to my knees. He makes a choking sound like he can't believe this is happening but that quickly turns into a moan as I take him in my mouth.

Fuck, he feels so good. His cock is thick and while I only got a few minutes to play with it earlier, I can see now that my mouth alone is not enough. I tease him a bit around the head and lick my way from the base to the tip a few times before taking him as deep as I can. Then I wrap one of my hands around his base and twist in rhythm with my bobbing. Robbie is panting and moaning my name and I need to reach down and touch myself with my free hand to relieve some of the pressure. Holy fuck, giving him a blow job got me so close to my own orgasm. I start to moan as well.

His hand finds my hair and fists it, and that little pinprick of pain makes me come almost immediately. I moan and gasp around his cock and his voice is rough when he bends over me and says, "Fuck, I'm close." His cock hits the back of my throat and I swallow around him but he doesn't come yet. I look up and see him hanging on, fighting his release. I pull out with a pop and continue stroking him as his hips stutter and he lets go of my hair to steady himself on the shower door.

"Fuck, you look absolutely wrecked," I rasp out and his eyes fly open and latch onto mine. I pick up the speed of my strokes and angle myself up more so that he can come all over my breasts. He groans out my name as he does and his body stutters and shakes until he slumps over me.

I stand up and guide him to lean back against the shower wall as I use the washcloth to clean myself. Robbie watches me through half lidded eyes the whole time, his fist clenched like he wants to take over and do it for me. But he's too tired and spent and I'm not the one that needs looking after right now.

I turn off the water, go up to Robbie and kiss him against the shower wall, leaning my full weight into him as I do, my palms flat against his chest. I can feel his heart beating fast so I slow our kiss down and bring my head to his neck. His good arm wraps around me in a tight embrace. We stay like that for another minute until we start to get cold. Then we towel off, put on underwear and I re-tie Robbie's sling. He lays on his back in bed and I curl up beside him, next to his good arm, gripping his fingers with one hand and holding on to his bicep with another.

"Hey, Olive?"

"Yes, Bobbert?"

He chuckles, "You're the best."

"No, you are," I say and kiss his shoulder. "Goodnight."

"Goodnight, love."

TWENTY-SEVEN

Robbie

WAKING up next to Olivia might be my favorite thing in the world. She's a big cuddler, which I did not expect. I think physical contact might be one of her secret love languages, because even though she doesn't seem to enjoy it from most people, she always melts when she's in my arms. She spent the whole night cuddling me and, if my arm wasn't in a sling, I would be spooning the heck out of her.

We were both so tired that we turned off our early alarms in favor of sleeping in. Even though that means our plans for the day are all jumbled, I don't want to leave this bed. I get up to use the restroom and when I'm back, Olivia is still asleep, her head on my pillow. She has a small frown on her face and I trace my thumb against her forehead to smooth it out. I let my hand wander a bit, tucking a strand of hair behind her ear and moving to her jaw. Her lips part and she lets out a soft sigh that makes me smile. *She's so perfect.*

Looking at her lips reminds me of last night in the shower and how incredible her mouth felt on me. Just thinking about it makes me hard again, but as much as I want to spend all day learning every shape and part of her body, we don't have a lot of time before we have to leave.

I gently wake her up and she blinks at me, then gives me a big smile. "Good morning, Olive." I bend down and give her a soft kiss, but as I'm pulling away, she follows, nipping at my bottom lip. I chuckle and stand up, wrapping my right arm around her waist and pulling her up to me, peppering her face with kisses.

"Mmm, why are we not still in bed?" she moans against my neck.

"We need to check out and get some food before we leave."

She sighs and looks up at me, stealing one more kiss. "So, we're really going to do this? Long distance relationship and all?"

"I'm all in if you are."

"Do I get to give you another nickname now?"

"Only if it's cute and affectionate."

"Oh yeah, like, baby?" she says, laughter in her eyes.

"Ugh, no. Never that." I shake my head and shudder.

"Okay, love," she says softly.

"Hey, that's mine. Find your own," I say and tickle her. She laughs and swats me away.

After a quick brunch, we go our separate ways and since she can't visit me for Christmas, I won't get to see her for another couple of weeks. Maybe this makes me a giant simp, but I already miss her. I only had her in my arms for one night, and it wasn't anywhere near enough. I want so much more, but I need to be patient.

WE SPEND the next week video calling every night and staying up way too late talking. She tells me about her day and how work has been, she catches me up on all the books she's reading while she travels from one game to another. I tell her about how I missed two games, but have been playing better since my sling came off. And I also tell her about how the cats are doing and how my mom and Alice ask about her every time they get a chance to.

And yet, it's not enough. Tomorrow is Christmas Eve and as I watch her tired face answer my video call, I realize that I want to be with her right now. To be cuddled on a couch, drinking hot cocoa, watching a holiday movie together. I notice her living room still doesn't have any Christmas decorations.

"Are you going to put up any garlands or a small tree or something?" I ask.

"No, I don't really decorate. I'll be spending Christmas Eve and Day at Grams', so I guess I don't see the point," she says on a yawn. "I'd only be putting them up and then taking them down. I don't get to enjoy them really."

"Are you spending the night at Grams'?"

"No, I'm driving to her place for dinner tomorrow night, then back again for brunch the day after," she says tiredly. Olivia is in her room now, laying in bed, one hand tucked under her head as she faces the phone. Her eyes are heavy and she looks like she might fall asleep at any point.

I glance at the clock and realize it's past midnight. I know she had a long day, traveling by bus back from Ohio. "Hey, Olive?"

"Hm?" She mumbles back, opening one eye.

"Goodnight. I miss you," I sigh and give her a small smile.

"Miss you too. I wish you were here." Fuck, I want to be. As I watch her fall asleep, I keep thinking that maybe I can be there. I know she doesn't want me to help her with money for tickets and that's the main reason she didn't come here for Christmas. But she didn't say anything about me going to her. I think she just assumed I wouldn't because my whole family is here.

I send my sister a text to ask her for a second opinion.

> How mad do you think Mom would be if I didn't show up for Christmas?

It doesn't take her more than a minute before she responds.

> Depends on the reason, I guess?

I should've known Alice was up at this hour, probably reading a smutty book.

> Do you think it would be crazy if I got a last minute flight to Minnesota?

Before I can type out more, I have an incoming call coming from Alice.

"Hey," I say as I answer.

"HOLY SHIT. Are you serious about going to Minnesota?"

"Yes. But I don't want to overwhelm her. You two have gotten close recently. What do you think I should do?" I ask and bite my thumbnail nervously.

"Well, when we talked earlier today she seemed a bit

sad, honestly. I don't know how many people she talks to outside of you and me, but I got the sense she was feeling a little lonely, too."

I bring out my tablet and start searching. "I found a flight that leaves at eight in the morning. It would get me to her house by eleven. Any chance you want to drive me and catsit for a couple of days?"

"I would never pass on the opportunity to leave my annoying roommates and this awful apartment. And to see my nephews."

I sigh, exasperated and say, "They're cats, Al. Stop calling them your nephews."

"Well, until you marry Olivia and have kids of your own, those adorable fur babies are your kids, therefore, my nephews."

"I just bought the ticket. I'm going to pack now."

Alice chuckles and says, "Alright Roro, get a few hours of sleep too. Oh, and make me a fancy coffee if I'm going to drive that early."

"Fine. But you gotta tell mom."

"Yes, I got your back big brother. Always."

"Thanks."

WHEN I LAND IN MINNEAPOLIS, I am running on three cups of coffee and pure anticipation at seeing Olivia. I managed to make a reservation for a car rental before I left, so I throw my duffel bag in the backseat of the SUV and look up the nearest Home Goods store around. I grab every imaginable Christmas decoration, ribbon, and a small artificial tree to put up in her living room. Then I drive to the grocery store and get all of her favorite foods, because I know she's just eating frozen dinners when she's not at Grams'. And I won't let my girl eat frozen pasta for Christmas.

By the time I pull into Olivia's driveway it's early afternoon, which means she should be awake by now. I load up my hands with as many bags as I can fit and head to the door. I ring the doorbell twice and hold my breath when it opens.

Olivia clearly does not expect to find me on her doorstep and after blinking away the shock, she breaks into a full grin and envelopes me in a hug. She's a couple steps above me so I have to tip my head up for her to kiss me. Once she realizes my hands aren't around her, she looks at the bags in my hands and her gaze flies back to me.

"Robbie, how are you here? What is all this?" she asks with excitement in her eyes. She looks like she just took a shower, her hair a little damp and she's wearing her comfiest sweater and leggings. She's so pretty, and soft, and *mine*.

"Merry Christmas Eve!" I say and she grabs a few bags from me and helps me bring them inside. I drop them by the entrance and run back to the car to grab my duffel and the small tree. When I close the door and put my items down, Olivia tackles me in another hug, and this time my arms close around her tightly. I breathe her in and feel myself relaxing. This is exactly what I needed. *My girl.*

We stand there hugging for a couple of minutes before she slowly pulls back and cups my face in her hands. "I can't believe you're here," she says softly, her eyes intent on mine.

"Is it okay that I am here? It's not too much?" *Am I too much?* I anxiously chew on the corner of my mouth as I wait for her reply. She's going to tell me to go home, that she needs some space. That I'm too clingy.

Olivia drops her hands from my face and I screw my eyes shut. Fuck, maybe I shouldn't have come here and intruded on her space.

TWENTY-EIGHT

Olivia

"HEY, LOOK AT ME," I say. Robbie's gaze slowly meets mine and there's so much fear and uncertainty in his blue eyes. I don't know where he went just now, but when he hugged me by the door a few minutes ago, all I could think was, *Finally, I'm home.*

This past week has been exhausting and all I wanted was Robbie next to me. Ever since we shared our feelings in Vermont, *hell,* ever since he kissed me at the airport almost a month ago, all I wanted was to spend time with him. To touch him, have his arms around me.

I think back to what he said. *Is it okay that I am here?* Of course it's okay. It's better than okay. *It's not too much?* The last time he was on my couch here he confided in me and told me how growing up people always said he was too much, too loud, too brash. I need to reassure him that I won't ever think that.

"Robbie, I am so happy you are here. It means the world

to me that you took a last minute flight and gave up your mom's famous biscuits and gravy to spend the holiday with me instead." He lets out a deep breath, but before I can lose my courage, I keep going.

"You're such a bright fucking light in my life and I'm so lucky to have found you. I know it wasn't easy for me to open up, but I did. You know why?" Robbie shakes his head.

"Because you made me feel safe. Sure, you bullied me into being friends, but even then you were looking out for me." He chuckles lightly and that gives me hope. "You are not too much. Not to me, honey." Robbie's shoulders relax and his hands find my wrists, holding tight. Like he needs to ground himself. I'll give him whatever he needs. *I'll be his fucking anchor.*

I bring my forehead to his and brush our noses together. "I'm in love with you, Robbie." I kiss the corner of his mouth, then his cheeks, his nose, his lips.

"Please tell me I'm not still on the plane, dreaming," he whispers against my lips.

I chuckle and shake my head. "Afraid not."

"Thank fuck," he says before capturing my mouth in a fierce kiss. He's not gentle this time, teeth biting at my lip, devouring me completely. He abruptly pulls back, eyes wide like he just registered what I told him, before saying, "I'm so fucking in love with you, I couldn't stand being away from you for another week."

I give him my biggest, most genuine smile and lean in for another kiss. He breaks this one too and this time I whimper my disapproval. The jackass just smiles at me and says, "I actually have food in the shopping bags. Let's put it away first."

Ugh, how dare he be responsible when I'm about to

climb him like a tree? Robbie gives me another quick kiss, then moves to the bags he brought.

"Seriously, what is in all these bags?" I ask warily. Did he buy the entirety of Home Goods?

"A tree, because it's finally time you put one up. Decorations, of course, and some presents too. Groceries, so you don't poison me with burnt toast." He gives me a wicked smile, teasing me.

"I'm not a monster, I would at least feed you some freshly made frozen mac and cheese."

His laugh is deep and wonderful and his dimples are making an appearance too. I really need him to stop with the bags, so I can continue my hike up Mount Robbie.

"Did you eat today?" he asks and I scoff. "Never mind, of course you ate, you'd never stay hungry for this long." He smiles again and I love how easy this is. How well he knows me. How at ease I am now that he's here.

"I had a bagel, so I could eat something, if you're hungry. We can order takeout."

"Absolutely not. I am making us fajitas," he says and pulls out a giant red bell pepper, an onion, seasoning, and some pre-marinated chicken from one of the grocery bags.

"When did you even have time to do all this shopping?"

"I was lucky that my flight this morning didn't have any delays. It gave me plenty of time to woo you."

"You do know I would have been perfectly wooed if you showed up empty handed, right?" I say, coming behind him at the kitchen counter and giving him a hug. "All I need is you." My head rests between his shoulder blades and I think once again: *I am home.*

Robbie turns and puts his arms around my shoulders, fingers combing through my hair. He bends down and gives me a sweet and lingering kiss. "I do know that. And I'm not buying you things to impress you. I just thought, cooking together has kind of become our thing. As for the decorations, we had a lot of fun putting them up at my house, so I thought we could recreate that moment." His eyes twinkle and he gives me an almost shy smile. "This time, no one will interrupt us under the mistletoe."

"This time, you don't need excuses to kiss me. You can do that anytime now that I'm your girlfriend."

Robbie's hand trails down from my neck to my collarbone, then follows a path to right above my heart, where he rests his palm. "Mine," he whispers, so much love showing in his eyes.

I cover his hand with mine. "Yours."

※

ROBBIE WAS RIGHT. Cooking together has become our thing, and for once, I feel like I'm actually getting the hang of it. We work together seamlessly and chop up the vegetables, sear the chicken, then slice it up. I'm even tasked with cutting the avocado, but once Robbie sees how I'm holding it in one hand and trying to cut through it with the other, he immediately stops me. Apparently "avocado hand" is a thing; one he'd rather not take me to the ER for.

After he garnishes our fajitas, we sit down to eat in a comfortable silence. I can tell he's tired because he gets quieter. He doesn't seem sad anymore though, and every time I catch his eye he gives me a wide grin.

"We have a few hours, do you want to take a nap before we go over to Grams' for dinner?"

"Can we decorate first?" Robbie asks hopefully.

"Sure. Let's do it." I smile and pull him out of the chair by his hand.

We decorate the living room surprisingly fast, considering we keep taking breaks to kiss and put our hands on each other as much as we can. The small tree has white lights and a variety of small, rose gold ornaments in it. There is mistletoe in the archway between the kitchen and living room, lights in the small tree and in the window, and other small trinkets around the coffee table. The soft, warm white lights make this place look so much cozier. Robbie was right, I should have done this much sooner.

"Okay, the last thing we have to do is make some bows," he says, unspooling a roll of rose gold ribbon.

"How do we make them?"

"Well we start by making loops. We want to make a big bow first and put it at the top of the tree." He cuts the ribbon and eyes it. "Here, give me your hands."

I put out my hands and he uses them to loop the ribbon around them, pinching it in the middle, then repeating the loops. I am so mesmerized by the movement of his hands, I don't listen to the rest. I want him to tie the ribbon tighter around my hands, push me up against the wall and kiss me senseless.

"Olive?"

"Hmm," I say, breaking out of my fantasy. He must see the blush on my face because he's smirking at me, blue eyes darkening.

"What were you thinking just now?"

Fuck it. "I was thinking you're doing it all wrong."

He quirks an eyebrow at me. "Oh, yeah?"

I nod and take a confident step towards him "You're supposed to tie me up with it, then use your imagination." I look at him through my lashes and watch his throat bob on a swallow. He doesn't say anything for a moment, just looks at the ribbon he's pinching between my hands.

Then he lets it all drop, except for the two loops around my wrists. He carefully, slowly pulls on the ribbon until my wrists are pressed together and my fists tighten in anticipation. He looks at me to make sure it's not too tight and I give him an assuring nod. He then ties a knot underneath, one that I definitely can't reach and undo myself and moves my hands so they hang around his neck.

I give him a kiss and without breaking it, he picks me up. My legs immediately go around his waist and he walks us to the couch. I can feel his eager hands on my thighs, gripping hard like he's trying to keep in control. I want him to unleash himself on me, give me everything he's got. I bite his plump bottom lip and he groans, his erection growing harder against me.

With more gentleness than I expect, he lowers me down on the couch and presses himself into me for a beat before taking my hands from around his neck and moving them up above my head. This feels too good, and I need more of him, so I lift my hips up into him and make him hiss.

"Patience, love," he whispers against my lips, then kisses me as he trails one hand back down my body, playing with the hem of my hoodie when he reaches it. He strokes his thumb over my skin and my eyes roll back in pleasure. Fuck, he's barely even touched me and I'm already ready to combust. He notices my reaction and continues his slow exploration. I throw my head back and take a deep breath and Robbie's mouth finds my neck, his teeth grazing gently, his mouth leaving sweet kisses on me.

I can't tell if the sound I make is a whimper or a groan, but I can't even be embarrassed about it when Robbie snaps his hips against me, hitting me in the right spot. We both exhale a sharp breath and Robbie pulls back and slowly lifts my hoodie until it goes above my head and reaches my forearms. He realizes he can't take it all the way off so he just shrugs and leaves it there.

When he returns to my body he presses soft kisses to the tops of my breasts, then drags his teeth until he meets my lacy bralette and pulls it down so my nipples are free. One of his hands moves to mine and he laces our fingers together. It's awkward since my hands are tied but I squeeze his fingers tightly, silently begging him to keep going. To kiss me all over. He wraps his mouth around my right nipple, using his other hand to pinch the left one and I am in pure fucking heaven. *Is it possible to orgasm from just kissing?*

"Yes," Robbie says in a low voice, then continues trailing kisses down my body until he reaches the band of my leggings. He hooks his fingers under it and looks up at me for permission. He looks thoroughly wrecked and I haven't even gotten my hands on him. I nod a little too eagerly and he gives me another smirk before pulling down both my leggings and underwear all the way.

"Take your clothes off," I say more huskily than I meant. Robbie obeys, pulling his sweater off in one swift move. When he reaches down to his pants and slowly starts unbuttoning his jeans, dragging down the zipper, his eyes not once leaving my body. He stands up and takes both his layers off, leaving him completely naked and beautiful. He kneels back on the couch but before he reaches for me, he pumps himself in one long slow stroke, eyes held steady on my face. I think I forgot how to breathe.

"Fuck, you're perfect," he says, bending down and stealing a kiss before moving his mouth between my legs. He doesn't give me any warning as he wraps his mouth around my clit, not so gently sucking on it. My answering moan is loud and my hips have a mind of their own as they lift up into him. He pushes me back down with one hand on my stomach, applying enough pressure there to keep me in place. Then he licks and teases me until I see stars.

He knows I'm close, yet instead of giving me what I need, he pauses and kisses my thigh. He follows it with a bite and a lick and then his fingers are gathering my wetness and coating it around. He slides two of them inside me and I need something to grab onto. I bring my hands down to his hair and try to grab at it, but I'm doing a poor job since the ribbon is blocking me. He chuckles and takes pity on me, unwrapping the ribbon and tossing it aside. I reach up and take my bra and sweatshirt off all the way, bring my fingers to his perfect dark blond wavy hair and guide him back to my clit.

His answering sigh lets a hot breath out on my core and my fingers pull his hair tighter. Robbie doesn't hesitate this time, devouring me like a man starved while pumping those two fingers inside me, curling them at the right spot. I don't know what exactly comes out of my mouth, but it's some series of *yes, please, fuck, right there* that I am surprisingly not ashamed of. My release hits me so hard, I immediately start to shake, my legs closing of their own volition.

Before my mind can start overthinking and worry that I may have suffocated him, Robbie groans against me. "Fuck, you get so tight when you come." I give him enough space that he can take his fingers out but don't wait to see what his next move is. I drag him up to me and kiss him hard, tongues clashing, bodies pressing further into each other.

"Did you happen to buy any condoms?" I ask and notice the blush on his cheeks. He did. That makes me smile.

"I may have picked some up," he says, hiding his face in my neck.

I laugh, "You're cute when you're flustered."

"I am not cute. Handsome maybe," he says, narrowing his eyes at me.

"You are super cute," I say, poking him in the cheek where his dimple usually is and he rolls his eyes. "You're also smart, funny, and incredibly kind. And I love you for all you are."

His eyes soften on me and he presses his lips against mine. "I love you too." I grin through the kiss and he mirrors it, and before we know it we're both laughing hysterically, naked limbs tangled up in one another.

When our laughter dies down I say, "Stop stalling and get the condoms, Bobbert."

"Yes, ma'am."

TWENTY-NINE

Robbie

I GRAB the condoms out of my duffel bag but instead of returning on top of Olivia, I put my arms around her back and behind her knees and carry her to the bedroom. The curtains are drawn up and the only light in here is from her bedside lamp. She's holding on to me, smiling and I can't help but return the smile as I place her down on the bed and crawl on top of her.

I can't believe this girl. I can't believe this day I've had. I keep thinking I'll wake up and realize it was all a dream, but it's real. She's real and she loves me. As soon as I reach her mouth she kisses me hard and her hands splay over my chest. She pushes both of us up and guides me down so I'm now laying on my back.

She moves to put her mouth on my cock but I stop her and say in a low voice I don't recognize, "Fuck, I'm not going to last long here, and as much as I want your mouth on me, I want to be inside you even more." Her eyes flash with desire and she reaches over and grabs one of the condoms. Once she carefully unwraps it, she rolls it on my stiff cock and just that small touch makes me twitch. *I am so gone for this girl.*

Olivia moves to straddle me and she slowly rubs herself on me in a way that makes my eyes roll to the back of my head. *Fuck.* She must see my tortured expression because she reaches down and aligns my cock at her entrance, but before she moves she looks at me for permission. There's love and desire in her gaze but some of her confidence from earlier, when she asked me to tie her up and have my way with her, wavers.

I can't have that.

"Are you going to be a *good girl* and ride my cock?" I whisper against her jaw as I lean in and slowly nibble at it.

"Fuck," Olivia responds while digging her short fingernails into my pecs and sinking down an inch at a time.

It seems like we're both holding our breath as she continues all the way until she bottoms out and when she does I say, "Look at you, taking me so well."

Olivia whimpers against my lips and holds on to me tight as she adjusts to my size. "Fuck, Robbie. If you keep telling me things like that I'll think I conjured you straight out of one of my romance novels." She chuckles and I join in. The fact that we can laugh and make jokes together in such an intimate moment makes me fall in love with her even more.

I squeeze her perfect round ass and say, "Must be one hell of a smutty book considering the things I want to do to you." She drops her forehead in the crook of my neck and starts a trail of kisses from my collarbone to my ear, where she slowly bites down on my earlobe. My hips move in a slow upward thrust and she bites down more.

Then, she starts moving and I lose all train of thought. All I can think about is her—how well we fit together, how tight she is, how she moves so confidently, taking what she needs from me. Her confidence is without a doubt the sexiest thing about her, especially since I know how hard it was for her to tear down her walls of insecurities.

She picks up speed and I let her keep the control for a bit longer, until she's ready for me to take over. Her breathing is ragged and she's fucking me so hard I need to fist the sheets and use all the control I have not to come. When she starts to slow down, I wrap my arms around her, one iron clad around her waist, the other holding the back of her neck. I devour her lips with mine as I thrust in at a steady pace, one that's not as fast as hers, but rather one that hits her deeper. I can tell she's close by the way she starts to clench around me, so I bring a hand down to her clit and rub her with my thumb.

The way she screams my name as she comes will forever be ingrained in my brain. Her right leg starts to twitch and I slow down my thrusts, but don't completely stop moving inside her. I catch her mouth in a searing kiss, not letting her fully come down from her orgasm. When I suddenly pull out, I catch a slight frown on her face and give her a smirk in return.

"Get down on all fours," I rasp out. Olivia's eyes widen but she immediately complies, smiling at me over her shoulder as she presents me with her ass in the air. Fucking hell. I caress a hand on her cheek and bend down over her to kiss her. The angle is a bit awkward but neither one of us cares. I bite her lip as I pull back and then slap her ass with a loud *thwack*. She inhales sharply and I soothe the bite with my tongue. "Too much?" I ask her in a whisper. She shakes her head, but I need to hear her say it. "I need your words, love."

"Not enough," she says, reaching an arm back, grabbing my head and twisting her fingers in my hair, pulling just enough to sting. Alright then, my girl likes it a little rough. Noted. I line myself up at her entrance and she lets go of my head so I can pull back. I slowly press on her lower back until she's in the perfect position, then I drive my cock inside in one slow thrust.

Olivia moans loudly and grabs the sheets in her fists. I keep one hand on her waist, fingers digging into the soft flesh there, while my other hand moves up and wraps her hair around my fist, pulling just enough to make her arch. "Such a good girl, taking me nice and deep." I pick up my pace and thrust into her in hard, punishing movements.

She's quiet for a bit and just when I think I went too far she says, "Yes, fuck me harder."

I let go of her hair to grab on to her waist for more balance and slam myself into her as hard and deep as I can. I feel her second orgasm as soon as it hits her and my own follows closely behind, my movements stuttering, until I fall in a heap on top of her. I'm mindful not to crush her, but I can't bring myself to leave her warm body yet.

We're both breathing hard and my heart feels like it might leap out of my chest and lay itself at her feet. She can do whatever she wants with it, I don't even care, as long as she takes it. "Are you okay?" I ask her.

"I'm fucking fantastic, but I'm afraid I won't be able to move for the next two days." We both fall into laughter and I finally do pull out and use the restroom to take care of things. I toss the condom, grab my duffel bag from the hallway and find some underwear and a shirt to put on. As I approach the bathroom, Olivia comes out, still fully naked, red marks on her body where I dug my fingers in. She looks thoroughly fucked and bright-eyed and happy. I take my shirt back off and put it on her as she chuckles. Then I give her a lingering kiss that she breaks off too soon.

"How about we take a nap for a couple of hours? When we wake up, we can head over to Grams'?"

"That sounds perfect," I respond and she smiles and leads me back to the bedroom where she drapes herself on top of me before pulling a blanket on top of us. I hug her tight and tell her I love her, then promptly fall asleep before I hear her reply.

THIRTY

Olivia

THE ALARM WAKES me up right away and I reach out for my phone on the nightstand to turn it off. A heavy arm is draped around me and I have to wriggle my way out of Robbie's grasp. I let him sleep a bit longer as I get ready and put grandma's presents in the backseat of my car. When I get back, Robbie is still out cold. I feel bad that he didn't get enough rest last night, but I am so excited that he's here. I know we confessed our feelings for each other when we were in Vermont, but seeing him so out of sorts tonight, questioning whether he made the wrong choice coming here, whether he was being too much, I couldn't help but tell him I love him.

I swipe the hair off his forehead and run my thumbs along his strong, thick eyebrows before leaning in and kissing him softly. "Robbie, are you ready to wake up?" He mumbles something in return and I take my time caressing his beautiful face, coaxing him to wake up. I kiss his nose and he opens his eyes then. I give him a smile and say, "Hey, pretty guy."

"Hey, gorgeous." He gives me back a lazy smile and kisses me.

Before things can go further, I pull back and motion to the door. "We have to get going. But if you want to stay and rest, I understand. I can tell Grams I can't stay long and bring you back some food."

"No way, I'm coming with you."

"Okay," I say with a happy smile on my face.

"But before we go, I have a present for you," he says, jumping out of bed and running into the living room.

I laugh and follow him, taking a seat on the couch. I saw the wrapped presents when he brought everything inside, but I completely forgot about them until now. What could he have gotten me?

Robbie hands me two boxes, one quite large, and the other about half its size. I look down at them, perfectly wrapped and tied with neat red bows.

"You really didn't have to get me anything. Showing up here was enough, you know?" I mutter as I carefully unwrap the smaller present.

"I know, but gift giving is one of my love languages. I just hope you like them," he says, rubbing the back of his head nervously.

As soon as the wrapping paper is off, I open the box the rest of the way and find a pair of brand new hockey gloves. They're bright red, and unlike my old ones that have too many holes in them, these ones are perfect. I can't help but give Robbie a bright smile, touched that he noticed I needed new ones. He's always looking out for me.

"Robbie, thank you! I don't even know what to say. I feel kind of bad I didn't get you anything."

"You don't need to get me anything, love. Besides, you didn't know I was coming. I'm glad you like them, though." He smiles and my heart melts a little more. "Now open the big one," he says, nudging it towards me with his foot.

Once I get through all the paper again, I realize he's gotten me more equipment. This one is a pair of black hockey pants, the same brand as mine, but a newer model. "Robbie, this is too much."

"Shut up, it's not."

I sigh but move closer to him on the couch and give him a tight hug. Tears prick my eyes as I tell him, "You're the best."

"Come on, let's get ready."

DINNER AT GRAMS was even better than I expected, considering I was bringing a surprise guest. Grams was ecstatic to have Robbie back and to tell him more embarrassing stories of my childhood. Her roommates joined us for dinner as well and we had a pleasant time. Robbie was quieter than usual, but looking at him I can tell it's just exhaustion catching up with him. Grams and I exchanged our presents like we always do at midnight, then Robbie and I headed back to my house where we both crashed as soon as our heads hit the pillows.

Christmas Day passes too quickly as we wake up late and have brunch at Gram's again. After we're done, we go ice skating at the outdoor rink downtown and head back to my place where Robbie insists on making us lunch. However, as soon as we get through the door, we never make it to the kitchen. We end up naked on the couch instead. As we lay there together I realize I don't want him to leave. Even though it's silly and I know I'll see him in exactly one week, I can't help but wonder what sort of couple we'd be if we didn't have these crazy jobs.

"What would you be doing if you weren't playing hockey for a living?" I ask him.

Robbie and I are tangled up on the couch and he's lazily drawing circles on my back. "Hmm. That's a tough question." He thinks for a moment and says, "When I was 8 or 10, I wanted to be a cashier."

I laugh. "What? No way."

"I'm dead serious."

"Why a cashier?"

"Well, every time my mom would take me grocery shopping, we always went to this local place. The kind of place that was in the same family for generations, you know? And it was the same cashier every time and she was so nice and kind to everyone. She'd always give me a free piece of candy, telling me I was her favorite customer. And I think that kindness really stuck with me. To me, she was helping people and making their day better. And that's what I wanted to do."

"That's really sweet, Robbie. You do help people, you know. You are a great leader to your team, they respect you and listen to you. Especially Ash. And you make every day better for me," I say and kiss his cheek.

He laughs and says, "Thank you, love. Although to answer your question properly, I would probably do something involving food. Michael owns a restaurant in downtown Grand Marquee and I would probably be his chef or something. Keep it in the family."

I gasp. "God, you would make an amazing chef. A sexy one too," I say and nibble at his earlobe.

"Don't start something we can't finish. I need to head to

the airport soon," he sighs in defeat. "What about you? What would you be doing if you weren't married to hockey?"

I smile against his chest before responding. "Realistically I'd be a waitress somewhere nearby. But if I had a choice, I would maybe coach. There aren't enough women in hockey, so I would work on changing that. Maybe start small, coach at the little league level, then move up the ranks."

"You'd be a wonderful coach. I know you say you don't like people, but I saw you with my nieces, and you are great with kids. You're patient and always have ways to explain things to them in terms they will understand. Have you given this more thought?"

"Not too much. Just—I guess if the next four years don't work out for me as a referee and I don't make it to the NHL, maybe I need to reevaluate some life choices."

"Well, no matter what you end up doing, you have my full support. I love seeing you kick ass." He smiles down at me and his words are like one of his bear hugs. He makes me feel safe and seen.

"I love you."

"I love you too, Olive."

THE WEEK between Christmas and New Year's is a bit of a blur. Both Robbie and I are busy with road games but at least we're in the same timezone so we get to have our nightly chat before bed. Keeping busy on the days off has been a challenge but I've been reading more books that Alice recommended to me. She and I have started to become really close. I never felt like I missed out on not having siblings until I met Robbie's family. The way they tease each other while also caring for one another is something I long for.

Robbie is at morning skate practice when I land in Grand Marquee the day before New Year's Eve, so Alice picks me up from the airport, all bright-eyed and happy.

"I'm so happy you're here! We truly need more women to join our family hangouts. I mean, it wouldn't hurt if Eli and Ash would bring a date every now and then. Make it more interesting for us, you know?"

"What about Jordan?" I say casually, looking for a reaction. Her cheeks go red instantly and her eyes are wide.

She sputters, "Yeah—I mean, of course—Jordan can bring whoever he wants. Why wouldn't he?" She chuckles awkwardly and I put my arm around her, giving her a side hug.

"I'm just messing with you. But you do realize we know, right?" The other night Robbie told me how he and Jordan met up with Alice to shop for party supplies and groceries. The New Year's party tomorrow is taking place at Robbie's house and a few more of his teammates are invited. Alice and Jordan were apparently stealing glances and being shy around each other.

"Know what?" she feigns ignorance.

"For all the romance books you read, I thought you'd realize by now that you and Jordan are totally a book trope."

"I have no idea what you mean."

"Come on! Brother's best friend? Friends to lovers? The last three books you recommended had those exact tropes. I know it's been on your mind. Besides, it's super obvious you two are crushing on each other."

She chews on her lip as she contemplates it. "Do you think he likes me back?"

"Are you kidding me? He's totally into you." She nods but changes the topic as she drives me to Robbie's place.

As soon as we get to his place, the cats immediately greet me. I spoil them and give them each their favorite treats before taking my bag to Robbie's room. I hope he doesn't think it presumptuous of me that I assumed we'd be sharing his bedroom. After his morning skate, he's coming back here with lunch for the both of us and we have some time to hang out before we head to the game.

I'm a little nervous to be here for the party tomorrow. Since he's inviting more teammates, we have to be careful around them and not divulge that we're in a relationship. His inner circle of friends knows and they can be trusted, but we're being cautious with everyone else.

I'm looking forward to some time to ourselves before the party. Robbie is so excited about it and has a whole menu planned out, so we'll all need to help out and make sure everything is ready. While he apologized that it wouldn't be just the two of us during my short trip here, I assured him it didn't bother me. I know how much he cares about his friends and he shows his love by hosting them and making them food, which I think is adorable. And delicious. No matter how anxious I get, I'd brave anything for him.

THIRTY-ONE

Robbie
New Year's

I WAS HOPING for more alone time with Olivia, but every time we've had a moment to ourselves, something or someone would intervene. First it was my brother Michael, needing to borrow some tools. Then, Ash, barging into my house like he owned it, complaining about not having a date to the party. Like he needs a date. He'll pick up someone regardless. While the party is not a huge rager, it's also not a small gathering. Every person I invited asked to bring three or more friends with them, so it will be packed in my living room. There will be plenty of hookup prospects for Ash.

"But I don't want to hookup," he whines at the kitchen island while Olivia and I mix together ingredients for various dips.

"Then what do you want?" I ask exasperated.

"A date. Like, someone to date. For longer than a few hours."

"And you thought waiting until the last second was a good idea to find a date?" I deadpan.

Olivia sighs and elbows me. "Ash, did you have someone in particular in mind that you wanted to be your date?" she asks gently. The fucker just pouts and props his head on his hand with a heavy sigh. I give Olivia an exaggerated look of, *Why the hell is he still here complaining?* but she just rolls her eyes at me and moves next to Ash, giving him a hug.

He hugs her back tightly then notices me staring and smirks at me over her shoulder. Ass. She pulls back and puts her hands on his shoulders, giving him a stern look. "Ash, I think you need to tell whoever this person is that you're pining over how you feel about them. I know it's not easy to open up to someone like that, but if you just hang on to those feelings and don't vocalize them you will regret it later."

I've never seen Ash like this before, so whoever this person is must have really made an impression on him. He looks so sad as he says, "But what if they don't feel the same way?"

"Then it's their loss, because you're amazing and you're going to do great things. But also, you deal with it. You move on. It won't be easy, but in time you'll get over them." Ash gives her a lopsided smile and hugs her again. No sign of a smirk on his face this time as he blinks back tears.

I wipe my hands, throw down the towel on the counter and join in on the group hug. "If you need a wingman, you know I got you, man."

AFTER THE GAME THAT NIGHT, both Olivia and I are so tired we go straight to sleep. We wake up tangled up in sheets, both cats sleeping at our feet, and it's perfect. I know she doesn't like waking up early but she wanted to help me with food prep, so I reward her by waking her up slowly, kissing her softly, working her up until she's panting and pulling me on top of her.

Soft morning sex with Olivia is even better than the tied up ribbon fantasy we recreated last week. We move in perfect sync and she digs her fingernails into my back as I bring one of her knees up to her chin. We find the perfect rhythm that has us both panting and whispering sweet nothings to each other until we're falling over the edge, lips pressed together, swallowing each other's moans of pleasure.

I'm hoping for more of these moments throughout the day, but soon after we start decorating and preparing food, my sister shows up to help. Even though she was supposed to come much later in the day. She must be bored. Jordan and Elias join us a few hours later and we all work together. The place looks incredible. Olivia and Alice put up lots of black and gold decorations and balloons. The dining table is decorated with a runner, some candles and greenery, and dozens of plates of party food. The kitchen counter houses all the alcohol, mixers, and other drinks. The cats are tucked away in my bedroom so they don't accidentally escape.

"Where is Ash?" I ask the group but they all just shrug. I invited my closest friends early so we can discuss the All-Star week break and our plans to go to my parent's cabin up North.

"Okay, we can fill him in later I guess. The cabin is ours

for the whole week, I made sure my parents didn't rent it out. We'll have to get lift passes at the ski resort, and I'm assuming everyone will bring their own equipment?"

They nod and then I say, "Olive, we'll rent you a snowboard and if you hate it, we have plenty of other things we can do. The resort near the cabin is huge."

"Sounds good. Besides having to teach me, I won't keep you away from the slopes, don't worry," she says in a chuckle.

"We're not worried, we all plan to take turns and teach you," says Elias.

We don't chat for too long before people start arriving for the party, and within an hour the place is packed and roaring. Music is blasting, courtesy of Jordan, the self proclaimed DJ. I introduce Olivia around to various friends and acquaintances but try my best to keep my distance from her. It's so hard to not reach over and grab her hand, or keep a casual arm around her shoulder, or lean in and kiss her perfect lips.

Ash shows up at some point and makes a beeline for the drink counter, lining up shots. I make my way over there and say, "Hey, man. Where have you been?"

"Hey Grandpa. I was home, getting ready," he says, looking around the room.

"You okay? What's with all the shots?"

"Liquid courage," he says and downs all three in a row.

"That was kind of a waste of shot glasses, you could have just poured yourself a cup."

"Where's the fun in that?" He smirks over at me, "Is Olivia nearby?"

"Don't piss me off tonight, Ash. Stop flirting with my girlfriend."

"Aw, but it's so worth it to see your murderous glare."

"So, I take it you didn't ask your person to be your date?" I throw back and immediately regret it.

His face falls and he takes another shot before saying, "Nope, guess I didn't." The next thing he says is so quiet I almost don't hear him. "He's here somewhere anyway."

I pat his shoulder and tell him, "I'm sorry. I'm being an ass. Come with me, let's play some darts or something. And maybe take it easy on the drinking, yeah?"

"Fine, Grandpa. I guess we can do something fun around here. It's a good turn out by the way."

"Unfortunately," I grumble and he laughs at me and pats my chest.

"You're such an old man."

THE PARTY WAS SURPRISINGLY tame and people left around two in the morning. We had a countdown at midnight and then Olivia and I sneaked off to the bedroom and made out for ten minutes, until Alice knocked on the door and told us someone was looking for me. After that we didn't get any more moments alone which is a shame. All I wanted was to press her up against the wall, hike up her dress and bury myself inside her. It's like I'm starved for her body and warmth. I haven't been this horny since I was a teenager.

Jordan was fine to drive and offered to take Alice home. She suggested they both stay and take the spare bedroom but he yelled out, "*No!*" and basically ran to the car. What an idiot.

Ash got progressively more drunk as the night went on and he's now passed out on the couch, a bottle of whiskey dangling from his hand. I saw him disappear around midnight, but I couldn't tell who he was with. I'm not sure if that interaction went well since Ash is in his current state. Poor guy must have gotten rejected.

Elias is trying to wake him up and take him home but I don't think that's an option. "Just let him spend the night here," I say.

"What if he has to throw up during the night? You want him to do that on your nice carpet?"

I wince and say, "No, but if you take him home he'll probably throw up all over his bed."

"I was planning on taking him to my place," Elias says and that takes me by surprise. Although, maybe it shouldn't. They live in the same building, across from each other. They're close and spend time together at parties and work events. Even our social media account loves their "bromance." Something seemed off with them tonight, though. I must be quiet for a while because Elias looks up and says, "What is it?"

I hesitate, but then say, "Nothing, that's just surprising. You two didn't seem to get along that well tonight. Is everything okay?"

"Yeah. It's not that we don't get along. I just don't like it when he drinks so much. It's hard to have a serious conversation with him." He shrugs but sits on the small patch of couch that's not covered by Ash's body. He reaches down and takes the bottle from Ash, then moves his arm up over his stomach so it doesn't dangle anymore.

"Can I ask you something personal?" I say quietly even though no one else is around to hear, expecting him to shut down. He surprises me again by nodding, but he's not looking at me.

"Why do you always take care of him?"

Elias exhales in a rush, relieved I didn't ask the real

question. He clasps his hands so hard they're white and says, "He's my friend. I care about all of you."

"That's a lie. I mean you care about us, sure, but you don't treat us like this. You don't cover us with blankets when you think we're cold. You don't bring us water when we're hungover. You don't rub our backs when we throw up because we drank too much. Should I keep going?"

"No." He takes a moment to gather his thoughts then softly says, "It's hard to explain. When I met him, I thought he was an idiot. Probably still is, but he's *my* idiot, you know?"

I smile and sit down on the chair to his side. He relaxes a bit more and continues, "I told myself I wouldn't make the same mistakes again. I know I never talk about my previous relationship. I was young and stupid and fell in love with a teammate." He looks up at me, waiting for a reaction. He won't get one. I just nod and encourage him to continue. He blows out a relieved breath and does.

"I was 24 when we started seeing each other. We were on the same team in Finland and we hit it off. Both of us wanted to keep it a secret, because let's be real, gay men in hockey are not exactly respected. There were very few openly gay players in the league, if any at all. So we did our best to hide it, and we did for two years, until a couple months before my trade here. I was ready to come out, but he didn't think I should. He basically told me I'd ruin my career if I did. So I asked him where he saw our relationship going. You know what he said?"

I swallow but shake my head and he continues. "Nowhere. He said I was a fun time for a while, but he would never even dream about being seen with me in public, let alone date me openly."

"So what's keeping you from telling all this to Ash? I

mean he's not exactly closeted. Sure, he doesn't publicly announce his orientation, but we all know he's bi."

"I just don't think I'd be good for him. He's got so much potential, and I've got a lot of baggage that he doesn't need to deal with. I don't want to put that pressure on him."

"I still think you should tell him."

"Yeah, maybe."

"You know what I think? I think he gets drunk on purpose so you take care of him. Because he's too scared to tell you how he feels and so he hides behind pretenses to be near you."

Elias doesn't say anything else, so I stand up. "You should take him to the spare bedroom and stay with him so he doesn't throw up all over my bed, yeah?"

"Yeah, okay," he says quietly, looking at Ash and brushing his fingers across his forehead.

※

OLIVIA and I don't get much time together the next morning before I need to drive her to the airport. We knew the trip was going to be short, we just didn't anticipate how little time we'd actually get to ourselves.

"What is it about us and airports?" Olivia says with a small smile as she looks up from where she's snuggled against my chest.

"We've perfected the act of PDA. Everybody gets to see us say goodbye to one another," I say, running my thumb across her bottom lip.

"I'm sorry we didn't get more time."

"Don't apologize. I had a lot of fun in the moments we did spend together," I say, lowering my head to whisper in her ear. "Especially this morning, against the bathroom wall, when you came so hard you almost woke up Eli and Ash."

"Shh, stop!" She halfheartedly swats my bicep, and I kiss her right below her left ear, the spot that makes her shiver.

"I love you and I'm going to call you every day for the next month. You're gonna be so sick of me."

"Never," she says with a smile before kissing me and heading for airport security.

When I get to the car I see a text from her.

> Love you too, Bobbert.

A MONTH APART

Robbie

I don't think I can take this anymore. Can I just jump on a plane and come see you?

Olivia

I wish. I'll be traveling all next week for games :(

What are you wearing right now?

Um, leggings and a sweatshirt?

Sexy. Tell me more ;)

We've been over this, Bobbert. Sexting is cringey, we can just video call later :*

What happened to my fun girlfriend?

> She's been apart from her boyfriend too long and now she's a bitter shell of who she used to be:((

THIRTY-TWO

Olivia
February

A MONTH apart from Robbie is pure torture. Especially since every time I hear his voice on the phone, it makes me want to cry. I want to hug him at the end of a long day, I want to kiss him senseless when I have one too many drinks and run my fingers through his soft hair. I want to dig my fingers into his back as he fucks me against the wall.

I haven't stopped thinking about that since I left Grand Marquee. I have dreams about it, remembering how I woke up and told him I was going to shower and pack. Robbie stayed in bed for another minute, then joined me in the bathroom, fully naked and *very* eager for me. The water was running but I hadn't entered the shower yet and before I could ask him to join me, Robbie pushed me against the wall and kissed me like he never had before. There was a sort of wild desire running through him and I was the only one he wanted, right then and there.

He lifted me up, his whole body pressing into mine. My legs wrapped around his waist and he found my clit with one hand and rubbed small circles until I couldn't take it anymore and started shaking around him, my teeth sinking into his shoulder. Then he got inside me in one thrust and fucked me senseless until all I could see was stars. I started screaming his name and he had to silence me with his hand over my mouth, so our friends couldn't hear us. When his thrusts got choppier and his breathing against my mouth got harder, I wrapped one hand around his throat and squeezed lightly. I'll never forget the noises he made as he came. *Pure fucking bliss.*

"Olive, you still with me?" Robbie chuckles on the phone. A blush spreads over my face and he smirks over the video call. *Busted.*

"Hm? I was just thinking about something."

"I know exactly what you were thinking of."

"I doubt it," I say, looking away to hide my smile.

"You. Me. Bathroom. Am I right?" he smirks and I shake my head and laugh.

"I can't wait to see you next week!" I say, changing the subject into a more tame subject.

"Me too. I forgot to tell you though, Ash and Elias got invited to the All-Star game, so they had to bail out of the trip up north. So it's just you, me, Alice, and Jordan."

"Oh, interesting. Do you think they'll finally get together?"

"Probably not. He literally acts like he doesn't know her when I'm around and I don't understand why."

"Have you tried talking to him?"

"Yeah, but he shuts me down every time. Or finds something convenient he has to do to avoid me. It's getting kind of annoying."

"I'm surprised he hasn't backed out of the trip then."

"He tried but I told him he has to be there or else," he says, voice low.

"Oh, sexy."

"Yeah? Do I need to start telling you what to do?"

"Only in bed."

"Fuck, Olivia. You're killing me here," he says and scrubs a hand down his face.

I laugh and tell him goodnight before ending the call and going to bed, dreaming of the things Robbie would order me to do.

THE NEXT DAY I have another game to officiate. The Vermont Vortices are playing the Minnesota Moose and while I'm happy it's a hometown game, I am dreading facing the Vortices again.

"Hey, Olivia, how are you?" one of the linesmen asks me in the locker room as we're getting ready.

"I'm good, Ben. How was your trip to the west coast?" I ask him, remembering he was in California recently.

"It was a lot of fun, my wife definitely enjoyed the sunshine. And Disneyland was a blast," he says and I nod my head and smile. Ben is nice, we've ended up officiating a lot of games together this season and I've been paying more attention in the locker room to the conversations around me.

Before, I felt like an outsider because I was new and I didn't know anyone, so I kept to myself and listened to music instead of making conversation with the linesmen and the other referee. But after a few weeks, it started to feel lonely, and I realized I needed to bond with my coworkers to better understand their mentality on the ice. After speaking to my mentor Jack about it, he also suggested I become more engaged off the ice.

"So Olivia, you're a local here, are there any good restaurants around we can go to after the game?" Jackson, the other referee asks.

"Yeah, plenty. My favorite is probably The Logan. It's mostly a bar, but they have the most amazing hot dogs and fried pickles."

"Sounds great, we can all head out after the game then. We'll wait for you so you can show us the way," Daniel, the second linesmen says, and for a second I'm stunned. They want to hang out with me?

Usually I take my time to shower after the guys are done, so I can have more privacy. They're willing to wait for me so we can have dinner together?

"Um, yeah, that would be great," I say, smiling down at my skates. Look at me, making friends. Robbie would be proud. I quickly send him a text to let him know the game is about to start and that I got invited to dinner afterwards and he immediately replies with a series of celebratory emojis. I love how supportive he is, even when he's being silly.

The game is pretty intense and it even goes into overtime, so by the time we're back in the locker room we are all tired and hungry.

"That was a great call on Mitchell, Olivia. I can't believe some of the shit that guy tries to pull every game. It's like he has no respect for other players, or the game," Jackson says and then Ben and Daniel nod along in agreement.

"That's because he doesn't have any respect for anyone. You'd be surprised how many times he verbally harassed me, but as much as I want to, I can't kick him out of the game every time," I say, opting for some honesty.

"That is fucked up, no wonder we don't have more women in this sport. Because of assholes like Mitchell," Ben says hotly.

The guys head out and promise to wait for me in the lobby, so I rush through my shower, braid my hair and make sure my hat is tucked over my ears before grabbing my duffel bag and heading out.

Once I'm outside the locker room, I immediately collide with a big, solid body. I look up, starting to apologize before realizing it's Mitchell. His face is red and angry, like always and his eyes are narrowed on me.

"Excuse me," I say, trying to sidestep him, but he blocks my path. "Can I help you?" I ask, trying to keep my tone calm.

"You can actually," he says, with a mean smile on his lips. "You see, I know something. Something you don't want to get out into the public."

"What are you talking about?" I ask, starting to get worried about this whole interaction.

"The last time you were in Vermont, you stayed at the Madison hotel. See, I was there to meet an old friend, and imagine my surprise when I saw you, of all people, hand in hand with the captain of the Manticores." He smirks down at me and my breath catches in my throat. He knows? *Fuck, he knows.* We weren't doing anything wrong though. Not really.

"Your point?" I say, standing up straighter, trying to show him I'm not scared, even though I am internally panicking. What if he tells my bosses? Makes a formal complaint? Would I lose my job, be reassigned?

"My point is, if you don't start making some calls in my team's favor, I will get you fired from the AHL," he says hotly, annoyed that I'm not cowering in front of him.

Screw this guy. Who does he think he is to fucking blackmail me?

"Are you seriously blackmailing an official to make calls in your favor? Your team must be awful if you need to stoop so low," I reply, balling my hands into fists. I've never been a violent person but I just want to punch this guy in the face. "As for getting me fired, you can sure as hell try, but your assumptions are wrong and you'll just look like an idiot when the AHL finds out you not only lied, but also blackmailed me."

Mitchell is fuming and moves closer to me to say, "You will regret this." I take a step back, but startle when I hear voices.

"Hey, what the hell is going on?" Jackson asks from behind Mitchell. Ben and Daniel are also there, the three of them looking annoyed as hell, arms crossed and glaring at Mitchell.

"Mitchell was just telling me what a great job we did tonight. Weren't you?" I pat his shoulder as I move towards the other officials and hide my shaking hands into the pockets of my coat. "Let's go, guys."

The four of us head out and leave Mitchell behind, probably fuming. When we get to The Logan, the guys try to ask me about that interaction, but I just tell them he was trying to pick a fight, keeping the blackmail information to myself.

I WAS SUPPOSED to call Robbie after I left the bar, but my phone died and I didn't have a charger in my car. While the night wasn't a complete bust, worry and panic started creeping in more on the drive home.

I can't fathom how Mitchell would stoop so low. Do I believe him, though? If he has any proof, he didn't mention it. That makes me think he's just desperate and bluffing. Still, he can cause both me and Robbie lots of problems down the road. How am I going to explain this to Robbie without him freaking out?

My house is dark and colder than usual when I get back. I take a look at my thermostat and see it's below 58 degrees. That can't be right, I always keep it at 65 all year round. I try turning it up but it doesn't work. As if the night couldn't get any worse, now I have to sleep in the fucking cold.

Frustrated tears burn my eyelids and all I want to do is let out my rage. I want a home that doesn't have a billion different issues to fix, and I want people not to hate me for doing my job, and I want two cats to cuddle me when I go to bed, and I want Robbie next to me.

I wanted Robbie at the arena tonight, helping me with Mitchell. I want Robbie now to deal with the broken thermostat so that I can just fucking catch my breath. This thought makes me irrationally angry with myself. Since when do I need a man to fix things for me, when I've always done things myself?

But wouldn't it be nice if we could tackle these issues together?

While I want to punch something, I don't. I cry myself to sleep in a pile of blankets so I don't freeze. I don't text Robbie. I don't even charge my phone. I just feel sorry for myself.

THE NEXT MORNING, I call someone to come fix the heat and spend the day with Grams. I get a call from Robbie and immediately feel better.

"Hey, Bobbert."

"Hey, love," he says, chuckling. I know the nickname is growing on him. "You didn't text me last night, I just wanted to make sure you got home safe."

I sigh and say, "I'm sorry, my phone died and then I—" I contemplate telling him everything now, about Mitchell and the heat and my meltdown, but I don't "I fell asleep." I pull my legs up to my chest on Grams' couch and feel like shit for that small lie.

"Okay, did you have fun at the bar?"

"Yeah, it was nice. I wasn't too bad at socializing."

"Of course you weren't. You're amazing."

I smile into the phone and close my eyes, wishing that he were here sitting next to me. I could really use a Robbie hug right now.

"The reason I called is that I found you a ticket for next week. There's actually a direct flight this time, but there's only a few spots left so we need to get it now."

"How much is it?"

"It's $400."

"What? Robbie, that's insane. That's $300 more than the flight with one layover."

"Well, yeah. But do you really want to deal with potential delays? Michigan weather is unpredictable. There could be rain, snow, even a blizzard next week."

"Are the weathermen saying there's a blizzard next week?" I ask, annoyed.

I can basically hear him rolling his eyes when he says, "No, but there is supposed to be snow, and you never know."

"Well, I can't afford the extra $300 since I had to get my heating fixed. So I'll take the regular flight," I say with some bite. I get that he doesn't have to worry about money like I do, but suggesting this flight seems crazy to me.

"Okay, so let me pay for it."

"Absolutely not!" I all but yell back.

He's quiet for a beat, then says, "Why not? At least give me a good reason."

"Because, that's too much money regardless of who is paying for it. I wouldn't feel comfortable with you paying for it. Can we please drop it now? I'm going to get the regular ticket today and forward you the details." I wait for him to push the subject more, but he drops it, albeit reluctantly.

"Okay. I miss you and love you and can't wait to see you next week," he says in a softer voice than before.

"Miss you and love you too. I'll be there in no time."

CABIN FEVER

Olivia

I'm so excited for our trip. I apologize in advance for being terrible at snowboarding.

Robbie

Forecast shows lots of snow, so we might end up spending a couple days just huddled inside the cabin.

What will we do inside all day?

I have a few NSFW ideas. And board games.

Who is going to watch Beans and Caramel while we're away?

My mom will stop by and feed them every couple of days, and make sure they have water and treats.

Tell your mom I said hi.

THIRTY-THREE

Olivia

IT'S A WEEK LATER, and my flight got delayed due to a snowstorm so I am stuck in Chicago O'Hare. This is what I get for skimping on the tickets and not getting the direct flight to Grand Marquee like Robbie suggested. Now I am frantically typing out messages to both Robbie and Alice to let them know the plan needs to be slightly delayed.

The two of them—plus Jordan—were going to pick me up at the airport then we were going to head straight to the Elliots' cabin three hours to the north. I keep glancing up at the screen but all it says is *DELAYED*. I've been waiting at the gate for half an hour and no one has come up to the desk to give us any information.

My phone rings and I see Robbie's name flash on the screen.

"Hey, babe. I'm so sorry, I don't have any updates yet," I say with a frustrated sigh. Why did this stupid storm have to come today? Just to wreck my plans.

"Can you find someone and ask?" he says with a bit of an edge. My brows furrow and I pause. Is he mad at me? For being stuck in an airport due to a snowstorm I have no control over?

"It's not going to do much good. Someone nearby tried and the worker just said to sit tight and wait for an attendant to come to the desk. My hands are tied, Robbie."

He scoffs and I wince slightly. He really is mad. "This wouldn't have happened if you just let me get you the direct flight."

"I'm sorry that I have principles, Robbie. Sorry for not letting you pay for everything all the time, like God forbid I ever pay for a meal once in a while. What does it say about you that you need to always be the one to provide?" Shit, it feels good to snap every once in a while. Screw him for being the only one who's mad. I am angry and frustrated too. We've been away from each other for a month and I miss him like crazy. I really don't want to have this meaningless fight, but at the same time I feel like it's long overdue.

Robbie is quiet for long enough that I can take a shaky breath and blink back the tears that threaten to escape. His voice is cool when he says, "There's a winter weather advisory starting, and if we don't leave in the next two hours we risk not making it up north."

"And what exactly do you want me to do?" I whisper yell through the phone. "Turn back time, get a different flight? Teleport myself there?" I'm being a bitch and I know it, but how the hell is it my fault that the weather is bad?

"I just want you here!" he yells and I wipe away the tears from my face.

Sniffling, I softly say, "I want to be there too, okay? I'll let you know as soon as I hear any news. And if I don't have any updates in the next hour, just go without me. I'll see if I can get a flight back home. Alright?"

"No, not alright, Olive," he replies defeatedly. "This is supposed to be our vacation. A full week of spending time together. Just—just keep me posted, I guess."

"Fine," I say meekly and he hangs up. And I stare and stare at his name on my phone and let myself cry more, because it's the first time he didn't end the call saying *I love you*.

An hour passes by with no updates and I text Robbie to let him know so the three of them can head to the cabin. It breaks my heart that I won't get to see him and have the rest of this fight in person. I want to see his face, to know if he truly does blame me for this trip going south, or to see if he'll hug me and apologize instead. I don't hear anything back from Robbie or Alice and that puts me in even worse spirits.

When an attendant finally does come she reassures us that we'll be able to take off in the next hour, which we do. As soon as the plane is about to leave the gate, I text Robbie again and let him know I'll text him when I land. Then I turn it off, turn my head to the small window and cry some more.

THE FLIGHT from Chicago to Grand Marquee was only 50 minutes including take off and landing, and even though there was a ton of turbulence, we landed in one piece. I'm not usually paranoid when flying, but with the storm, I did question all my life choices and why I even got on this plane to begin with. I should have just gotten a return flight home from Chicago and not even come here. But I didn't have my luggage with me and maybe deep down I was also hoping that Robbie would still be here to pick me up.

I feel so lost right now. Robbie is mad at me, Mitchell is probably going to get me fired, and I'm starting to question if a long distance relationship was a good idea. Would we have been better off as just friends, without all the added baggage? *Was it all worth it?*

I drag my little carry-on and approach the baggage claim area, hoping that my luggage didn't get lost with the delay. I know this airport like the back of my hand now, and so I walk with my head down, avoiding the looks that people give me when they see my swollen face and puffy eyes.

I shake my head at my traitorous thoughts. Of course it was all worth it. *Robbie is worth it.* I love him, and I'm willing to fight for him. But is he willing to do the same?

My gaze snags on a pair of black winter boots as they stop and stand next to me. The scuff on the top of the right foot looks exactly like the one I accidentally gave Robbie's boot when I wore it in the garage last time I was at his house. I tripped and scuffed it on a piece of metal and I immediately panicked thinking he'd get mad. He didn't. He'd laughed and said, "Love, they're just a pair of shoes. I'm just glad you didn't fall."

I blink away more tears just thinking about him and I slowly look up at the man next to me. He stares back with a look of sadness and exhaustion on his face that mirrors mine. I manage to give him a small smile and say, "You still came."

Robbie's shoulders slump and he lets out a sigh before slowly approaching me and wrapping me up in a hug so tight, I can barely breathe. But I don't care, I hang on to him just as tightly and nuzzle my face in his chest. He's bundled up in a warm winter coat and I want to burrow myself in there with him. "Of course I came. The trip is not worth it without you there, love," he says in a ragged voice while wiping away some of my tears.

The luggage arrives and we head to his car. I notice that he brought the Jeep and not the truck this time. He usually prefers to drive the truck in the snow. We don't say much on the drive to his house and I wonder how awkward this week will be if all we do is fight and ignore each other. I don't like this feeling one bit, not being able to tell him every single thought I have, not knowing how he feels about skipping the trip because of me. I know he said it wouldn't be worth it without me, but that's not true. He loves going up to the cabin every year, and Alice and Jordan would have been there too.

When we get to his house, everything is quieter than usual. Not even the cats come to greet me and that brings another wave of sadness. So I just walk straight over to the couch and lie down. Robbie crouches and pushes a strand of hair away from my eyes.

"Olive, we need to talk," he says, serious but in a soft tone.

I sit up slowly and look anywhere but at him when I say, "I'm sorry you're missing out on the trip. I messed up your plans and it's all my fault. I'll reschedule my flight for tomorrow or something and I can leave you be."

Robbie's fists clench and he sits next to me, turning me slightly so I can look at him. I still avoid his eyes. "Why do you think I want you gone?"

I close my eyes but my shoulders slump as his hands are holding me. I all but melt into him, my head leaning on his shoulder. "Because, I don't deserve you. I just feel like I'm always going to mess things up and you'll just leave me."

Robbie grips the back of my neck and pulls me closer to

him so that I'm now crushed to his chest. His heart is beating fast.

"Because you didn't say I love you," I whisper.

"When?" he asks gently.

"On the phone, after we had our fight."

"Oh, love. Can you look at me, please?" he pulls back and gently tilts my chin up so I can see his face. "I'm sorry about earlier," he says, and I can see the regret in his eyes. "But I need you to listen to what I'm about to say."

I nod and he continues. "Earlier, I was frustrated at the situation and I took it out on you. That wasn't fair, I get that. I know you can't control the weather. I apologize for that. As for the end of the call—well, I was angry. The comment you made about me always paying so that I feel superior in the relationship really pissed me off. Because that's not true. I know that I've grown up privileged, but I need you to understand that me offering to pay for your food, or flights, or anything else you need is not something I do to get validation.

"I genuinely want to help, and I'm trying to do that by showing you that you're not alone in this relationship. It's not fair for you to have to pay for every flight just to come see me. And if my schedule allowed it, I would come see you a hell of a lot more often. So yes, I was angry and I hung up. That doesn't mean I don't love you or that I want you gone." He sighs and grabs my face in both his hands, bringing our foreheads together. "*I love you all the time. Even when I'm irrationally mad.*"

"I love you too." I sniffle. "Can I kiss you?"

"One more thing, before we make up. If you need more affirmation that I am here to stay, I'll give that to you. But I need you to understand that I'm not perfect, and I'll make mistakes and get frustrated. And we'll fight again, because that's what healthy couples do." He looks at me and I feel like he sees my soul down to its core. "So promise me, if you're ever angry or annoyed, you'll tell me what's on your mind, and that you won't hold it all inside."

"I promise. And I'm sorry too. I should have handled that phone call better instead of snapping at you. We were both frustrated and I just felt bad for making us miss the trip."

"It's okay, I meant what I said earlier, all I want is to spend time with you. Besides, maybe now that Alice and Jordan are alone together they'll finally admit their feelings for each other."

I gasp and my eyes widen. "They went to the cabin?"

Robbie smiles. "They did. I gave Alice the truck and they left just in time to avoid some of the bad snow. I made her promise to call me with updates when they arrive."

"Hmm, I do have to say, I'm low-key happy to have you all to myself."

Robbie pulls me in his lap and my legs move to straddle him. Then I kiss him softly, almost shyly at first, until he deepens the kiss and shows me exactly how much he missed me. Our clothes end up in a heap on the floor and we don't move off the couch until the cats finally find us and scream at us for food.

THE STORM KEEPS us inside for most of the week, which neither of us complains about. Alice texts me with some updates but she won't make any comments when I ask about Jordan. Robbie stocked up the fridge and pantry before picking me up at the airport so the whole week we experimented with new recipes, watched TV together, and ended up having sex in almost every room of his house. Those poor cats have seen too much.

Last night we were talking about hockey and I happened to mention the Vermont team and how heated the last game was with them. Robbie got so mad just hearing about Mitchell again, reminding him of how he punched Ash at the beginning of the season and almost got him in trouble for it.

I was a coward and didn't mention my own confrontation with Mitchell, but I think I have to tell him. Robbie has been nothing but honest with me and always asks me for my opinion when making decisions, so it's only fair I do the same.

"Hey, babe, can I talk to you about something?" I say, approaching him on the couch where he is reading a book, dark frame glasses making him look sexy as hell, just like I knew they would.

"Yeah, what's up?" he says, bookmarking the page and putting the book aside to give me his full attention. God, I love this man so much.

I nervously spin the ring on my right hand and sit down by his hip where he is lounging. "So, I meant to tell you this earlier, but I've been putting it off because I know you'll get mad."

He studies me with a furrow in his brow and says, "Tell me."

"Well, about a week ago, I had that game at home that I officiated. Remember, we talked about it last night and you vented about how much of a dick Mitchell is?" He nods and clasps his fingers tightly in his lap. "Well, after the game, he was waiting for me and he cornered me at the arena." I glance up at Robbie and see his jaw harden and his nostrils flare. He's pissed.

"Did he lay a finger on you?" he asks through gritted teeth.

"No, of course not. He's not stupid enough to do that," I say and pause for a moment, taking a deep breath. Robbie doesn't get the chance to relax before I say, "He basically blackmailed me."

"What?" Robbie's expression is shocked but also concerned and he grabs my hands in his. "What do you mean he blackmailed you? With what?"

I swallow and say, "He knows about us. Apparently he saw us at the hotel in Vermont last time we were there. He said he happened to be there and saw us holding hands. Either way, he told me he knows and that if I don't start favoring his team more in the remaining games, he's going to tell the AHL and get me fired."

"That fucking asshole. He needs to be taught a lesson," Robbie says.

"Absolutely not! Doing that would just prove him right."

"How are you so calm about this? Your career is on the line if he tells everyone."

"The thing is, I don't know if I believe him. He didn't say that he had proof, and if he did, he didn't dangle it in my face. Which makes me think he's bluffing. Even if he did see us at the same hotel, in the same elevator, holding hands or whatever, it doesn't mean anything. It's just his word against ours," I say confidently.

"And if he does have proof?" Robbie asks warily.

"Then, I will accept whatever verdict the AHL gives me. I'm not going to break things off with you just because some idiot in Vermont has a small dick and an even smaller brain."

Robbie bursts out laughing and I can't help but join

him. "Honestly, the only reason I didn't tell you is because I didn't want to worry you. I'm confident we can put up with him for the next couple months and then once you're retired we don't have to worry about it."

"But you still have to be in the same games as him, unless he gets traded to another division. Aren't you worried he'll try to retaliate further?"

"No, I'll be smart around him. Not let him rile me up. Beat him with kindness and penalties."

Robbie chuckles and kisses me. "That's my girl."

"As for you, are you sure about retiring?" I ask, watching his face more closely. I really don't want him to give up hockey for me.

He smiles and says, "Hold that thought. Let me go get my tablet." He comes back and pulls up a presentation for the nonprofit. "Alex and I met last week, and we put this together." The presentation is very thorough and talks about how they will collaborate with the Grand Marquee Manticores to set up auctions and fundraising events. "Things are becoming more official. Alex is doing most of it, but as soon as the season is over and I'm available, I plan to join him."

"This is great, Robbie! You're really excited for it."

He gives me a bashful smile and I can see he's going to be perfect at this. "Yeah. I really am."

WILL YOU BE MY VALENTINE?

Robbie

Will you be my Valentine?

Olivia

The answer is always yes. And also, that's a week away...

I was thinking about catching a flight and spending a couple of days with you. Our schedules line up. I'd like to take you to dinner if you'll let me.

How did I get so lucky? You're thoughtful AND considerate. Swoon.

Yes, I will definitely be your Valentine :)

Love you, always.

Love you the most.

Impossible.

THIRTY-FOUR

Robbie
March

WE HAVE a month and a half left in the season, and that's if we don't make it to the Calder Cup. Right now we're in the wildcard position which is great for us and the closest we've come in years. On the one hand, I'd be so excited to play in the Cup, but on the other hand, I don't want this season to be extended so I can spend more time with Olivia and start focusing more on the nonprofit.

A week after the All-Star break, I flew to Minnesota to see Olivia and spent Valentine's Day together. I didn't surprise her this time, but I did take her to a nice restaurant and got her a new ring to replace the one she always fidgets with and turns her finger green. The new one is a simple rose gold band with an infinity symbol on it. When I handed her the box at the restaurant Olive said, "This better not be an engagement ring, Robbie. I love you, but we haven't been together long enough for that kind of commitment."

I laughed and assured her it was just a token of my affection, and maybe a promise too of what's to come. I agree with her, we've only known each other for a few months, it would be way too early to think about marriage. But I do know in my heart that she is the one for me and I know Olivia feels the same.

Tomorrow night is another home game and we are playing the Vermont Vortices. I've been dreading this game ever since Olivia told me about Mitchell cornering and blackmailing her. My blood boils just thinking about it, but I promised Olivia we would handle this like professionals and not let our feelings affect the game. I'd be more than happy to clock him in his stupid face and knock him out on the ice but that will certainly get me suspended if I do it with intent to injure.

Olivia is traveling from Ohio after officiating a game there, so instead of picking her up at the airport, I meet her at the bus station and we head straight to the game. My whole family got tickets and they are super excited to see us both on the ice. The few times Olivia has spent time with my family, they've gotten along great, which makes me happy. I know my mom can be a bit of a helicopter parent, but Olivia doesn't seem to mind the fuss and attention.

I drop Olivia off at the arena's back entrance then go park the car so that we're not seen entering the building together. I suggested we do this just in case Mitchell is looking for proof to report us.

I head to the locker room and start to get ready, then go out for warm-ups with the rest of the team. Michael brings my nieces down to the glass and I wave and do some tricks for them before throwing them each a puck. They don't come to the game often, but when they do, I make sure they have a fun time. They're both wearing my jersey and waving excitedly at me. I got them seats in one of the upper level boxes that has the best view of the ice. When I skate away from the glass, I see Mitchell hovering on his side of the ice, smirking at me. I lift my chin up and then promptly ignore him.

The first period is rougher than I expected. Mitchell and his goons are coming in hot and keeping the pressure on us. They've managed to draw two penalties so far and I swear every time Mitchell is on the ice, I see him talking shit to Olivia. It's messing with my head and I'm definitely distracted and angry, which gets me a couple of penalties as well. The whole crowd is booing at Olivia and the other officials as she escorts me to the box.

"What has gotten into you?" she asks out of the corner of her mouth.

"That guy is a prick, what the hell has he been telling you?"

"I can handle it, Robbie. Beat him with kindness, remember? Just focus on the game and win instead."

Fuck. I know she's right but my skin is buzzing with too much anger and I'm having a hard time controlling it.

With only a couple of minutes left on the clock, I come out of the box and intercept a pass, taking my shot at a breakaway, except before I can wind up and take the shot, I get hit in the face by someone's stick. Olivia blows the whistle and skates up to me, checking for blood. I turn around and spit a mixture of blood and saliva at Mitchell's feet. Fucker split my lip, he better get a double minor penalty for high sticking.

Olivia makes the call and sends Mitchell down the

tunnel, but not before I hear what he tells her. "You're a goddamn bitch, and you're going to pay for this."

"You talk to her like that again and you'll be the one paying for it," I say in a low voice.

During intermission, I am too fired up and I pace around the locker room, then decide to go and find Olivia. I need to talk to her.

She's outside of the locker room, tucked into a dark corner looking as anxious as ever. As soon as I get to her, all my anger melts away, concern taking over. "What's wrong, Olive?"

She stops fidgeting and she gives me a look of, *I can't say anything here.* So I lead her to a more secluded area where no one will find us for now.

"I'm freaking out, Robbie. What if he does tell someone about us? He might not have proof, but enough people on his team see the way you protect me and stand up to him when he's being an ass."

"Yeah, but I would do that for any referee, because he doesn't have a right to insult any of you. Even in the heat of the moment, you might make a bad call but that's no excuse to be verbally assaulted."

"But, what if this is messing with my head and my ability to make sound decisions? What if I'm biased now and I always call out his penalties because I know what to look for? What if no one takes me seriously anymore?" Her eyes are filled with tears and I take her face in my hands.

"Olive, of course everyone will take you seriously. Are you kidding me? Just because he made you doubt yourself and your abilities doesn't mean he's right."

"But what if I'm not strong enough to deal with it all?" she whispers and her bottom lip wobbles.

"Love, you are the strongest person that I know. Just

look at you and how much you've accomplished all on your own. You've never had a good support system behind you and yet you never gave up on your dream. You worked hard and proved people wrong when they said you couldn't do it, that you weren't tough enough.

"I need you to know how proud I am of you. You are level headed, fair and impartial, and you are not afraid to make the tough calls. You are exactly what this league needs. Someone who won't back down when threatened. I know you've never had anyone in your corner before, but I've got your back. Our friends do too."

Olivia laughs and turns her head to kiss my palm. "That can't exactly work out there on the ice. You having my back."

"Of course it can. Fucking hell, if anyone even looks at you funny, I will board the hell out of them."

"You can't do that, Robbie," she says, scolding me with a small smile on her face.

"Sure I can. I'm retiring, so it's not like my career is in jeopardy. Besides, if I do, you can just send me to the penalty box. Call it *the love penalty*."

She laughs again and gives me a quick kiss before we have to head back to the lockers. "Thank you for the kind words." I squeeze her hand and reassure her that she's got this.

THE SECOND PERIOD is a disaster of massive proportions. Mitchell continues to harass Olivia but she keeps to her word and ignores him. She's playing it smart so that if he tries to escalate it and call her any names in front of the other officials, they would intervene. My shifts don't line up with his as much since one of our guys got hurt last period and hasn't come back to finish the game. Otherwise, I would absolutely keep my word and check him into the boards as hard as I can for even daring to speak to her.

The majority of the period is littered with penalties, the most recent one including Ash and Mitchell. When Mitchell tripped Ash, my little hothead friend dropped his gloves and started a fight. While I know this hurts the game, I'm glad he did it. Mitchell deserved that punch to the face, not just for what he did to Ash, but also for how he's treating Olivia. When I skate up to the penalty box to give Ash his gloves and helmet, I make sure to skate by Mitchell's box as well and give him a glare. The asshole glares right back and the look on his face is pure hatred.

Good. It's a matter of time until he snaps and hopefully he does something that gets him suspended.

I head back to the bench and watch as our guys prepare to be on the power play and hopefully score a goal so we can take the lead. My head keeps a steady movement between following the puck, looking at the clock, and keeping an eye on Mitchell for when he comes out of the box.

We still haven't scored.

Five. Ash continues to sit in the box. He'll be in there for the rest of the period.

Four. I look over at Mitchell and see him standing up,

getting ready to come out of the box. He glares at me, then moves his eyesight on Olivia.

Three. Olivia is over in my team's defensive zone, where the Vortices are attempting to make a play.

Two. Jordan snatches the puck away and gets a breakaway..

One. Mitchell comes out of the box and heads straight for Jordan. Olivia is skating up right behind them both, trying to get the right angle on the play to see what they are doing. Mitchell transitions so that he's skating backwards towards his net, then attempts to trip Jordan which makes him stop his pursuit towards the net. The two of them are just kind of locked in on each other as Jordan handles the puck and looks for someone to pass it to. Mitchell's eyes dart to Olivia who is by the glass behind Jordan.

Then, Mitchell charges at Jordan as if he'll check him and Jordan retreats backwards toward Olivia, who is trying to move out of the way. Except she's not fast enough. Not when Mitchell is headed toward her at full speed. I always thought that when something crazy happens, time would slow down. Like how sometimes people describe being in a car accident and remember every detail because it happened in slow motion.

Mitchell checking Olivia into the boards is fast. One moment she's standing up, and the next she's flat on her back with Mitchell on top of her. And I swear my heart stops.

My view is blocked by the linesmen and the other ref approaching and if a whistle is going off, I don't hear it. I jump over the bench wall and skate up to them in a daze, and it feels like everyone in the whole damn arena is collectively holding their breath. You could probably hear a pin drop on the ice, but all I hear is the rushing in my ears.

Because there, on the ice, Olivia is on her back with no helmet on. There is blood coming out from the back of her head and she's not moving.

The team physician is walking out and my teammates are gathering around us to keep people's view blocked.

And all I see is *red*.

Mitchell is just standing there and I move so fast no one has a chance to stop me as I rip his helmet off and punch him in the head hard enough that he goes down on the ice. I should stop here, but I don't. I get on top of him and continue to land more hits on his face and gut. The fucker doesn't even fight back.

Two sets of hands have to pry me off of him and I hear Ash and Jordan talking over each other, telling me to calm down.

"How the fuck am I supposed to calm down when she's fucking bleeding and unconscious because of him?!" I yell at them. As they pull me away from Mitchell I see that a stretcher has been brought out for Olivia. Fuck. I need to see her face.

I try to move closer to her but Bob, the second referee stops me in my tracks. "Elliot, what the hell was that? You realize you're out of the game and will definitely get suspended, right?"

"I don't care. How is she?" I say in a commanding voice.

Bob straightens and a look of understanding passes over his face. He gets closer and whispers, "Doc said the head wound is not too bad, considering. But she may have broken a couple ribs. She was just coming back to when they brought the stretcher."

My head whips up and I see them opening the glass doors over by the zamboni area to take her out of the arena. I skate up to them despite Bob and my friends' protests. I see

Olivia looking around, probably confused as hell and get closer to her.

"Olive!" I say, loud enough that she hears me and looks over, eyes going wide.

"Robbie," she says, and the team physician and the EMT slow down so that I fully catch up.

"What hospital are you taking her to?"

"St. Mary's. A few blocks away."

I don't take my eyes off of Olivia for a moment but I give her the best smile I can muster and say, "I'll meet you there, love." She nods back with tears in her eyes and I breathe a sigh of relief at seeing her awake.

When I skate back to the tunnel, I don't look at any of my teammates as I walk to the locker room, take my equipment off, and plan to head out to the hospital. Coach tries to stop me but there's no chance in hell.

"Elliot, I appreciate your sense of righteousness but did you have to pummel the guy?"

"He deserved much worse," I say and leave him gaping after me.

THE SHORT DRIVE to the hospital still somehow feels like forever. When I park the car, I quickly check my phone and see tons of messages and missed calls from my family and friends. I open up the text from Alice and quickly type a message telling her what hospital I am at. Then I call Elias as I walk into the lobby, heading to the ER.

"Robbie, thank God. Where are you?"

"Hospital."

"Is she okay?"

"I don't know yet, I'm trying to figure that out," I say as I reach a shaky hand and press the third floor button in the elevator. Only now I realize my knuckles are split and bloody after what I did to Mitchell.

"Okay. You do that. We told Coach you and Olivia are friends and that Mitchell took it too far, obviously. But, Robbie, I don't think even Coach can do anything to get you out of a suspension."

"I seriously don't even care about that right now, man."

"Okay. Well, we're headed into the third period soon, and I don't think Mitchell is coming back out either. So, at least we won't try to finish the job."

"Look, can you do me a favor after the game and bring me and Olivia some clothes? I'm sure she'll want something clean to change into."

"You got it. We'll be there, just text me the details."

"Thanks," I say and hang up as the elevator dings and I walk out to the ER lobby. It's surprisingly quiet for a Friday night. I guess the bar fights haven't started yet; it's too early.

I walk up to the nurse's desk and ask for Olivia.

"Your relationship to the patient?"

I hesitate before blurting out, "I'm her fiancé."

"Well, Mr. Fiancé," she says and raises her eyebrow like she knows I'm full of shit. "From what I see she's still being checked out. But if you want to take a seat over there in the waiting room, I will let you know when I have updates."

I run a hand over my face and wince as I try to flex it. I think I may have broken a finger. "Please, is there anything at all you can tell me? Can I go in with her? She might have a concussion and need someone to fill in the details of what happened."

She looks at me pensively and asks, "You were at the hockey game where she got hurt?"

"Yeah, I saw it happen, " I say shakily, blinking away

tears. I look down at her name tag. "Please, Janice, let me see that she's okay."

She looks at me and takes a deep breath before shaking her head. Fuck. I feel so goddamn useless right now. Janice starts typing on her computer and I go to turn around but she stops me by saying, "I think we need to get that hand of yours checked out ASAP. You may have some broken fingers."

I turn around and bite the inside of my cheek so I don't cry in front of Janice. "Thank you."

Janice leads me to one of the small consultation rooms and tells me to hang tight, but when she leaves she doesn't shut the door. Instead she leaves it wide open and gives me a wink.

I sit there on top of the medical chair and stare out the door like at any moment I will see Olivia. And I do. She's laying down on a rolling bed as they take her out of the room straight across from mine. I jump down from the chair and reach her in just a few steps.

"Excuse me, who are you?" the doctor pushing Olivia's bed says, affronted.

"No, it's okay," Olivia says at the same time I say, "I'm her fiancé."

Olive's eyes dart back to mine, wide and tired, but with a hint of amusement. I grab her hand that somehow looks smaller than ever and say, "Are you okay, love?"

She squeezes my fingers and I keep the wince to myself this time, but the doctor notices and sighs. "Alright, I'm headed to the MRI machine so you might as well come and we can check your hand as well."

"What happened to your hand?" Olivia says, looking down.

"Nothing you need to worry about right now."

A nurse comes and brings my chart and takes a scan of my fingers. I have a broken middle finger that needs a splint, which somehow feels appropriate.

The MRI confirms Olivia has two broken ribs and a concussion. Our doctor orders a CAT scan as well to get a better look at her head. When we head back to the exam room, they let me stay with her until they get the final results and can clear her for going home.

Hours later, we walk out hand in hand only to be met with a sea of people. My whole family is here, joined by my friends. When they see us, they immediately surround us and pepper us with questions.

"Olivia, honey, how are you?" my mom asks.

"Is your middle finger broken?" Ash says with a cocked head and a smile on his face.

"Do you have a concussion?" Alice asks.

"Guys, slow down!" I say and look over at Olive, making sure she's not overwhelmed. But my girl is smiling wide with tears in her eyes.

"You all came to check on me?" she asks shyly.

A chorus of replies assure her that yes, they did come here for her. I squeeze her hand and she laughs. "Thank you all. I'm fine, but two of my ribs are broken and they'll take about six weeks to fully heal. As for my head, I did get a few stitches, but the concussion is not severe."

"Here, I brought you both some clothes. It's cold outside," Elias says. He hands us both hoodies and sweatpants and we put them on. I help Olivia with her hoodie when I see her wince from the effort to raise her hands.

"I'll drive you both home and take the truck back to my place," Alice says, and I am so fucking lucky to have this amazing family. I am even more happy that they came here for Olive to show her their love and support. It means everything to me. I hug them all and promise to give them more details in the next few days. For now, I just want to be home with my girl and make sure she's taken care of.

"Let's go home," she says, leaning her head on my shoulder on the ride down the elevator.

"You're staying with me until you heal, okay?"

She nods and says, "I'm tired of always taking care of myself. Do you think the cats will cuddle me even more now that I'll be bedridden?"

I chuckle and kiss the top of her head. "I'm sure they will."

THIRTY-FIVE

Olivia

THE PAST WEEK has been the most stressful time of my career, and yet I've been able to find peace in the quiet days with Robbie and the cats. Not one of them has left my side since we got back from the hospital. Robbie insists on making me food every day and attending to my every need. He's washed and braided my hair, helped me get dressed, and held me as I cried the first couple of nights. While I felt useless in the beginning, I'm starting to get used to him tending to me. He's spoiled me this week and I'm not sure how I'll go back to doing things for myself.

I don't remember much from the collision with Mitchell. One moment I was watching the play, and the next I was down on the ice. My helmet must have come off during my fall and I hit my head pretty hard. Robbie begrudgingly filled me in on the rest of the details, grimacing the whole time. I can't imagine how hopeless he must have felt, seeing me unconscious and not knowing if I was okay.

What I do remember is bits and pieces from the arena and the hospital. And I remember Robbie, the way he skated up to ask where they were taking me, how he showed up outside my exam room and told everyone he was my fiancé.

My head is telling me that he made a mistake by attacking Mitchell. Robbie got suspended for 10 games which means he won't be able to play for the rest of the season. My heart is soaring because it knows Robbie would do anything for me, even give up the last of his career for me. He's told the board that he doesn't regret what he did and that he would have done it regardless of the referee being a stranger or a friend.

In the past week, I've been waiting for news. The AHL thankfully covered my medical bills since I got hurt during a game. They are also investigating Mitchell's foul play. The cameras caught the angle where we collided, and there was clear intent to injure me. I decided I wouldn't press charges, but that a hearing should take place and that Mitchell should be held accountable one way or another.

I called Grams and told her about my injury and that I planned to stay with Robbie for the first couple of weeks while I start to heal. I plan to take a flight back home and check on the house as well as pack more clothes to bring back to Grand Marquee. Robbie plans to fly out with me and help, and he's all but wrangled me into living with him for the next five weeks.

I hear my phone buzz somewhere on the counter top and start to stand from the couch, but Caramel doesn't want to move from my lap. A moment later a hand pops into my view and passes me my phone. "Thank you."

"No problem, love," he says and bends down to kiss the top of my head over the couch. The past few days, in between taking care of me and driving me insane, I told him to start focusing on something other than me, so he started looking over paperwork for the nonprofit. "Hello?" I answer the unknown number and as soon as I realize who it is, I break out into a sweat.

"Miss Wilson, my name is Jackson Veritas and I'm with the American Hockey League's Player Safety Committee. How are you feeling today?"

"Doing better, sir. Thank you."

"That's great to hear. I won't keep you long, Miss Wilson, I just wanted to let you know that Dustin Mitchell has been fined for his actions during last week's game. On top of that, I believe he was also let go by the Vermont Vortices."

"Wow, I don't even know what to say."

"Well, we certainly hope you will return next season, you have been an incredible asset to the AHL."

"Thank you, sir."

I'm still holding the phone to my ear long after the call ends and staring out towards the living room when Robbie comes and sits next to me.

"Hey, what was that call about?" he asks, nervously looking me over, expecting bad news. I blink back tears of relief and give him a smile.

"Mitchell got fined, and fired apparently."

Robbie's eyes widen and he gently hugs me so as to not hurt my ribs. "That's amazing news."

It really is. I was fully expecting Mitchell to tell the board about my relationship with Robbie and try to get me fired. In the end, I guess I was right. He was bluffing about having evidence.

"So, what are you going to do next?" Robbie asks, holding me on the couch.

"You mean if I survive five weeks of you babying me?"

He snickers and I laugh, lacing my fingers with his. "I think I'd like to stay here, with you, during the offseason. Do you think your brother is looking to hire someone at the restaurant?"

Robbie is quiet for a moment and I look up to see his contemplative face. I can almost hear the gears turning in his brain. "Actually, how would you like a job at the nonprofit?"

I slowly sit up straighter and give him my full attention. "Are you serious?"

"I was actually talking to Alex earlier and we could use someone with a marketing background to help us get started. I know it's not something you love, but you do have a degree in it. We might be able to hire you full time as we start out, then find someone else to take over when the new season starts and you return to officiating. You plan to return, right?"

"Of course. But what if I'm not good at sports marketing? I mean, I'd have to start brushing up on things right now."

"I'm sure you'd be amazing at it. And we might not be able to pay you as much as other people in the field, but it would be a bit more than you'd make at a restaurant."

"That would keep me here, until at least September," I say, heart pounding.

Robbie looks at me and gives me a lopsided smile as he says, "Or maybe even longer."

"This could work well with my master plan of stealing your cats away," I mumble and see the bright smile on

Robbie's face take shape. "So, do I need to find my own place if I move here?"

"Don't you dare," he says, and captures my lips with his, making my head spin. I love him so much I can't even think straight sometimes. I can't believe he chose me. I can't believe he wants me. *I can't believe he loves me.*

THIRTY-SIX

Olivia
   Six months later

I GRAB the last box from the living room and look around the empty house. I have so many good memories here from when my dad was alive. Happy memories of us watching hockey together and him helping me with homework as best as he could. I have sad memories too, of holidays spent alone and lonely nights when all I would do is sit quietly at home and avoid people.

I've been renting out the house for the last five months, but when the tenants decided to leave early and I found out Grams fell and broke her hip, I decided it was time to sell. I'm using the money from the sale to get Grams set up in a nice assisted living community in Grand Marquee which is only a 10 minute drive from Robbie's house. No, *our house*.

I've been living with him since March and I've never been happier. The nonprofit youth hockey foundation is taking off wonderfully. Robbie and Alex not only manage the day to day tasks, but they also coach the little kids. When I'm not helping on the marketing side, I'm down on the ice as well helping out.

The NHL offered me a five year contract to referee at the AHL level and I accepted. This is exactly what I hoped out of my career and I am well on the path of making it to the NHL, despite all the setbacks life tried to throw at me. I'm lucky to have a partner who understands my dream and encourages me to pursue it every day. And if it doesn't work out, I always have the foundation to return to.

While this is Robbie's project, I couldn't help but feel included as well from day one. When I'm not traveling for my job, I plan to continue working part time at the foundation. There's something really magical about seeing the smiles on those kids' faces when they come in for practice.

It reminds me of my early days in the little leagues and how hard my dad tried to make ends meet. I've talked to several parents and guardians and most of them are in similar situations, which is why we are planning to host a variety of donation events to help pay for kids' gear. Thankfully, Robbie's connections with the team are still strong and they are more than happy to partner up with the foundation and give back to the community.

Robbie comes up behind me and puts an arm around my collarbone, pulling me back into his chest. "Are you ready, love?"

I nod and take one last look at the house. "I'm ready. Let's go home."

EPILOGUE

Olivia
Six years later

I'VE ONLY BEEN on the ice for ten minutes and my legs are already killing me. This is what I get for getting older, I guess. I told Robbie I needed to get on the ice more during the offseason, but he insisted we needed a long vacation somewhere warm. So we spent the last two weeks in the Bahamas, in pure family bliss.

One of the Toronto players takes control of the puck and moves toward the Detroit net. As he gets closer, he passes the puck to another player and takes up a position to screen the goalie. He keeps moving closer to the goalie until he is inside the crease and his stick is blocking the goalie's glove. When his teammate shoots, the goalie can't move in time to make the stop. The player screening him falls back and knocks him down into the net.

I blow the whistle and motion that there is no goal. Then I skate up to the box and make sure my microphone is on when I call the penalty. "Toronto, number #22, two minutes for goalie interference. There is no goal."

A chorus of cheers rings out in the large arena, and I skate back to the goalie. "Eli, are you okay?"

He pulls off his helmet and sprays water on his blond hair. "All good, Olive." Elias smiles and winks at me.

I turn around and almost collide into Ash as he skates up to check on him as well. "He's fine, get back in the face-off before I give you a penalty," I say with a small smile on my face.

"Yes, mom," Ash replies but does as he's told. These two are something else.

DETROIT WON 3-0 THIS AFTERNOON, and while I have to be impartial on the ice, I have to say that I am damn proud of this team. Elias got called up to the NHL about four years ago when one of the goalies got injured and was out long term. He proved himself by being a hell of an asset to the team so they kept him on. He is now the primary goalie for Detroit. Ash got called up as well a few months after Elias and fluctuated between the NHL and AHL for that entire season. During training camp the following year, he showed more promise and eventually got a contract in the NHL.

As happy as we are for them, we do miss seeing them on a regular basis. Which is why I can't wait to go out to dinner with them both while in town.

As soon as I leave the locker room, I head to the player entrance. My two favorite people in the world are there, wearing referee jerseys with #13.

I'm accosted by a tiny human with dark blond hair and

green eyes as she jumps in my arms. "Mommy, I saw you on the ice!"

"You did, baby? How did I do?" I say, twirling her around.

"Daddy said your skating was choppy." My adorable four year old doesn't understand the concept of a filter. I bite my lip and hold back a laugh and I see Robbie choking on a cough. "I did not say that, love. She's lying."

"Mhm, I'm sure."

"Are we going home?" Valerie asks, bouncing up and down in my arms.

"We need to say hello to Uncle Eli and Uncle Ash first and get some food. Then we'll go home."

"Okay," she says and then wriggles around until I set her down.

Robbie's gorgeous face replaces my view. How is he even more handsome now than he was six years ago? The silver hair he's gotten in the last few years blends in perfectly with his dark blond hair which is now shorter on the sides and longer on top. And I love running my hands through it. He also looks incredibly sexy wearing my jersey.

"You did amazing, love. Is the NHL everything you expected?" Robbie asks, knowing I was nervous and excited to officiate in the NHL for the first time ever this week.

"It is. Although I'm going to miss you both once I start traveling."

"We'll miss you too, but we got it handled. Plus if you're gone too long, we can always come visit you."

I smile at my perfect husband. "I love you."

Robbie chuckles. "I love you too, Olive." He leans in and gives me a sweet kiss, his thumb caressing my jaw.

We get interrupted by a loud text and Robbie sighs as he looks down at his phone.

"How are the wedding preparations?" I ask, knowing Alice has been driving him insane.

"Jesus, I can't wait for it to be over already. She's such a bridezilla."

"I made sure I wasn't working that whole week so we'll be there at her every beck and call." Robbie groans but I laugh. I get to be Alice's maid of honor at her wedding up north and I am beyond excited. She's become my best friend in the last few years and there's nothing I wouldn't do for her.

Ash and Eli join us in the lobby and we all hug and congratulate them on their wins.

"How's my favorite niece?" Ash asks Valerie while grabbing her and flipping her upside down.

She's giggling uncontrollably but manages to say "Good, uncle Ash."

Robbie scoffs and says, "I think you mean your only niece?"

"Well, if Alice gets her way she'll have a whole football team of kids once they get married. Val will definitely have competition then. Won't you Val?" he asks my toddler and snuggles her.

"Are you excited to be the best man?" I ask Ash.

"Hell yea, I have a speech they will remember for the rest of their lives."

Elias sighs and shakes his head at this. "Not sure why he wanted Ash to be the best man. It will be a disaster."

We all laugh and head out into the crisp October air. I love my found family that somehow keeps expanding.

The End

ACKNOWLEDGMENTS

When I started writing this book, I never thought I would have the courage to publish it. I've always had an overactive imagination, I've always been a daydreamer, but I've never written down any of my ideas.

To be honest, this book would not be possible without the endless support from my husband, Aidan. He won't ever read this book, so I can safely praise him here without inflating his ego. Thank you for letting me talk your ear off and teaching me all about hockey. You're the best. *You're my Robbie.*

To my family, sorry you had to find out about this book from Instagram, and please skip those smutty chapters.

Thank you to my ride-or-die, Emma. You're the first person that gets to read my nonsense, and for that, I apologize. It's messy and unpolished, but somehow you always come back for more. *Kiss loveh.*

I have to thank my alpha readers, Chelsey and Leanne. You are both such amazing hype women, and I probably wouldn't have made it further than that alpha draft without your support and honest feedback! You'll be getting future book snippets from me whether you like it or not (sorry not sorry).

To all my beta readers, you are all so sweet and amazing, and I am so grateful you decided to give me a chance. I've promised you all I'll be naming future characters after you, and while it might take me a few books to do that, I will keep my promise!

Thank you to my lovely editor Ciara for always putting up with my memes and random messages. Those dang Oxford commas and dialogue tags could not have fixed themselves.

Lorissa, my amazing cover designer, thank you for bringing my characters to life. I am in awe of your talent and so happy we got to work together.

I also wanted to thank my friend and fellow indie author A.K. Isaacs, you are so sweet. Thank you for always giving me tips and answering my questions about indie publishing and your own journey!

And lastly, this book would not exist without YOUR support! Thank you, from the bottom of my heart. Thank you for reading and sharing and hyping me up!

www.ingramcontent.com/pod-product-compliance
Lightning Source LLC
LaVergne TN
LVHW010310070526
838199LV00065B/5511